Praise for *A Death in Florence*

"Great story with wonderful descriptions of Florence! Reflection on a life of missed opportunities to be caring to those who matter."
—Gustav Koven

"This interesting book provides local information that can only be learned by living there for a long time. It makes me want to be a long-time visitor on my next trip to Europe. I liked it and recommend it."
—Anthony Kilburn

"Beautifully presented in all its Italianate splendor in both glorious and gory detail. Dante comes alive through this semi-recreation of his life, centuries later."
—Frederic Todd

DESERT ELECTRA

DESERT ELECTRA

A Novel

BRUCE MOSS

*To the memory
of my dear son Greg
lost to cancer*

Chapter One

Anna wondered if there had been a mistake. Again she squinted at the signature on the painting. Yes, it read *D. Kunstler*. When she last checked his website she had seen only desert landscapes, picturesque pueblo villages and serene American Indians, like most of the work in this Santa Fe art gallery.

But this subject matter—what would have motivated the artist to paint such a thing as this? Was it a celebration of death? A mockery? Was the artist ripping himself open to show the world his scar tissue, the result of a calamity? The skeletal figures and body parts twisted in space as if they were being blown by some malevolent wind. A skull-like head glanced at her over its right shoulder, the nearly amputated forearm barely suspended by tendons and ligaments. A headless, legless torso hung in middle space, its stomach muscles bulging purple. Wispy, emaciated figures floated against a sulfur background. For Anna these paintings from the artist's *Wraiths* series were sickening her.

Anna couldn't imagine even the most disturbed patient in her psychotherapy practice producing such work. Nor was the artist just any artist. He was her *father*, the father she had never known. She had lost her mother and brother years earlier, and

Kunstler was her only living relative. She had tracked him to New Mexico over considerable time and distance. She would need to find a way to meet him. She wouldn't tell him right away that she was his daughter, of course. She would first have to judge what kind of man he was, especially in view of his disturbing artwork. Would such a man be capable of a grandfather's love for her children? She would have to find out, not only for her own sake, but for that of Tommy and Katey, who were upset enough about the divorce as it was.

Certainly, the paintings carried no hint of what might have attracted her mother to Kunstler nearly forty years ago, conceiving with him a daughter named Anna. Had her mother been attracted to danger and darkness? There had been no sense of that in the few memories Anna cherished of her mother, Kate, who had died when she was only six.

For thirty-two years she had tried to imagine what her real father was like, ever since that traumatic night in the Italian farmhouse, just short of her seventh birthday. The family, including her little brother Thomas, had gone to live in Florence during Anders' sabbatical year from the university. For six years she had understood Anders to be her father. But one night, awakened by shouting, she had crept from her bedroom to the top of the stone stairs. Her mother and Anders were arguing in the hallway below. It was frightening. They seemed about to attack each other over Anders being with another woman. Again she recalled the chill of the stone step through the seat of her little pajama bottoms as she hugged her knees and shut her eyes, as if blinding herself would stop up her ears. Getting back at him, her mother sounded angry and bitter... *"at first I thought Anna was yours. Or I told myself she was. I realized only later, as she grew older. It was her nose and her mouth. David's mouth, David's nose..."*

Why, she'd thought, hadn't she been told? There had been something terrible about it all, her face going prickly with shame and confusion at overhearing such a thing. And then, her mother's voice again..."*You want to kill me, don't you? Of course you do. I've done the one thing a husband can never forgive. Well? What's stopping you?*"

The very next day Anders, with her mother in the passenger seat, had driven head-on into an approaching car on the *autostrada*. As a child she hadn't been told the details of the accident, apparently to spare her feelings. But she'd heard enough to have nightmares for days afterward, with visions of her mother, trapped and dying, in the car's crushed metal.

In her mind there had been only one explanation. Anders had murdered her mother. Even a six year old could tell that. They had had the fight. He had been the one driving. The fact that he had been badly injured, that he'd had to spend weeks in the hospital, only proved that Anders had risked his life to kill her. So it was as a little girl that Anna understood that men, when pushed, might kill their women. It was foolish of her mother to have dared Anders. "*What's stopping you,*" her mother had shouted at him. Did she have no regard for her own safety—or for her children's? Had she been *so* angry?

Not long ago, Anna had come to understand her mother's rage when she caught her own husband carrying on an affair—with one of her own patients. That ended the marriage for her. After working out the separation agreement, Anna had taken the children and driven from their home in Columbus, Ohio, to Anders' *casita* in Tucson, to stay there while looking for a place to live. Was it strange that she would seek even momentary refuge with Anders, this stepfather who had been so indifferent to her in his role as her father? What had she wanted from a man she'd held responsible for her mother's death for so long? Had it been her need to confront Anders with his guilt—and in so doing, come to terms with her ambiguous feelings, sexual and otherwise, towards men?

She remembered the expression of alarm on Anders' face, last October, when he opened the door of his *casita* and saw her standing there. She couldn't have predicted that her appearance on his doorstep would have such an effect on him. She'd told him she only meant to stay with him long enough to find a place of her own. Yes, she had eventually confronted him about his womanizing past, emotionally fueled, she supposed, by her own husband's betrayal. But she hadn't anticipated that after little more than two weeks Anders would claim that he couldn't bear being with her and her children in his little home. He had fled her to Italy, ill as he was, dying in Florence the day after he arrived. His hurried will left everything to her, including a sizable bank account. Had he suspected that he might die in Italy? He had withdrawn only enough funds necessary for his trip. She was left to assume that the inheritance was evidence of his guilty conscience. Yet she had felt guilt of her own. Hadn't her presence made him so uncomfortable that he was forced to leave his own home?

It was only after coming across Anders' journal, after he had left, that she learned the identity of her real father. *"David"* and *"Kunstler"* appeared in a number of its pages, revealing how much Anders had brooded over his rival. The wound her mother had given him that night so long ago in Italy had been deep.

With her father's name, and some of her detective work, Anna had been able to find his website, which revealed the name of his gallery and examples of his art. There had been no photo of him, and little biography. Would she be able to find in Mr. Kunstler a man she might call something close to a father—and children's grandfather?

Anna closed her eyes for a moment, took a deep breath, and moved on to Kunstler's acrylic wash, *Fear*. It was a frontal portrait of a balding man wearing European-style tinted glasses. He was sitting at a table with his sleeves rolled up, his bare elbows planted on the table surface. His fingers were locked below his chin, so that at first glance he seemed merely caught in contemplation. But there was a twist to the half-open lips and a leftward roll of the eyes behind the lenses, the whites showing, as if he were confronting a sudden threat. Could this have been a self-portrait? If so, what might have been the threat?

Anna shook her head and moved on to the next work, a Kunstler drawing behind glass that was another of the *Wraiths* series. A skeletal female figure floated against a glowing orange-red background. She was naked except for a trace of red miniskirt; her sunken chest and featureless face were overlaid with gray-green blotches. Could this have been a distorted image of her mother, the Kate of Kunstler's passion from long ago, with her nose, eyes, and mouth smudged to conceal her identity? Was the painting an expression of anger? Grief?

As Anna stared at the drawing she was startled to see a face materialize on the drawing's glass—a heart-shaped face with full lips, a prominent forehead, hazel eyes, a delicate nose— her *mother's* face. Anna shut her eyes and struggled for balance, willing the vertigo away. Had these intense thoughts of her mother called up a vision of her features from long ago?

Anna opened her eyes again. Her mother's face was still there. But, no, those features were *her own*. It was *her* reflection on the drawing's glass. Her mother, as she remembered her, had been almost the same age as she herself was now. Most galleries seemed to use non-reflective glass, but the glass over this drawing was reflective. Had Kunstler insisted on it, meaning to bind the viewer's reflection to the gruesome material, to convey the woman's devastation in a shocking, personal way? But why would he have done that? If Kunstler had had Kate in mind—somehow learning that her life had been smashed out in Italy—had he tried to convey his own horror?

Wandering as if in a trance, Anna left the back alcove that contained Kunstler's haunting work. She now found herself in a section of the gallery that showed more typical Western scenes and portraits of American Indians—subject matter that Kunstler's website had led her to expect. Though she had learned something of Western art during the months of her search, she didn't recognize any of these artists' names.

One painting was of Indian children gathered around the entrance of an adobe home. It was titled, simply, *Children*. One little boy, dressed in leather britches and soft-fringed boots, had an especially poignant expression, as if he had lost someone dear. Anna thought of her little brother, of the years with him that had followed the accident that had taken their mother away. She and Thomas had often been left alone, evenings, with the housekeeper, while Anders had been off with one of the women he pursued in those days.

Lost in a flood of confused feelings, Anna returned to the Kunstler alcove, barely noticed the click of heels on the hardwood floor behind her.

"If you have any questions about our artists," came a woman's voice, "I'll be happy to answer them."

Chapter Two

Anna's thoughts flew like startled birds. She turned to find a heavily made-up, middle-aged woman standing behind her. The woman was wearing a lemon-colored Western-style shirt and a gray calf-length skirt set off with a turquoise-studded Concho belt. Ten minutes earlier she had glanced up from her desk as Anna entered, undoubtedly to size her up: was she a likely prospect—or just a vacationer who'd wandered in on a day in mid-June with little intention of buying anything?

"His work is wonderful, isn't it?" the woman said, with the coolly alert manner of a sales veteran.

"I have to say I was expecting something different, " Anna began. Her experience of her father's work felt so personal that the saleswoman's question seemed beside the point. Yet the woman might be helpful, she realized, in her effort to meet him. "I checked Kunstler's web site before I came in, and found only Southwest desert landscapes, Native Americans, and pueblo villages—like most of the other art you show here."

"That's interesting. How did you hear about our artist?"

"I recalled his name from something a relative wrote some time ago."

"I see," the woman said. "I'll have to remind the gallery owner to update Kunstler's home page. The artist stopped doing the Western and Indian work some time ago. Now he does these," she said with an expansive gesture of her hand.

Anna pointed to Kunstler's work, *Fear*. "Would this by any chance be the artist's self-portrait?" She felt self-conscious, as if asking this stranger to verify her damaged family tree. Again, she sensed the woman studying her, trying to fit her into a profile—this tourist in the denim skirt and sandals, with her fluffy, cinnamon-colored hair: was she someone who might spend a good deal for a David Kunstler work?

"A resemblance? Possibly, when he was younger. I don't often see him now. Mr. Kunstler rarely visits the gallery." She shrugged. "But his work *is* special, don't you think?" Her tone was confidential, as if searching out Anna's tastes.

"Well, yes, it *is* special," Anna said. "There's an honesty about the portrayal. You get the feeling that the dark details aren't contrived."

"They're not contrived at all, considering his background. As a child he spent much of his youth in Germany—part, actually, in a Nazi extermination camp. These stabs of black and the distorted figures carry hints of the harrowing things he must have experienced." She glanced at Anna. "But the work transcends the macabre, don't you think?"

Anna tried to absorb the information: *her mother fell in love with a survivor of the Nazi camps?* Was he Jewish? Russian? Gypsy? Something else? Half her genes were his, if her mother was speaking the truth about her affair all those years ago. She found herself recoiling, as if she could suddenly smell the tragic, decomposing bodies she'd once seen in pictures. There had to be something almost heroic in her father's emerging alive from such horror. "It's all so unexpected," she said, taking a step back.

"Well, I wouldn't claim that his art flies off the walls. But you might be surprised at the range of buyers of his work," the woman said, smiling at her.

"Really?"

"There are shrewd collectors—those who know which art will appreciate in value, and which won't." The woman cocked her head and appeared to study *Fear* and its balding, dark-lensed subject. "A banker from Cincinnati bought one. Even an Italian museum director. A woman from Maryland bought one of his just two weeks ago. So did a German tourist. You never know. Art speaks variously to different people...*chaque à son goût*, as the French say."

Anna smiled, wondering whether to believe such claims. And there was that French phrase. "You're referring to *taste*?"

"Naturally, the French expression refers not to good or bad taste," the woman answered quickly, "only that taste varies. Kunstler's images touch people differently for reasons that may have nothing to do with the artist's impressions of life and death."

Yes, Anna thought again. The gaunt female in the *Wraiths* series had her wondering about her father's taste in women. Had he been after the fashion runway sort? Had he been after the erotic vulnerability that love can demand of a woman? Still, there was male vulnerability in *Fear,* too, something men usually tried to hide. She thought of her soon-to-be ex-husband. Sanderson's professorial restraint had really been a protective distance he'd adopted. Yet that restraint, she reminded herself, had promised her a measure of the freedom to be herself.

The thought of Sanderson made Anna turn away. Something about the mutilated figures in these drawings was triggering the sense of betrayal and anger she'd felt eight months ago, when she'd discovered her husband's affair. She had always taken pains to live her life on an even keel, keeping her emotions at bay, just in case. Life was unpredictable, and you didn't want to be surprised and upended at a vulnerable moment. Losing her mother so suddenly and painfully had ingrained that in her. Marriage with Sanderson had been a comfortable if staid eight-year existence. He'd had his professorial career, and while Tommy and Katey were in daycare or at school, she could have her small but absorbing psychotherapy practice.

Standing there, Anna felt the nakedness of those mutilated figures in Kunstler's art. They seemed to mirror the rawness she'd felt after the betrayal. A visceral pang would gouge her stomach without warning. Now that the children were away, she missed bathing Tommy and Katey before dinner, toweling their wet, wriggling bodies before slipping them into their pajamas. She missed the children's chatter over dinner, even their squabbling over small things.

In her memory there were times when Sanderson seemed less objectionable. In the early years he would compliment her on how nice she looked on a given evening. He was attentive, almost romantic when it mattered. There were moments when she could almost believe, looking back, that her home in Columbus had been something she'd always wanted. But then her anger would return, even as she knew that the fault couldn't have been all his.

Yesterday she had put the children on a plane back to Ohio. Sanderson had agreed to keep them for two months, until mid-August. This temporary loss of her children was clouding the exhilaration she had hoped to feel in beginning the task of reorienting herself, the chance to reorganize her life along new lines. So far, Sanderson had been reasonable. Of course he had young, blonde Heather by his side to comfort him.

As if on cue, her memory called up that tear-stained face from Ohio: a young woman who had come to her for therapy. Petite, pale, blonde, with huge brown eyes, Heather was in love with a married man who refused to divorce his wife. He was stringing her along, she claimed. A woman yearning for an unavailable man—it was an old story, often repeated. Anna had explained that she had a full schedule and saw patients only Tuesdays and Thursdays. Heather persisted. She somehow "knew" that *only* Anna could help. Nobody else. She had such a wonderful reputation. Yes, one hundred dollars an hour could be managed. A patient's motivation being half the battle, Anna agreed. How could she have known?

It had been last September when Heather cancelled her morning appointment at the last moment. Anna had decided to use the hour to pick up a few groceries at the Giant Eagle Market. On the way there, she happened to pass Sanderson driving in the opposite direction in his blue Camry. A woman was in the passenger seat. Sanderson had been talking to her as he passed, too quickly for Anna to make out who she was.

Curious, Anna had made a U-turn at the next intersection and followed them. Their car had pulled into a motel and parked. Anna had slipped into a space nearby and watched as Sanderson and Heather hurried out of the car and into the motel. They were so preoccupied with each other that they never spotted her, fifteen yards away. She couldn't believe what she was seeing. *Heather*—her patient, with her *husband?* She felt her face on fire.

She had driven home in a daze, running a red light, barely avoiding an accident. Shock struggled with disbelief as disbelief disintegrated into mental paralysis. What should she do? Pretend she'd seen nothing, and continue with her marriage as if nothing had happened? Her mind snagged itself on the motel. Their trysting in that mundane motel somehow fit—the banality, the sordidness.

That evening she had waited for Sanderson to come home. When he arrived at eight-thirty, she'd asked, in a determinedly small voice, "So, how was your day?"

"The usual," he'd said as he hurried up the stairs to change his clothes.

"Dinner is ready, Sanderson. I don't want it to get cold. Why don't you change afterwards?"

"I'll be just a minute."

She followed him up the stairs. "Why in such a hurry to get your clothes off?"

He turned and looked at her. "What do you mean?"

"I mean you're in such a hurry. Almost as if your clothes are dirty," she said, surprising herself with a strange laugh.

His face reddened. "I don't know what you're talking about."

"Motels are filthy," she said, the words spilling from her mouth.

The color left his face. "I don't know what you're talking about."

"I went for groceries this morning when Heather cancelled her appointment. You and Heather passed me in your car. Naturally I was surprised. I did a U-turn..."

"We were just..."

"Having a conference in that motel?"

Sanderson flew into a rage. "What are you doing, spying on me? Who the hell do you think you are?" He slammed his fist into the wall—and hunched over from the pain.

"I'm your wife. At least I thought I was."

The next day she couldn't help studying her five foot six, thirty-eight-year-old figure before their full-length mirror. *My body has its curves,* she remembered thinking. *And my curves are firm, not flabby.*

Standing there in the gallery, months later, in her denim skirt, crisp white blouse and wedged sandals, it still bothered her: was she still attractive? Men's glances lingered on her face and figure, didn't they? Her curves were still...

"Excuse me..."

Anna flinched. She had almost forgotten where she was, looking at her father's artwork.

"Are you thinking about the prices of the Kunstlers?" asked the gallery woman.

"No, no. I was just wondering what motivates people to..."

"Excuse me?"

"Just that I wonder how we can fathom such distressed subjects. We wake up in the middle of the night wondering why someone did something to us."

"I know what you mean. It's why a person chooses one work and not another. Sometimes one that costs as little as a couple of thousand," she added in a helpful tone, "can carry a message that is a tribute to both artist and investor."

How smoothly she slipped in that price, Anna thought. Yes, she had to pretend to be a buyer. "I admit I'm interested in this portrait. But to have his work hanging in my home I would really like to know more about the artist."

"I understand," the woman said, nodding. "Do you live here in Santa Fe, or are you visiting?"

"I've just moved to the Pojoaque area."

"Well, I understand that Mr. Kunstler lives near Las Trampas, on the High Road to Taos. Of course our whole area is simply drenched in art history. *Los Cinco Pintores,* and the rest," the woman said, leaving the phrase hanging.

"*Los Cinco...?*"

"Bakos, Ellis, Mruk, Nash and Shuster were known as The Five Painters after their 1921 show at the New Mexico Museum of Art, as it was known in those days. You can just imagine what their work brings nowadays."

"Oh?"

"Sometimes in the hundreds of thousands."

"I confess I'm not an art collector," Anna replied. "I'm just attracted to this particular artist's work. Kunstler's."

"Well, if you buy one of his because you love it, you can't lose, can you?"

Anna decided to be direct. "Would it gain me an introduction to the artist?"

The woman sighed. "He's *very* reclusive."

"Again, I would like to know more about him. Perhaps I could talk to the gallery owner?"

"He's not here, but I could inquire further for you about Mr. Kunstler. I do have a brochure I could give you." She smiled. "I'm Jane Wilcox. If you'll give me your phone number...excuse me, your name is?"

"Anna Croft." Anna *Summers,* her mother's name, she reminded herself, when she got around to officially changing it. "Will the gallery owner be in tomorrow by any chance?"

Ms. Wilcox's smile faded. "I'm afraid Mr. Sharpe won't be in until next Monday."

Anna guessed Jane Wilcox would have preferred to wrap up the sale herself. But there was no question of a purchase, at least not now. She thanked Jane for the brochure, and walked out, letting the door close behind her. How convenient it would be, she mused, if she had Jane's access to the artists. She stood in the bright sun and read the glossy brochure…*David Kunstler is a contemporary artist whose work includes drawing, painting, monotypes and sculpture. Born in Germany, much of his evocative work was shaped by his childhood experiences during the war. A piano prodigy, he survived the Holocaust to emigrate to America where he studied music at a New York conservatory before moving on to the study of painting and drawing at several top New York art academies. He has exhibited in Paris, Berlin, New York, Tokyo, San Francisco, Chicago, and Santa Fe. The artist presently lives in Northern New Mexico.*

Anna glanced up from the brochure, lost in thought. So, he was a pianist before he was a painter. It was all so strange. And he studied music in New York, where her mother also studied when she began what she hoped would be her piano career. Was it possible that he studied at the same place—at the Manhattan Conservatory? Could that have been where they met?

Chapter Three

Curious about other art galleries in Santa Fe, Anna found over the next week that although some specialized in Western and Pueblo art, others showed abstract and expressionist work. By comparison, her father's painting was unusual for its apocalyptic tone.

As for the galleries themselves, Anna read in a guide book that most were once earth-floored adobe or territorial-style homes that Hispanic families had owned and passed down from generation to generation. Living space was added over centuries, warrens of small rooms to accommodate new children and elderly relatives. By mid-twentieth century the art entrepreneurs were arriving in force. They bought up the old houses, knocked down the interior walls, gave them an inviting sheen, and set up shop. Many old New Mexican families, some descended from the original Spanish settlers of the 1600s, moved away as real estate prices and property taxes skyrocketed.

Anna stopped one day on Canyon Road to gaze at the broad leafy crowns of thick-trunked cottonwoods that stood over some of the galleries like grizzled sentinels. What had the street looked like when the trees were young and the street was dirt, a place where children could play? She read that in the old days, woodcutters, their burros laden with piñon wood from the Sangre de Cristo Mountains, used to sell it door-to-door along *El Camino del Cañon*. Beyond the gallery roofs to the northeast, Anna could see the mountain peaks of this Southern end of the Rockies. The snow had melted from their summits, leaving brownish-green patches above the tree lines that she guessed were wind-scoured grasses—a crabbed life restoring itself after winter.

The Blood-of-Christ mountains, or Sangre de Cristos, as the Spanish named them, made Anna think of the Tuscan Apennines. She had seen those again when she'd had Anders buried near Florence. They were mountains she'd known as a child, visible from the farmhouse they had rented during the year of Anders' sabbatical. She could remember her mother, exhausted after hours of piano practice, sitting on the low wall in front of their *casa colonica* farmhouse, lost in thought, staring through the summer haze at the mountains. What had her mother been thinking so deeply about? Could she have been lonely, recalling vanished days and nights with a lover named David?

In her third week, out for a walk in town, Anna's thoughts were interrupted by a reedy voice. Staring at her from a few feet away was a teenage girl, her dirty blonde hair straggling out from under her red wool cap.

"Excuse me, but my car just ran out of gas," the girl whispered. "Could you spare ten dollars so I can get back home to Albuquerque?"

Before she could answer, Anna noticed a skinny boy in a dark gray hoodie eyeing them from a corner of a building on her left. A hoodie on a warm spring day? He looked away as she spotted him. She understood. The girl would appear more sympathetic if her boyfriend made himself scarce. Not gas, *grass* was probably what they wanted to buy.

Anna smiled at the girl. "I'm parked just down the street. You'll need a ride to the gas station if your car is out of gas. Do you have a container to put it in?"

The girl shook her head.

"That's all right, they probably sell them at the station. Let's go," she said, starting in the direction of her car.

The girl didn't move. She glanced at the skinny boy with the hoodie, who jerked his head at her. "That's all right," the girl said, backing away from Anna. "We don't have time."

At their age, they *should* have time, Anna reflected, as the girl and the boy vanished around the corner. But if they had chosen the drug road, the girl was right—they might have little time. Young people didn't understand that death reaches out and touches us at any moment. Her own brother hadn't understood that…poor Thomas, having his whole life to live, succumbing to heroin. Then there was Anders, her stepfather, enraging a jealous Florentine into killing him, his womanizing catching up with him.

It had been on a rainy afternoon last November that Anna buried Anders next to her mother's tomb in Greve, a town near Florence. She and a Florentine Contessa, who had once been Anders' lover, stood in the rain under their umbrellas and watched the cemetery attendants lower the casket into the grave. Anna couldn't keep her eyes from wandering from the casket to the small faded photograph set into the nearby marble tombstone. It was a picture of her mother, Kate Croft, taken at about her own age. The image had filled her heart with old sensations of yearning and dread.

As a child, when her mother was killed, Anna had felt the panic of not knowing where to turn. She had been two years younger than her own daughter, Katey, was now. Losing her mother that year had marked the end of being tucked in at night, safe against the darkness. Even then, she'd known Anders to be unreliable. She would be the one to look after her little brother, who at four was too young to comprehend the catastrophe. He'd thought his mother would be home soon from the village to run her hand through his tousled hair.

Anna had sworn early on never to marry an Anders. She'd promised herself that *she* would have a long and happy marriage. But now that she had left Sanderson Blackwell after eight years, she had to admit to herself that she had very much married an Anders Croft. The emotional slog of hammering out the separation agreement over the winter was over. A psychotherapist with insight into these matters, she had nonetheless become one of the many whose lives had become messy, in the end paying to see a therapist like herself. The coming divorce was necessary, but such a defeat.

Putting Katey and Tommy on the plane to Ohio for the agreed two months with her estranged husband was harder than she had expected. She had been so busy preparing them for the trip that she had almost forgotten to emotionally prepare herself for the coming weeks without them. She'd had to hold back her tears as she showered them with kisses.

Training her emotion and energy on searching for her biological father had in some ways become a relief from the heartache of divorce. Was that part of what her quest was about, to fill a void that had opened up within her? At times it seemed too melodramatic a project for the reasoning professional she considered herself to be. Was she bent on creating a new Anna through a new father, righting life's errors? She still had no idea what sort of man she might discover, but she hoped he might be a good grandfather for her children. Would she know, when she and he came face to face, if he was at least safe? She planned on being cautious in approaching a transplanted European artist who drew and painted such desperate images.

The challenge would be how to arrange a meeting with him. Not even buying one of his expensive paintings would guarantee her an introduction. What other tactic could she use? Would she be able to find in herself the cunning of the animals of the Navajo legends, tricksters of the book she's been reading to the children at bedtime? Was it time for her, a health professional, to learn to scheme, as Heather did, to get what she wanted? Anna laughed at herself. How life could come full circle. Hadn't she always thought scheming beneath her? Must she deceive like Coyote, who brought Death into the world by promising both First Man and First Woman immortality if the rock hidden under his blanket would float in the nearby river?

Finding her car, Anna climbed in, started the car, and drove slowly up the street, pausing once to allow a group of heedless tourists to wander across in front of her. She had bought the low-mileage Subaru Outback in Columbus for the trip west. It had so far proven itself at off-road driving in the desert. But she'd chosen it mainly for its carrying capacity and—the children in mind—for its safety. Yes, safety. What car had Anders been driving with her mother on the *autostrada*, years ago? Wasn't it an Alfa Romeo—a small, fragile sports car—that ended her life?

Turning right from Canyon Road onto Camino del Monte Sol, her first thought was to drive up the hill past where, according to her guidebook, sanitariums had housed tuberculosis patients in the 1930's and '40's. Men and women from the East had arrived in droves, it said, for the cure of the dry desert air. Across the Atlantic, she knew, Nazis were setting up camps surrounded by electrified fences to imprison enemies of the Reich, including a boy named David Kunstler.

On impulse, she turned off Monte Sol onto Acequia Madre. She followed the road as it twisted right, then left, squeezing between old adobe houses. She was cruising with her windows down, hoping the breeze would help quell the periodic pangs she'd been feeling at being separated from Tommy and Katey. She slowed the car at the faint sound of a piano being played nearby. The piano notes were coming from a long, one-story building on her right. She pulled into its gravel parking area. Nobody seemed to be around to mind her parking there. She turned off the motor and listened. It was a piece by Beethoven, a theme and variations sonata, one of those her mother once played. Gliding arpeggios floated out of the building's open windows. The piano sound made her think of her father and her mother—both pianists, studying music in New York. Really, mustn't that have been where they met?

Two years earlier, little Katey had begged for piano lessons after seeing a young Korean girl perform on TV. The old upright in their Jacona rental had turned out to be just the thing for her—a little out of tune, but fine for practice. As for Tommy, he had no obvious musical talent, at least not yet. He enjoyed scrabbling in the dirt, collecting bugs and worms, frogs and toads. Now he had a feral kitten. He'd brought Ma-i home a few weeks ago from one of what he called his 'venture walks' in the neighborhood. Finding the kitten had cheered Tommy up for a while. The coming divorce had touched him more than Katey. After arriving in Santa Fe he'd entered a world of his own, separate from his mother and his sister, demanding not more affection, but less. Anna hoped it was only a phase.

But what was happening in Ohio? Were the children safe? Was Sanderson at least paying attention to the four-page, single-spaced letter she'd sent, detailing the children's schedule? Did he understand the importance of their bath before a seven o'clock dinner, and their bedtime no later than eight o'clock? She wrote of Tommy's nightmares, omitting divorce as their probable cause, if only to keep the hatchet buried. She had insisted that Tommy have his little yellow rabbit with the brown button eyes when he went to bed— also suggested that Sanderson have the rabbit talk to him in a squeaky voice. She reminded Sanderson that ventriloquism was a parenting art.

She wrote that he should ignore Katey's compulsion to line up her shoes in a neat row at the foot of her bed. Also, that he must resist correcting her obsession about spacing her clothes in her closet the exact same distance apart. Their daughter, she explained, coped by creating her own kind of certainty in an uncertain world. Finally, she reminded Sanderson to keep up payments on the Baldwin upright so that Katey could practice when she was with him.

In her letter to Sanderson she made no mention of Heather. Would she have moved in already, appropriating *her* house? Once again, the thought of the interloper's deceit was enough to make Anna seethe—her coming to her as she had in the beginning, begging to be her patient. There'd been hints. Why hadn't she guessed? At one point in therapy, Heather had described to her the obsessive sex she was having with her married lover, complaining that though the older man was good in bed, he was too possessive. How, she'd asked Anna, should she deal with her lover's jealousy? Anna had warned of the allure of a married man, that she might be hurt. Married men were a bad bet, she'd advised. Anna would never forget the strange, secret smile on Heather's face.

Tiring of the piano music, Anna started the car and backed out. She drove slowly down Acequia Madre until she approached a crossing at an elementary school. Yellow lights were flashing. A gray-uniformed guard, middle-aged and stocky, was monitoring the cars' 15 MPH speed with a warning eye as he delivered children, one by one, to their parents' waiting cars. The scene reassured her that New Mexico would be a safe place for her children, whether that happened to be in Santa Fe or Jacona.

She decided to call Ohio that night just to check on things.

Chapter Four

Anna took the highway home later that afternoon. On the way, she picked up milk and a dozen eggs at the Pojoaque market. Noticing the many Hispanic foods on display, she made a mental note to try cooking *posole,* a Southwestern dish made with hominy and pork.

She left Pojoaque, taking a secondary road west that led her past a number of massive hills of compacted, rust-colored volcanic ash. Her guidebook called them *barrancas,* Spanish for ravines. The book explained that a huge caldera lay eighteen miles further northwest. When a series of volcanoes had erupted in the area between sixty thousand and a million and a half years ago, they had forged many of Northern New Mexico's surface features, including the *barrancas* and the Jemez Mountain Range. The central caldera lay nestled in the Jemez, asleep but not dead. Its lava domes occasionally bulged into view, and its vents sometimes steamed. With its next unpredictable eruption, it might demolish everything for hundreds of miles in all directions.

A part of Anna missed the fresh rain and greenness of an Ohio spring and, years before that, the choruses of spring peepers in the wetlands of her North Carolina childhood. This Western desert had no obvious pulse of life, but she was

beginning to find in the spare folds of the land and the sil-
houettes of the buttes and mesas a different kind of beauty.
The stark simplicity of the land matched the directness of her
New Mexico mission: to find a man named David Kunstler.

She continued driving on the blacktop that ran beside the
nearly dry arroyo that edged the *barrancas*. After two miles,
now in Jacona, she turned right, easing into and up the other
side of the roadside arroyo. Two chestnut-colored quarter
horses watched her from her neighbor's corral. Long-tailed
black and white magpies, perched on the horses' backs, were
picking off flies, thirsty for blood in the dry afternoon heat.
Anna drove down a narrow dirt drive for several minutes,
and slowed as she reached what was, for the time being, her
home.

She noticed Lant Wolverton working on the glass-paned
front door of the small, four-room guesthouse she had rented
from him and his wife. Lant and Betsy were splitting up, and
Betsy has already moved into Santa Fe. They'd been discussing the terms of what they called a friendly divorce. Their
example gave Anna the sense that hers was only one in a
wave of couples all over America that were on their way to
divorce court.

Anna drove past Lant and parked at the far end of the
guesthouse near the clothesline, a rope strung between a
metal pole and a Russian olive tree. When she had moved in,
she'd asked about a clothes dryer. Lant had told her there was
no need for one. Clothes dried in no time in the dry desert
wind, he'd said, not mentioning that her towels and sheets
would wind up as stiff as cardboard.

Anna switched off the ignition and waited, the tips of her
fingers on her carton of eggs, as she watched Lant in her rear
view mirror. He had stopped scraping paint off the door and

was staring in her direction. Was he again using the condition of her front door as an excuse to talk to her? When she'd signed the lease in April she had told Betsy she valued her privacy. She had repeated that when she moved in. Anna was wary of his interest in her. In her experience, men who were divorcing were often needy and anxious to prove themselves. Had she found Lant attractive, her attitude might have been different.

Through her windshield she studied the sagebrush and low-lying cactus. The sun was well past its zenith, deepening the flesh color of the desert's sandy folds and ridges that stretched up toward the *barrancas*. She would have liked to be alone with the desert. She felt a twinge of regret, wishing for the calm of solitude so soon after having put the children on the plane. Why couldn't Lant have been someplace else, or at least in his house, forty yards distant?

"That cat of yours has been havin' a heck of a time scratchin' on the door," Lant drawled as Anna walked toward him, carrying her eggs and milk. He had stopped scraping and was leaning against the doorframe. The thumb of his left hand was hooked on his belt and he was holding a putty knife in his right hand. Tall and rangy, he had on a dusty black Stetson, a blue denim shirt, worn jeans and scuffed brown cowboy boots. His looks reminded her a little of an aging Willem Dafoe, but his face had none of the actor's expressiveness.

Lant pushed his hat back and smiled, showing his stained teeth. "He must be gettin' itchy, left all alone in there."

"Solitude isn't so bad," she replied. "In the wild, his mother would have had to leave him at times to catch food." She was now almost in front of him, waiting for him to step aside so she could go in. "Besides, it teaches him self-reliance."

"Well now, who wants a self-reliant cat? Better a self-reliant man." He stared down at her with his squinty brown eyes. Was he waiting for acknowledgement of what he seemed to assume was his cowboy charm?

Anna pretended not to notice. "I have found in life that self-reliant men are not always so reliable. Lant, may I get by and put my eggs in the refrigerator?"

"Sure thing," he said, without moving. "You know, when I first laid eyes on you I told myself, Lant, that new tenant of yours—that Anna—she's a real firecracker. She's pretty and she's got class and nobody's going to push her around. I like that in a woman."

"I'm glad I've made such a good first impression. It's easier when tenants and landlords get along."

"Truer words were never spoken. Yes ma'am, I hope we're going to get to be real good friends."

Something about Lant had Anna imagining that he would wipe his face with his sleeve after a plate of barbecue. She had no idea if he ate barbecue, it was just the image she had of him. She shifted the carton of eggs to her other hand. "Lant, just one small thing. Did Betsy mention to you that my privacy was important to me?"

At mention of Betsy's name, his grin faded. "She told me something about that. But I chalked it up to Betsy's being her usual jealous self. When we were together, every time a woman so much as smiled at me she'd get a little crazy."

"Well," Anna said, "I treasure my solitude. Really."

"There were times I didn't know whether Betsy was jealous of me or jealous of the other woman," Lant said, twisting his head around to spit tobacco juice in the dust. "Sometimes I wonder why she wanted to get married in the first place."

Anna sighed and took a step toward the door, but he didn't move.

"Marriage is a funny thing," he said. "You think you love someone, and after the fun's over you take a good look at her one fine morning and realize you don't know why you're even there." He raised an eyebrow. "Ever happen to you?" Anna had told Betsy of her divorce, and Betsy had probably told Lant, in which case he might have been checking if it would profit him to fish in these particular waters. "Marriages end for many reasons," she said quietly. "I have two fine children, and they're a blessing. As I told Betsy, I want privacy—both for myself and for them when they're here with me."

"Said like a lady," Lant said, squinting down at her. "But your little ones aren't around now, are they? Gives you a chance to ease up on yourself and have a little fun."

The kitten was mewing on the other side of the door. It must have heard her voice. "Lant, I'm tired and I want to get these things in the refrigerator. Would you mind stepping aside?"

"In just a minute. Almost finished here." He turned to the door and ran the putty knife along the edge of a glass pane. "Got to get this place sparkling. We're selling the place, you know. Going get top dollar for it. In a couple of weeks Betsy'll be bringing buyers around." He peered at her over his shoulder. "Betsy told you that, I hope. Respecting your privacy and all."

Betsy had mentioned the possibility of the house and guesthouse being shown for sale. "Yes, she did. But she said the summer season was usually quiet."

Lant made a sucking sound with his lower lip. "I'm between real estate offices right now or I'd show it myself. I'm well known around here after all these years." He turned and stared off into the distance. "I'm the kind of man who if

I see an opportunity, I make it happen." His eyes went squinty again. "Could be oil, could be cattle, could be real estate. No difference to me."

Anna wondered if Lant really had a job. She guessed he probably hadn't worked for years. Betsy probably got tired of that.

"I've fixed up the main house," he said importantly. "Patched the stucco outside, new coat of paint on the inside. Why don't you come on up and take a look? I could mix up some margaritas."

"I don't drink during the day, Lant. Would you mind letting me in?"

Lant didn't move, instead lit up a cigarette. "We're asking a ton o' money for this place," he said.

She wondered if she should just push past him. "And I'm sure you'll get it. Now…" But she didn't want to touch him— nor did she want *him* to touch *her*.

"We'll be looking for around a million." He checked her out of the corner of his eye. "This is a pretty select community. Upscale, you know. House comes with fourteen acres and the guesthouse, with its good rental income." He tipped his Stetson at the guesthouse as if respecting its healthy income stream. "But you already know about that," he said with a wink.

Anna laughed in spite of herself. Something about him was so predictable. He had to be casting for a replacement for his departed sugar-mommy. "If the time comes that I decide to put down roots in New Mexico, I'll be sure to let Betsy know."

A flash of anger crossed Lant's face. "You don't need to talk to her. I'm the one you need to talk to." He stared down at his cigarette and flicked off the ash. "Betsy has no conscience—she'd sell you a house you'd regret. New Mexico real estate is full of tangled codes and ownership rights going back to the original Spanish land grants. Newcomers get taken all the time. I'll make sure that doesn't happen to you." His voice dropped to a whisper. "I'll take good care of you, Anna."

The kitten's mewing was more insistent. "I'm sure you would, Lant, if that time ever came. But right now it's time for me to feed the kitten. Excuse me," she said, as she brushed by him and unlocked her front door. She opened it a crack, careful not to let the kitten out, then slipped inside, locking the door behind her.

Chapter Five

Anna scooped up Ma-i and stroked his fur. The kitten twisted and nipped at her finger with his sharp little teeth. "We won't let Lant hurt you," she whispered. She pressed him to her cheek. Ma-i began to purr. "We'll be on guard when he's around." Tommy had found the gray, tiger-striped kitten in the *arroyo* on their third day there. They'd named him Ma-i, the name for Coyote in the Navajo tales.

Anna had a soft spot for kittens. She'd never forgotten when, as a child in Italy, visiting neighbors, she had watched a farmer's wife chloroform three of them. "Why, why…?" she'd asked, as the kittens in the big jar with the saturated cotton slowly stopped squirming. *"Son' cattivi…"* the *contadina* neighbor had answered, raising her finger in warning. Knowing little Italian, she'd thought that *cattivi* must be the Italian word for cats. That was puzzling. Her mother had explained later that it meant wicked or nasty, and that some Italian peasants' feelings toward cats came from the old days when cats were thought by some to be witches in disguise. "It's sad for the kittens, some people having such old ideas," her mother had said, holding her and running her fingers through her hair.

She surveyed the interior of the adobe guesthouse, now

her home, with a pleasure that hadn't faded over the weeks. Each of its four main rooms connected in series with the next, which some city-dwellers might have called a railroad flat. The floor was red brick, while its walls were white plaster. The ceiling's whitewashed beams, or *vigas,* supported a roof insulated with sod, a centuries-old protection against the heat of the summer sun and the cold of winter. Sometimes, as she sat reading, tiny nodules of dirt from overhead cracks fell on the pages of her book.

The old upright piano that came with the place sat in the entry room, its brown varnish speckled, its brand name long vanished. Now that Katey was in Ohio, the piano was silent. The entry way opened into the kitchen, which in turn opened into a dining room that doubled as her office. In its corner sat an armchair, while nearby was an antique Italian trestle table. She had retrieved both pieces of furniture from Anders' *casita* in Tucson. The table's surface still bore a few circular traces from Anders' glasses of bourbon.

The next room was the children's. At the foot of a double bunk bed was a low table where Katey and Tommy did their drawing and watercolors. Their red-painted dresser stood against the wall next to the blue and white children's ward-robe.

The last room was hers. Beside the bed was a small table with her landline phone and a small lamp with a pretty brown Southwest-style base she'd bought in town. Against the opposite wall stood her 19th Century Italian dresser, carved from walnut, also brought from Tucson. Anna remembered Anders and her mother buying the dresser and the trestle table in an antique store on the outskirts of Florence some thirty years earlier. They were the only furniture she could call heirlooms.

Each of the two bedrooms had a raised *kiva* fireplace, with their traditional horseshoe-shaped openings. Lying in front of each fireplace was a tiny, mysterious heap of ash. An old Anglo woman with a beaded Indian headband had come by in mid-May and convinced Anna it was necessary to discourage evil spirits from lingering on the newly-occupied premises by burning smudge-sticks—small bundles of bound sagebrush. According to the woman, such spirits from the ancient past had been known to enter children's ears and give them night-mares. She had insisted that the resulting ash heaps remain undisturbed for at least a month to convince the spirits that the exorcism was genuine. After the sage smoke had cleared, the woman offered also to protect the three of them from the Taos Hum. The Hum, she explained, was a Pentagon-engi-neered stream of electromagnetic pulses engineered to force those within a 100-mile radius of Taos to support any current or future U.S. wars.

Anna had felt it prudent to make peace with such an inhab-itant of New Mexico so early in her stay. Katey and Tommy had watched, awe-struck, as the woman moaned and flailed her arms in the general direction of Taos. For several min-utes she recited what seemed to be incantations, before she finally fell silent. Then she held out her hand. Anna placed the agreed-on twenty dollars in her palm, incredulous at what she'd just witnessed.

As Anna watched the woman's old Chevy pickup clatter back up the far side of the *arroyo*, she wondered how the woman knew that Anna had moved into the guesthouse. It was unsettling to think of a network of such people spreading news of her arrival. In any case, Katey and Tommy said that they didn't want spirits crawling into *their* ears. Anna had to explain that the lady was not to be trusted, that she simply had to be humored. The children nevertheless begged her not to move the ash heaps. Now that they were in Ohio, it was time to sweep them up.

At a quarter to four—quarter to six in Columbus—Anna remembered that it was time to call before Katey and Tommy had their baths. Who, exactly, would be bathing them? Certainly not her ex-husband.

Sanderson answered, sounding distracted and stressed. His voice was pitched higher than usual. "The children are right here—wait a minute."

She heard him growling at someone—the children had probably been upsetting him.

"Katey will be here in a minute. Incidentally, my parents want to know how to pronounce the name of this town you're living in. You spelled it P-o-j-o-a-q-u-e."

Anna had a vivid image of Sanderson's elderly parents, retired and living in Florida. They had been peeved that she had decided to move west, taking their grandchildren so far away. Not that they had come to Ohio to see Katey and Tommy more than once a year. "Phonetically," she explained, "it's pronounced *Poh-WAH-kay*. Emphasis is on the middle syllable. But the neighborhood I'm in is Jacona, pronounced *Ha-KO-na*."

"Sorry I asked," he said. "The children are fine and I have your letter. Heather's got everything under control. Here's Katey."

"Hi, Mommy. We've already had our baths. Heather did it. She uses a sponge instead of a washcloth. She got soap in Tommy's eyes and made him cry."

Anna gritted her teeth. "Sponges and washcloths are both fine, sweetie. Have you had dinner yet?"

"No, we were about to, when you called."

"So you're fine?"

"Yes, we're fine," Katey said, her tone slightly impatient, as if wondering what her mother expected.

"Wonderful, honey, now let me talk to Tommy. You go have your dinner. Mommy loves you."

"You always say that."

"That's because I mean it." Through the phone Anna felt the turbulence filling the house she had recently called her own.

"Hi, Mommy!" Tommy's voice had an urgent quality. "How is Ma-i?"

"Ma-i is fine, honey. I miss you and so does Ma-i."

There was a brief silence. "How do you...how do you *know*?"

"How do I know what?"

"How do you know Ma-i *misses* me?"

"I can just tell, sweetie. He goes from room to room, looking for you."

"Oh."

"And Tommy, dear—when Heather gives you a bath, close your eyes tightly so soap won't get in them."

"It hurt, Mommy."

"I know. Now, darling, let Mommy talk to Daddy again. I want to ask him..."

There was a click. Tommy had hung up. Or had it been Sanderson? She'd wanted to ask if Heather still had her job, and if so, who was watching the children.

Anna sighed and hung up. He had said, *Heather's got everything under control.* Best, she decided, to leave things as they were, at least for the moment.

That evening, Anna tried to relax in the brown leather armchair as she leafed through the children's book of Navajo tales. She was trying to put aside her feelings of loneliness and loss after talking to Sanderson and the children. What was that prayer for serenity? *God grant us the serenity to accept the things we cannot change…the courage to change the things we can, and the wisdom to know the difference.* A tiny voice in her head asked yet again—should she have stayed with Sanderson for the sake of the children? Stupid question—love had disappeared. All she'd lost was the chance at a soulless marriage—the opportunity to tolerate a wandering husband. How would she have advised one of her patients? To stick it out? She felt anger rising in her gorge. Did her patients feel such anger as she dispensed her calm advice from a safe therapeutic distance? Her life had certainly taken a sharp turn, and it was humbling.

A picture in the book attracted her attention. A Navajo child was gazing up into the branches of a piñon tree. A mountain lion was glaring down at him. Would the animal attack? Would the child be saved? She turned the page, then another, to a picture of Coyote as he watched First Man and First Woman making the stars for the sky. But Coyote was up to mischief. He would soon scatter the stars, destroying the best-laid plans.

"So *he* was the one," Anna whispered sardonically.

She closed the book and stared up into the darkness of the overhead *vigas*. Would David Kunstler enjoy reading to his grandchildren? Would he even like the idea of *having* grandchildren, assuming he had none besides Katey and Tommy? He might be so wounded by the Nazi camps that he was emotionally eclipsed. So many questions. Would he be angry that she had searched him out? Would he be understanding and kind, or flinty and gruff? He might be happily married, of course. Or alone, too damaged to live with anyone. She shifted in her chair, and the leather squeaked. Would she have the patience to find out what he was like before telling him she was his daughter? What if he made sexual advances? Not knowing, he might consider her fair game. What then? So much would depend on how she handled things.

Contemplating so many variables was starting to fog her brain. It had been a long day. She got up and opened the window in front and the one in back to let in the warm breeze. Returning to the padded leather of the armchair, she found she couldn't stop her eyes from closing. She felt herself drifting off...drifting...dreaming...*odd shapes...they began flitting around the room with shrill cries—disembodied spirits laughing...small shadows separated and converged at high speed, dive-bombing like swallows, coming closer with each pass as the ceiling lamps rocked from the force of their mischief and the Taos hum rumbled and the shapes disappeared...now yips sounded just outside the window, coyotes after a rabbit, poor thing disoriented by the high-pitched yelps, unable in the dark to tell the direction, the panicked searching for a juniper for cover, crouched and terrified, the ceiling lamps rocking...rocking...*

Anna woke with a cry, lunging forward in her chair, as if to escape...what?

Above her, the ceiling lamps *were rocking*. Had it all been real?

She kept staring at the lamps. What was real and what wasn't? She was aware of a light breeze touching her face. Was it the night breeze through the open windows that sent them rocking? No wonder the coyote yips sounded so loud, with the back window open. She took a deep breath. The kitten was crouched at her feet, staring up at her, wide-eyed. The fur on his arched back was standing straight up.

Anna managed to get up to close the back window. Return-ing, she whispered to Ma-i, "Come here—I won't let them hurt you."

The kitten backed up, his ears flattened. Anna leaned for-ward, scooped him up, and began stroking under his chin. Usually this put him into a trance. But he nipped at her, his tiny hind legs churning, digging at her hand. Was he still terrified by the coyote yips? Anna kissed him, as she kissed Tommy and Katey when they needed calming—the way her mother's lips had brushed across her face when she was a child.

Ma-i was still not purring, even after soft stroking. He was on the alert, vigilant. Anna sighed and set the kitten on the floor. She slipped into the flip-flops she'd learned to wear to avoid the painful goat-head thorns she and the children occa-sionally tracked in from outside. She padded to the kitchen, grabbed the bottle of red wine she'd opened for dinner, and poured herself a glass. So much, she mused, for the smudge sticks keeping spirits away.

She stopped to listen. There it was again, that sound in her dream—a low, vibrating hum from the front window. The Taos Hum? *Really?* It had been there all along, but now it was louder. She went to the window and peered into the darkness. She made out the silhouette of a low-slung car a dozen yards away. Its lights were off. Had it been there long? If Lant had visitors, why had they parked here, she wondered, instead of at the main house? She backed away, went into the next room and sat down. As she considered whether to call Lant—of all people to have to call—she heard the car's engine rev up. Its wheels crunched on the dirt and gravel. She set down her glass and crept back to the front window. The car, with its red taillights and vibrating hum, was disappearing.

Chapter Six

At ten o'clock the following Monday morning, Anna found herself walking up the steps to the Sharpe gallery. She was wearing a peach blouse and a pair of gray linen slacks—no jeans for *this* occasion. Her stride in her elegant summer sandals was firmer and more purposeful than usual, in part to hide her nervousness. An idea had been bouncing around in her head for the last few days. Mightn't she make herself useful to Mr. Sharpe, with her expertise in psychology? Among the many people passing through his gallery, she might be able to spot the likelier prospects by asking the right questions.

She could work for him long enough, she thought, to find a way to meet David Kunstler. She could volunteer to be a sort of girl Friday, picking up paintings, delivering them and so on. If she met her father and things went well, she might decide to stay in Santa Fe with the children. She could then start a practice in counseling therapy, or even find a mental health position at a hospital in Santa Fe, or Albuquerque, an hour south.

Within minutes of entering the gallery, Jane Wilcox introduced her to Donald Sharpe, a tall, gaunt, fidgety middle-aged man whose salt-and-pepper hair tumbled to his shoulders.

Standing there in jeans and a leather vest over a white collared shirt, he had barely time to acknowledge Anna over the top of his tortoise-shell reading glasses before his attention was diverted by the entrance of a well-dressed Asian couple. Sharpe had apparently been expecting them. He dropped Anna with a muttered "See you in a few…" and escorted the couple down a short hallway that apparently led to his office.

Sharpe's brush-off irritated her. Did he mean—a few *minutes*? *Hours*? But she realized that the Asian couple might be important collectors. They might be newly arrived from China with money to spend, searching for an unusual American acquisition to impress friends back in Shanghai or Beijing.

Anna nodded to Jane and slipped into the Kunstler alcove. She went straight to the *Wraiths* drawing of the skeletal woman with the red miniskirt. Kunstler, she saw, had made her rib cage stand out from the canvas almost in relief. Was this the sort of art the Asian couple might be interested in? Anna hoped so, feeling the stirrings of a vested interest in her father's success.

By the time Anna left the alcove, Jane had returned to her desk and was going over some papers, perhaps resigned to the idea that Anna would buy only from Donald Sharpe, if she bought at all.

Twenty minutes later, Anna approached Jane again. "How long do you suppose they'll be?" she asked.

Jane glanced up. "Their meeting? You never know. Maybe a few minutes, maybe hours," she said, shrugging.

Was she implying that Anna would not be waiting if she had bought one of the Kunstlers from *her* last week? But Anna had come this far and waited this long—another hour or so wouldn't matter to her. She decided to spend the time imagining she was a buyer, comparing her father's work with that of the others on display. As she moved around the room, she again found most of the paintings to be variations on the Southwest Art she had found in books and on the Internet. Much of the work was by artists whose names were unfamiliar, though their styles were not. Some oil landscapes were thickly layered with heavy brush strokes in browns and greens, while others gleamed brightly. Several used strong acrylic colors in patterns that reminded her of the towering red formations of volcanic tuff lining the steep road that wound its way toward Los Alamos.

Again she wondered why Sharpe included the mix of traditional Southwest art and the avant-garde work—including her father's—under the same roof. Did it pay for a gallery to be eclectic? Did it broaden the appeal to more prospects? She had much to learn. As she studied a painting whose layered horizontal elements combined into what seemed a hallucinogenic parody of an O'Keeffe, Anna heard raised voices from the office down the hall. Men were almost shouting at each other. A woman's voice broke in. There was silence, then a male voice...

"...got to factor in the risk, you understand? No changing the price on this..." There was no trace of an accent, so Anna assumed it was Sharpe. She glanced over at Jane, but if Wilcox heard the voices she gave no sign. She was probably used to the noise of back-office haggling. Risk—Anna heard the word again. What risk was Sharpe talking about?

Whatever it was they'd negotiated, Sharpe and the Asian couple reappeared. Stalking over to Jane's desk, they muttered between themselves for a few moments before the couple left. Anna watched Jane nod in her direction and whisper something to Sharpe. In seconds he was at her side.

"May I help you?" he intoned, his voice rich and authoritative. "I'm Donald Sharpe. I understand you're interested in a David Kunstler?"

Anna was amused at her sudden status as a potential customer. "Yes, I'm interested in Kunstler's work, but I'd like to know more about him before I can think of buying something."

"Forgive me," he interrupted politely, "but we prefer to think of it as *investing* in art." His voice had become low and indulgent. "Works of art are like stocks, or gold, except that you can see and enjoy them on the walls of your home. I think of myself as an investment counselor. It's my job to be candid about the value of a drawing or painting. Selling art is not like selling cars that lose half their value the day after the sale." His eyes narrowed. "Any investment I recommend will increase in value and last a lifetime," he said, his brown eyes fixing her over his reading glasses.

Unfamiliar with the art market as she was, Anna couldn't help wondering about such a sales pitch. It was hasty and pretty glib. Sharpe's manner reminded her of one of Anders' graduate students, years earlier in North Carolina, when she was only seventeen. His name was Vaughn—he'd been brilliant and knew it. One day, Vaughn showed up at their house when Anders was on campus teaching a class. Tall and brash, he'd stood there in the doorway, his eyes devouring her through his horn-rimmed glasses as he discoursed, rapid-fire, on a weird subject she can't recall. His hands had twitched nervously, as if they might suddenly reach out and grab her. When she'd made her lack of interest clear, Vaughn became obnoxious. In so many words he called her a birdbrain. Afterward, when Vaughn had continued his conferences with Anders, she did her best to avoid him.

Anna studied Sharpe now, and decided it was worth letting

him know she was not a birdbrain. If her plan had any chance, he would need to respect her.

"I understand," she said, "but I research anything before I invest *or* buy. I would like to know more about Mr. Kunstler—an overview of his work perhaps. Any stylistic changes, his life, where he lives and works." She could feel Donald Sharpe's bright eyes assessing her.

"He lives and works in Northern New Mexico. Didn't Jane give you a bio sheet?"

"She did. But I wouldn't mind a more complete picture of the artist—more about his career, for instance." She kept her eyes on his, making it clear she knew what she wanted and would not be brushed aside.

"Well," he sniffed, glancing at her breasts, "if you're finding it difficult to evaluate Kunstler's work, may I offer you the benefit of my extensive experience?"

Attracted to her or not, Sharpe clearly wanted the upper hand. "That would suit me," she said. "I've always been a demanding student."

"Good," he said. "I have a PhD. in art history, and I have chosen to represent Mr. Kunstler's art because it is top drawer."

"I see." He was trying to impress her, she thought—a good sign.

"Jane tells me you've just moved here. Might I ask what brings you to Santa Fe?"

"Actually, I live near Pojoaque, in Jacona. I left Ohio with the idea of opening a practice here. I'm a psychotherapist." There would be no hint of what really brought her to New Mexico.

"Here to tackle our Santa Fe neuroses?" His tone sounded sarcastic.

"Something like that," she said. "Though I doubt Santa Feans have a monopoly on neurosis."

"As always, it's a question of degree. But we're good at self-medication. The usual alternatives to alcohol, for instance."

"I see you have a sense of humor. Drugs and alcohol only make things worse."

"Worse?"

"They unfortunately facilitate denial." She looked away at the thought of her dead brother. "My job is to help people avoid that."

Sharpe had begun rubbing his chin. "You sound quite the professional. What kind of psychotherapist are you…a psychiatrist?"

"No, I'm a counseling psychologist. I take a cognitive approach to therapy."

"Well, there are plenty of self-styled psychotherapists in Santa Fe. And plenty of patients. Our city attracts people who don't fit in elsewhere."

"Creative people? Like Mr. Kunstler?"

"He doesn't fit in either—not after the camps."

"How *did* he survive that?"

Sharpe shook his head. "It's a long story."

"I wouldn't mind. I wouldn't even mind meeting him."

He raised an eyebrow. "As the first of your new patients?"

"No, I…"

"Kunstler's too productive for me to risk having him shrunk."

"I know there are those who think psychotherapy dries up creativity. It doesn't. But that isn't why I'd want to meet him."

Sharpe scratched his head, studying her. "Why, exactly, is it so important that you meet him? Usually, if someone wants to meet one of our artists, it's *after* buying the artist's work. They want to learn more about their investment."

Was Sharpe getting suspicious? She smiled benignly. "Yes, I might become a buyer. But as a psychologist I can also say that I have a professional interest in this man, given the kind of work he does." Anna hesitated. "If you like, I could make a partial payment on one of his works as a token of good will. The *Fear* painting, for instance." She said this knowing well that even a thousand dollars would tax her budget.

He kept studying her. "So you say you're a counseling psychologist?"

"For over fourteen years," she said. He hadn't jumped at her bait. Did she miss something redeeming in Sharpe? After all, he was *not* Vaughn. Beyond her initial impression of his hunger for a sale, was there some element of thoughtfulness submerged there? She turned away as if to examine one of the nearby modernist landscapes. Red and ochre shapes oozed into each other while shadows resembling crouching humans lurked in the foreground of a rectangular mass set against a static black background. Frowning, Anna tried to make sense of the painting.

"You're looking at a Mezada."

"Oh? The small adobe—one of the small church buildings where the Penitentes store their…?"

"…carvings of Doña Sebastiana, *La Muerte*?" He chuckled. "You're asking if that's an adobe *morada*? No, but I see you're up on your Southwest guidebooks."

Yes, she had seen pictures of the wood-carved Doña Sebastiana —the skeletal Death Angel in her cart, an arrow fitted to her drawn bow. The Catholic sect known as the New Mexican Penitentes kept her locked in their *moradas*. "It must have been your pronunciation that threw me," she said with a smile.

"Now, now," he said, shaking his head. "Back to Diego *Mezada.* He is a reclusive Hispanic artist but his fame is spreading quickly. I've priced Diego's Adobe Pattern #23 at only twenty-eight thousand, but a year from now I'll probably have to price it at close to fifty thousand. The reason? This winter, our art museum will be installing his Adobe Pattern #12 in its permanent collection."

"Then I imagine Mr. Mezada and certain art collectors will be very pleased this winter." She paused. "I've always found it fascinating."

"What's that?"

"High-risk gambling, and the people who make those kinds of bets. Not everything goes up all the time. Not even artwork."

"Especially not artwork. That's why it's so important that I identify a work's intrinsic value." He swept a few hairs off his forehead. "And convince my clients of the truth of my analysis."

Anna frowned, as if deep in thought. "Wouldn't it be useful if you could identify which prospects are risk-takers and which are not?"

"Sure. But most of my clients are collectors, and I keep them collecting."

"But what about the ones you don't know about? The ones who walk in the door and browse?"

"The walk-ins?" He stared at her. "You say you're a psychologist. What kinds of questions would *you* ask to gauge a stranger's risk tolerance?"

Anna's heart beat a bit faster. "Questions that would reveal overconfidence."

"And that would tell you...?"

"In the context of the gallery, whether a person with an

inflated ego might act rashly to demonstrate superior intelligence—to Jane, for instance. They do it usually to hide their insecurity. Of course one can be fooled. What might seem a reckless comment could be informed by a solid knowledge of art."

"So how would you tell one from the other?"

"By asking the right questions. And instinct, based on my experience of people."

"That's how I work. Gut instinct." Sharpe looked away, working his jaw. "Let's say you wanted to spot people who're *not* here to buy. Those who'd just waste our time."

Anna frowned. "What sort of people do you mean?"

"Tourists with their hands in their pockets. Window-lickers who think I run a museum."

"People who want to enjoy art but not buy it?"

"Something like that." Sharpe scratched his head. "Tell you what. I've got a couple of ideas I want to throw at you. Why don't you come by tomorrow afternoon and we'll pick up where we left off. Say, around three?"

"At three?" she said, thinking quickly. "I could be here."

"Good." he said, turning and walking down the hallway to his office.

Chapter Seven

Driving home from Santa Fe, Anna found herself suddenly dizzy. She realized she'd been hyperventilating. Pulling to the side of the highway, she turned off the engine. She closed her eyes and tried an old Zen trick. She imagined geese floating on the surface of a lake. All was serene, the water still. On a signal they all flew up, leaving the lake's surface rough and rippling. Slowly the water calmed, returning gradually to mirror stillness. As Anna relaxed, her breathing deepened and became more regular. Minutes later she pulled the car back onto the highway.

Over the decades since losing her mother she had occasionally had these anxiety attacks. They'd increased in the weeks before she left Sanderson. But why now? Was it about working for Sharpe? Her pitch to him had been strong. If he hired her would she be able to follow it up with enough time to contact her father?

Or was her anxiety about the chance she *would* find her father—and was afraid of what she might find? Still, if her father had been badly damaged by his time in the camps, mightn't it be her destiny to help him? Her training and experience would qualify her to at least try. Psychotherapy was not like performing an appendectomy, with a clear-cut result. Early on, she had lost a patient, a young woman named Elaine, who after only six months of therapy had swallowed a bottle of sleeping pills. Elaine had been dead for three days by the time a neighbor found her. For months after that, Anna's patients had felt to her so fragile. The impact of Thomas's suicide, years earlier, had become fresh. She had tried alternating rest days with work days. No, she'd discovered she was vulnerable in ways she hadn't imagined.

Back home in Jacona, Anna decided to relax by reading the book of Navajo tales. She closed it after ten minutes. The tales only reminded her of Katey and Tommy's absence. It had been so quiet since they left. The gathering shadows in the guesthouse triggered memories of the children playing. Even their shouts seemed to echo faintly in her ears. She put the book on a table and lifted the sleepy Ma-i from the floor. He complained as she carried him into the kitchen. She poured a saucer of milk and watched his tiny pink tongue lap it up.

It was only six-thirty. Reading the few pages about the desert adventures of Coyote, Skunk and Gray Rabbit had made her restless. She felt the urge to hike. In Ohio, after she had put the children to bed and Sanderson had retreated to his study, she used to go for walks in the park trails around Columbus as the light was fading. The calm of a dying day had somehow comforted her.

From her guesthouse it was only a minutes' walk past Lant's house, then a few hundred yards to the road, then on to the *barrancas*—which were claimed as ancestral by the neighboring San Ildefonso Pueblo Indians. When she'd moved in, Lant Wolverton had mentioned that the San Ildefonsans had become stricter about trespassers on their sacred land than in years past. But reading about New Mexico's geology had heightened her curiosity about those *barrancas* beyond the road and the riverbed. She wanted to see the eroded red peaks and ravines of volcanic ash and siltstone up close, wanted to feel an ancient volcanic eruption's fossilized detritus under her feet.

There were still two hours of decent light left, close as it was to the summer solstice. She took a quick check in the bathroom mirror. Her red curls were still fluffed from the morning. Her blue denim shirt was open at the throat, showing a sliver of skin. Her hazel eyes, inherited from her mother, blazed back at her. It was Anders who used to claim she had inherited, too, her mother's impetuousness. Perhaps that was true, she thought, but how threatening could a solitary thirty-eight year-old woman be to the sovereignty of Native Americans?

Anna walked into her bedroom, reached for her boots, sat down, and began lacing them up. Within fifteen minutes, her water bottle was filled with cool water, and her blue canvas backpack was strapped on. Soon Anna reached the black asphalt road and began walking east. The broad riverbed alongside the road was dry except for a trickle cutting through the middle of the pale swath of sand.

The air was cooling from the afternoon heat. An old gray dog—a scrawny mix of terrier and spaniel, she guessed—broke out of the bushes and limped quickly away on its three legs. Anna saw that the dog had no collar. It glanced fearfully over its shoulder at her, and stopped as if to size her up. It seemed on the verge of approaching her, but instead ran off and finally disappeared downstream behind a clump of trees. Anna wished she knew the dog's name, if it had a name. She could have called it, showed that she meant well.

After reaching a certain point she crossed the riverbed, passed through a line of cottonwoods, and came up against a barbed wire fence. On the other side were the towering *barrancas*. Did the Pueblo post sentries? She stopped to look and listen. There was nobody in the landscape that she could see, no one silhouetted on the barren peaks. She took off her backpack and set it next to the fence. Bending the bottom strand down, she carefully ducked through. She reached through for her backpack, slipped it on, and headed upland. To the west, in the direction of the Pueblo, the sun had dropped lower in the sky, throwing shadows on the ravines in front of her. Far in the distance, a dog was barking. A vehicle passed on the road she'd just crossed, downshifting for the long curve. She watched it slow and park behind a clump of roadside bushes. It seemed to her that almost everybody in rural New Mexico owned a white pickup.

Anna soon discovered that what had looked like seaside sand dunes were no such thing. Over millennia the ancient sandstone, siltstone and volcanic ash had been compacted into something like cement beneath a thin surface of sand and fine gravel. As she climbed, the naked ridges and ravines made her think of the stories of Coyote and his tricks. The Navajos, the book said, couldn't help projecting their own weaknesses and longings onto that cunning animal. Coyote's enemies, having killed and cut him into small pieces as punishment for his tricks, had forgotten that the tip of his nose and the tip of his tail were immortal. Anna imagined him trotting up these hilly wastes after he'd reassembled himself, sniffing the air with his long nose for scent of rabbit, his lean body grim and mangy, his mind ever at work scheming his way to his next meal. Surprisingly, it was Donald Sharpe's image that popped into her head—there he was, peering down at her through those lenses perched on his long nose.

Anna spotted a peak to the north and decided to head for it. Peaks in the *barrancas* were not much higher than four or five hundred feet, but they were steep and the sand was slippery. The top layer kept giving way as the cleats of her boots penetrated only a fraction of an inch with every step. There were few landmarks in the badlands—no trees, not even stunted piñon or juniper—only the smallest of ground-hugging cacti. The climbing and descending was tiring, but the lonely peaks and ravines entranced her with their haunting beauty. It was as if she was losing herself in an extraterrestrial landscape. Even the lowering sun seemed as if it might have been from another solar system.

She soon found a lone large rock and sat down for a sip of water. A small gray and brown lizard scurried up the slope a few feet away and hesitated. She would never have noticed it if it hadn't moved. Its eyes swiveled and stopped, then swiveled again as its bulging eyes inspected her. It seemed to ask who she was and what she was doing there. Her mind wandered. When did she ever feel so unconnected, so weightless, in her life? Was it after her mother died, when she felt rootless and adrift?

Anders had been a different person after he recovered from the accident that killed her mother. He and Anna would look at each other, as if thinking, *You're not my daughter…you're not my father.* And of course she wasn't his daughter. But why did he have to be so lecherous? Like the afternoon she and Thomas, back from school early, walked in on Anders doing something confusing to Soledad, the housekeeper. Lying on her on the living room rug, her dress pulled up over her head, what was Anders doing that she was groaning so?

In those days, Soledad had been teaching her and Thomas how to make *quesadillas* and *tacos,* and *tamales.* She had become like a new mother to them. Anna had been nine, and only later did it occur to her that this must have been sex, not punishment. Yet the seeming brutality of it tolled like a bell deep within her. Something had been settled. Men would prey on you. They were not to be trusted. Anders had claimed, when she confronted him in Tucson years later, that he remembered doing no such thing—that it couldn't have happened. As if she'd had no brain to register what her eyes had seen.

Anna took another sip of water. The lizard seemed to be playing a waiting game. It crouched as still as the pebbles around it, all but invisible. A black beetle was now skittering down the slope. As it neared the lizard it veered away. The lizard was unperturbed, still studying the large creature sitting on the rock. Anna replaced her water bottle in its case. She sighed and stretched her arms wide and high. The beetle, now near her foot, raised its rear end almost vertically. Was it feeling threatened? Hadn't she read that stinkbugs do that? Anna laughed, rose to her feet, said goodbye to the lizard and the beetle, and resumed hiking uphill.

She traversed an eroded hill, then another, and then another. But the far-off peak she had set her course by seemed no closer. The landscape was beginning to create the illusion of ocean waves caught at mid-crest. Out of the corner of her eye she could almost catch their swing and sway. It was eerie. By the time she had covered the distance to the base of the peak she had set her eye on, she was breathing hard. She began to climb the several hundred feet to the top, but it was steep. She suddenly slipped and slid as the sand gave way under her boots. She fell forward to break her slide, bruising and cutting her hands.

Finally clawing her way to the top, Anna stood and surveyed her surroundings. To her surprise she found she had reached the highest point of a long ridgeline that ran off to the north and out of sight. For hundreds of yards in all directions, Anna saw greater and lesser eroded ridges and hills similar to the one she'd just climbed, with nothing to tell one from the other. What was it about the volcanic land that kept it sterile, that kept trees and bushes from even *trying* to grow there? She stared westward at the mountains of the Jemez. Somewhere near lay the restless fourteen-mile-wide caldera, invisible from where she stood. She tried to imagine the series of titanic eruptions, heaving up and reshaping the land, blasting rock and ash as far as what would become Oklahoma and Kansas.

The sun, with its growing nimbus of clouds, had dropped further toward the distant skyline. A screech startled Anna, sending the hair up on the back of her neck. She whirled, but saw no one, near or distant. She squinted at the sky. Far above wheeled two hawks, painted orange by the late sun's rays, calling to each other. They were being blown by the high winds from one patch of sky to another, first appearing small, then large. Anna felt a pang. This mated pair—hadn't she once hoped to have a marriage like that? Two people, soaring and free, their lives connected by invisible love? How naïve. The stuff of fairy tales. Should such ideas be put into children's heads, setting them up for crushing disappointment? Navajo tales didn't end with *happily ever after.* Which reminded her—what stories were being read to Katey and Tommy just then in Ohio? She checked her watch to calculate Ohio time, but her wrist was bare. She'd left it—the one anniversary gift from Sanderson she valued—on the table at home.

She swung the pack off her back and rummaged through it for her cell phone, with its digital clock. Her fresh socks were there, a pack of Kleenex, the zip-lock bag of trail mix, even a flashlight. But no cell phone. She felt prickly all over: she must have left it in her handbag. How could she have done that? She always kept her phone with her. The phone with its compass would have been useful now. She shivered and scanned the stark sand hills around her. They looked more identical than ever. Which direction had she taken to get here? The sun was gradually being hidden behind a blanket of clouds moving in across the horizon. She could tell its general location by its glow, but she wouldn't be able to see it from the bottoms of the ravines. She had to get moving. Without her phone she'd need to make it back before dark. She wriggled into her backpack and set off.

After what seemed like half an hour, Anna felt the first tendrils of panic. She choked it back. When she was on high ground, the darkening hills rippled away in all directions. When she worked her way down the hills' steep flanks, the angles and folds of the ridges and ravines seemed to shift as well, disorienting her and making the slope she'd just descended appear new and unfamiliar.

The air had begun to cool, and when she stopped to get her breath, her own sweat chilled her. Her mouth was dry from nerves, not thirst. Still, she stopped for a sip of water. Putting away the bottle, she noticed her bootlaces had come loose. Bending over to retie them, she felt the pounding of her heart. She had to stay calm, she told herself. After double-knotting her laces, she straightened and looked around. Was it her imagination, or had the light just faded a click?

Minutes later, Anna heard piercing yips like those she'd heard the other night outside her guesthouse. Coyotes were hunting somewhere beyond the *barrancas*, perhaps a quarter mile away. They might have come upon a rabbit that had made the mistake of creeping out from under a juniper to nibble a hummock of grass. She stopped and listened. The yips sounded almost like laughter. Would coyotes, detecting her presence and emboldened by their numbers, be hungry enough to attack her? Would they go for an Achilles tendon to try to take her down? She had never heard of their attacking humans, but she'd been in the West only eight months and knew little about such things. Except that their teeth were razor sharp. A Tucson neighbor's Jack Russell terrier had been lured away by a coyote last winter. It had been gone only a moment. The coyote's teeth had girdled the terrier's throat like a straight razor, severing the dog's carotid artery.

As she hurried in the fading light it was becoming harder to watch her footing. Her cleats kept slipping on the sandy surface . She had to move faster. She broke into a jog, the kind of lope she'd employed years ago around her high school track. But she was no teenager. She was a woman not far from forty trying to conserve her strength while escaping a strange wasteland. The coyote yips sounded closer. She had to avoid panic. She needed the energy that panic might steal.

Breaking into a downhill jog, she dodged small rocks that were appearing out of nowhere, their gray shapes blending into what was now an ash and sandstone surface. She suddenly tripped. She caught herself, tripped again, lost her balance and fell in a near cartwheel, her right shoulder hitting the ground first as she tumbled over and over, feeling the sharp pain of rocks hitting her ribs, her back, and her right knee.

Anna lay there, stunned, trying to focus on her knee. The pain was sharp. It worried her more than the pain in her back. But just then—was that a low laugh she heard? A man's laugh? Was she hallucinating? She propped herself on one elbow and squinted into the gloom. Nobody. But hadn't something moved, as she looked, halfway up the hill? She couldn't tell. She began to shake. Was it an Ildefonsan, enraged at her trespassing? But why would he have laughed? What might he do to her?

Anna shifted into a sitting position. She found it hard to breathe, her ribs hurt so. Perhaps they were only bruised, not cracked. But her knee—would she be able to walk? She sat, listening. It was strangely quiet. Slowly, shakily, she got to her feet and tested her knee. It hurt, but if she favored it, she felt there was a chance she could make it back to the fence line.

Then, not far off, she heard them. The coyotes. They were in full cry. She pulled off her backpack and groped inside for the flashlight. Her hand closed on it, and it worked. She might need it soon, she told herself.

A small rock rolled downhill past her. She stared, straining her eyes, but saw no one. She began to hobble in a direction she could only guess at, climbing yet another steep incline, shifting her weight always to her left leg in a series of clumsy hops. Her heart was racing, and she was drenched in sweat by the time she staggered to the top of the near ridgeline. She shook the fog from her head. Were those the tops of trees, fifty or so yards away? The cottonwoods she'd passed by the riverbed?

Anna began a stumbling, stuttering half-run down the side of the ravine. Filled with fright, she couldn't stop herself. She had forgotten her knee. All she could think was to escape the coyotes and their sharp teeth.

In the gloom she almost ran into the barbed wire fence. She felt for the bottom strand. She pressed it down and began to push through. Halfway, she became stuck. Her backpack. It was caught on the middle strand. She tried to squirm free, but couldn't move forward or back. She lunged and forced herself through, ripping her backpack. She staggered to her feet just in time to see the white pickup—the one she'd noticed earlier—moving. It was pulling out from behind the bushes across the road. In seconds it had accelerated around the curve and was gone.

Anna scrambled down the bank past the cottonwoods to the dry riverbed and limped across to the road. Behind her, closer now, she heard the chorus of yips. Were they only after rabbits? And that solitary gray dog that ran from her—how long could the poor thing survive on three legs in a world of hunting coyotes?

Chapter Eight

Anna lay in bed, staring up into the darkness at the faint outlines of the *viga* beams. Her ribs were hurting less now, but her knee still throbbed with pain. She had wrapped ice cubes in a kitchen towel, and was icing it. She'd resisted the idea of going to the ER in Santa Fe, trying to convince herself there was no ligament tear. But finally she had phoned Lant's wife, Betsy, not knowing anybody else, for the name of an orthopedist. Betsy had recommended one, and Anna planned to call his office in the morning for an appointment. She was grateful the divorce mediator had insisted that Sanderson keep her and the children on his health insurance for three years.

Her thoughts returned to the *barrancas*. Had she really heard a man laugh when she fell? Was it an Ildefonsan, enjoying seeing a trespasser take a spill? And there was that white pickup. But New Mexico was full of pickups, old and new. Even Lant owned one.

Anna shifted her weight. She had a pillow bunched under her knee, raising it to diminish the swelling. The ice was melting and the water was running down her calf. What if she had *really* been injured in the fall—hitting her head on a rock and suffering a concussion, or worse, a cerebral hemorrhage? In any case she would no longer go walking on other people's property without their permission. Especially that of Native Americans, with their deep-seated resentment about white Europeans having seized their lands so long ago. What had she been thinking? What if she'd been attacked? She'd forgotten that even in these times a woman alone was vulnerable to attack. Two small children depended on her. She needed to control herself.

But there was the gallery appointment tomorrow. How would she manage? She didn't want to appear disabled. She would simply explain to Sharpe that she had tripped and fallen, and let it go at that. No need to go into detail. The doctor would check her out, she'd limp a bit, but in a few days she would be fine. That was what she would tell Sharpe. Most of the gallery work would involve sitting, anyway, wouldn't it? That was, if he offered her the job.

Above the sound of the night wind sighing through the half-open windows, Anna heard a far-off chorus of coyote yips. Out there in the desert, a rabbit was running in circles, confused and fearful.

———

Early Tuesday, Anna showed up at the doctor's office. It was tucked away in one of the sprawling stucco professional buildings that in recent years had sprung up in the vicinity of the main hospital. Inside, it was air-conditioned and cool, a relief from the growing heat.

After handing a woman her insurance card and filling out other forms, Anna went to sit in the waiting room. She felt conspicuous, wearing nothing more elegant than a strawberry-colored tank top and wheat-colored jeans. She normally dressed nicely for doctor appointments. But yesterday she'd forgotten to pick up her clothes at the cleaners. A man and a woman—Native American, she assumed from their broad, sunburned faces and long black braids—were sitting quietly on the other side of the room. Occasionally their attention wandered her way. Were they Ildefonsan, Anna wondered? *If they knew she had violated their land...* But what was her mind up to? As if her knee sprain was retribution for trespass.

Anna picked up a magazine. On the cover was a picture of a soap opera actress holding her new baby. Anna's thoughts turned to the e-mail Sanderson had sent her that morning. It seemed things were not going well between Heather and the children. Katey and Tommy wouldn't obey, and they talked back. Anna was not surprised. She knew Heather well, of course. Young and inexperienced, she would not know how to handle children. Heather would complain to Sanderson, and he would end up doing the disciplining, something he always hated. The children didn't used to act this way, he'd written. As if Sanderson had spent enough time with them to know their baseline behavior.

In the email, Sanderson had demanded to know what Anna had told the children about Heather. That Heather had broken up Mommy and Daddy's marriage? That she was to be treated no better than a babysitter? If that continued, he wrote, he would have to send Katey and Tommy back to New Mexico early. Such a threat, Anna mused, as if sending her own children back to her would be an onerous burden. It was obvious, she reflected, returning the magazine to the table in front of her, that Katey and Tommy resented their father's being with a woman not their mother. She knew that feeling. Her own mother had been dead little more than a year when Anders showed up one evening with one of his female graduate students.

Of course, if Sanderson *were* to send the children back early, she would have to hire someone to look after them while she was at the gallery, at least until school started. A Hispanic woman would be fine, if she could find one. In those long ago days when Anders had been teaching or away, it was Soledad who'd been warm and caring, like a real mother.

Lost in the labyrinth of the old days, Anna jumped when a short, sharp-eyed nurse called out her name. She tried to control her limp as she followed her down a long hallway, playing down the seriousness of her injury to herself, if to no one else. She was there only as a precaution, wasn't she?

The nurse led her into a small room with an examining table, a stool, a chair, and a stainless steel cabinet. "Dr. Randler will be here shortly," she said before leaving and closing the door behind her.

After sitting in the chair for ten minutes, Anna wondered if she hadn't been forgotten. She had nearly memorized a framed, colored diagram of the knee's anatomical structure posted on the wall facing her. Why did studying it seem to make her own knee hurt even more?

Finally a young man in a white coat entered with the short, sharp-eyed nurse. The man was dark-haired, thirtyish, with broad shoulders and an engaging smile. He was holding a clipboard.

"Hello, I'm Dr. Randler," he said briskly. "And this is Ms. Peck. I see from this that you've hurt your knee. Before I do an examination, why don't you tell me what happened," he said, seating himself on the stool as Ms. Peck stood nearby.

The doctor seemed at ease, Anna noted. His brown eyes seemed to convey intelligence and compassion. "I was out walking in the desert, yesterday," she began. "I fell and twisted my right leg. When I managed to get up, my knee hurt, and walking was difficult. Back in my house, I iced it and it felt somewhat better. But the pain still makes it difficult to walk."

"Yes, icing can help. Did you take an ibuprofen, or aspirin?"

"I took two Advil."

"Good. So, you were out in the desert this time of year? I hope you were wearing sun block for the UVs."

""Oh yes, the ultra-violet rays. But it was late afternoon."

"Still, we're at seven thousand feet here in Santa Fe's high desert. Judging by your red hair and fair complexion, you probably burn easily."

"I do, but the sun was low." She thought she saw a sparkle in his eyes—was he teasing her about her pale complexion? "Anyway, I thought I'd better have my knee checked. I had a friend who had a motorcycle accident. His ACL tore and he didn't realize it. It atrophied, and naturally, without an ACL…"

"…his knee kept going out, I suppose. Well, let's have a look at *your* knee. Please come over and lie down on the examining table if you would."

Anna rose, came over, and seated herself on the edge of the table. She leaned down to roll up the right leg on her jeans. Except that it didn't roll—it was too tight and narrow to roll up past her calf. Again, she should have picked up her clothes at the cleaners.

"Well, I'm afraid they'll have to come off," Dr. Randler said, rising. He nodded at Ms. Peck. "I'll be back in a minute."

They left, and the nurse returned moments later. "You'll have to change into these," she ordered, holding out a pair of paper pantlets.

Anna peeled off her jeans and slipped into the pantlets a minute before Dr. Randler re-appeared. "If you'll lie down on the examining table," he asked. "Now stretch your legs out this way..."

Anna had a flash of her first time with a doctor as a little girl in North Carolina. She must have been four or five. She had been having bad colds and her mother thought she might have tonsillitis. After examining her throat the doctor had decided to give her a complete physical. Mortified, she'd refused to take her clothes off. Her mother had insisted and she had no choice. There she'd sat, humiliated and in tears, in front of a strange old man staring at her through his thick glasses. His stern expression had told her that he must have been mad at her for not trusting him. In Italy, several years later, the doctors were much nicer. What did they call her? *Carina Anna*—darling Anna.

"If you'll lie back now and extend your legs straight out," Dr. Randler was saying. "That's right. Now I'm going to take your foot like this..."

He gently pulled her foot and turned it slightly from side to side. He did the same with her other foot, apparently for comparison. He probed her right knee with his fingers. The sensation was rather pleasant, until he hit a tender spot that made her jump.

"I'm sorry," he said. "You can sit up now, if you like." He returned to his stool, sat down, and wrote something on his clipboard. "I don't think you've torn anything, but I'm going to order a CT scan instead of an x-ray, just to be sure your anterior cruciate ligament is intact—unlike that of your motorcycle friend. X-rays aren't reliable with soft tissue." He rose and turned to the nurse. "Anna can get dressed. I'll be right back."

When he returned, she had changed into her clothes. She said, "I hope I won't need surgery."

"I doubt you will," he answered. "But if you do, you might be on crutches for a while." He gazed at her thoughtfully. "Do you have someone at home to help out?"

"Not these days. Even if my ex-husband were home, he wouldn't have been much help."

"I see. Some men don't always find helping automatic." He smiled. "Actually, when I was in medical school my girl-friend at the time wasn't very nurturing either. I guess a person's gender doesn't tell you much about…but I'm sorry," he said, glancing at Ms. Peck, who has been quietly rearranging items in the steel cabinet. "I didn't mean to get personal." He winked at Anna.

Anna was silent. Yes, Dr. Randler was getting personal. But she found him attractive. Did he sense that? Was that why he began talking about an old girlfriend? Anyway, this was the closest Anna had been to being attracted to a man since Tucson, where she had been too busy wrapping up Anders' affairs and finalizing divorce terms to think about romance. At least until a good-looking young trainer at the health spa paid her more than adequate attention—as if a Stairmaster required constant supervision.

The spa trainer had asked her out—the only time last winter that she had hired a sitter for the children. After dinner at a Mexican restaurant they had sat in his sports car on a hill overlooking the frosty moonlit desert. He had taken the occasion to explain how 'athletic sex' provides the proper molecular balance for a chemically healthy body, not to speak of its development of positive karma. "It's all written there in the Sanskrit of India," he said. He went on about the health-giving properties of two naked bodies touching, not to speak of the *personal metabolic ecology* of the sex act.

On some level the experience had been absurd and on another it was touching. The twenty-something year-old had apparently thought he'd discovered a novel approach to seduction. How could she have begun to explain to the youngster that sex can sometimes lead to a dark place, where betrayal can replace love, and pain will overwhelm joy? Nevertheless, with a sitter at home minding the children, she had contemplated the prospect of a few hours of physical pleasure. At least until the trainer, frustrated because she was slow to react, asked her if she was "frigid." That might have worked with an insecure sixteen year-old, but not with a soul-damaged, soon-to-be divorcée. She couldn't recall her sarcastic reply. Whatever it was, he'd become sullen, and brought her straight home, thrashing his car through the gears. She'd decided not to do any more dating. She quit the spa—it was too expensive anyway. Walking and bicycling would do well enough when she needed to work off any excess erotic energy.

Anna found herself back at the admission desk. Her follow-up appointment with Dr. Randler, the woman told her, would be the folllowing Monday afternoon, after her morning appointment at the hospital for the CT scan.

Driving away from the hospital, Anna calculated she had time to stop by the cleaners and pick up her clothes—then go home to change for her afternoon appointment at the gallery with Donald Sharpe. Again she worried—would Sharpe have a problem with her limp? Would he wonder if she'd be capable of showing prospects around the gallery?

Chapter Nine

After picking up her clothes at the cleaners, Anna drove into town and stopped off at a local bookstore, Collected Works. If she was to have a better idea of what her father may have experienced in the camps she needed to do further research on the Holocaust. The idea that human beings had been packed into cattle cars and shuttled to camps designed and built by other humans for their extermination had always been difficult for her to stomach, much less comprehend.

Primo Levi's *Survival at Auschwitz—If This is a Man* was the first book on her reading list. Levi had been a Jewish-Italian survivor of one of the worst death camps. When Anna asked the attractive, grey-haired lady behind the desk if she stocked the book, the lady stared at her. Perhaps Anna didn't seem to her to be the sort of person who would ask for such a book.

"Yes, somebody ordered that book some time ago and never came by to pick it up," she said to Anna. "I think I know where it is." She disappeared among the rows of shelves and returned minutes later with the book in hand. "Quite a disturbing book," she said. "Can I find anything else for you?"

"There will be others, but not right now." Anna looked at her watch. It was 2:30.

She paid for the book and in minutes was in her car, headed for Canyon Road, mentally preparing herself for her meeting with Sharpe.

———

Sharpe's office style turned out to be his personalized version of a pueblo interior, with its overhead *vigas* and *latillas*—Ponderosa beams overlaid with a layer of diagonally set aspen or juniper poles. A weathered Spanish colonial table, cluttered with papers, served as a desk. His credenza, with its scarred top, seemed fashioned from what might have been a centuries-old church door from Mexico. Sharpe's only nods to modernity were a swivel chair and a large computer screen. Thick cables ran to a floor-standing server.

A dark leather couch with red and white diamond motif pillows sat against the wall opposite the desk. An *araña de luces* chandelier hung from the ceiling. Anna noted its similarity to ones she had seen in pictures of colonial-era churches. Original, or made of antique wood, its four candleholders had been replaced with flame-shaped light bulbs.

"Let's pick up where we left off," Sharpe said, sitting at his desk, as he waved Anna toward the couch.

"Thank you, but if you don't mind," she said, smiling and choosing a chair with a straight back that stood by his desk. "Couches relax me too much. I'd like to stay alert and give you my best attention."

He leaned back and fixed her with an appraising gaze. "I like your frankness—good attitude."

"As I remember," she said, "we were talking about your

gallery's walk-ins—how a psychologist like myself might be able to sort out buyers from non-buyers."

Sharpe frowned. "That's right. But it isn't always about buyers." He began tapping a pencil on his desktop. "Competition here can get pretty fierce. Galleries spy on each other. They can raid each other's artists," he said. "Then there are the art thieves who case galleries to check their security. There've been some recent thefts in town."

"Such thieves might be detectable," Anna said brightly. "They can show signs of nervousness, or restlessness."

"It's not that easy. Someone who looks like he's figuring how to cut a painting out of the frame, roll it up, and get it out of there, could be an out-of-town collector studying a painting for its quality."

Anna nodded. "Of course."

"Lately there's been something else," Sharpe said, lowering his voice. "A few galleries have been calling the police, claiming the competition's been dealing in stolen art. You know, just to harass us. So the police send undercover agents around to check." He tapped the pencil on his desktop. "Needless to say, I don't deal in hot art, but I like to know when the authorities are sniffing around. Police can be bribed, like anybody else. Even when you're innocent they can cause trouble—like leaks to the local media that you're being investigated. That can hurt sales. Paperwork, lawyers, time wasted."

"I understand."

"I have to watch my back. It's part of doing business." Again his eyes were assessing her. "But if you can read people as you say, you might be able to help. You know, spot these clowns—pick them out from the rest. Undercover cops too. What do you think?"

In truth, Anna was intimidated. Would she be out of her

depth? Selling art was one thing, looking out for thieves and undercover police quite another. Was there really such nefarious activity on Canyon Road? One would never have guessed by appearances or reputation. Was Sharpe obsessively suspicious? The fears he was exhibiting made her wonder. She shifted in the chair. "Well, I'm reasonably confident I can help you."

Sharpe laughed. "Reasonably? Now I've got you scared. Listen, it's not as if you have to approach any of these people. I'd be here and I'd do any approaching. You'd just be selling art and letting me know if someone doesn't seem quite right."

"I understand. So you'd give me an overview of your artists and their work? I'd want to appear professional and competent."

"I'd teach you what you'd need to know. More important is your knowledge of human beings." He paused and locked eyes with her. "Think you'd like to work for me?"

She watched him bounce his pencil on his desk. Her mind was racing. Wasn't this exactly what she wanted, the key to finding her father? She wouldn't have to work in the gallery for years, only until she managed the introduction. Would she be able to find someone to take care of the children when necessary?

She smiled. "How many hours do you have in mind? And the compensation?"

"I'm thinking of Friday evenings and weekends, when we get most of our walk-in traffic."

"It's an attractive idea," she said, relieved that it would be only a few days a week.

"I could pay you fifteen an hour plus fifteen percent of our margin on anything you sell." He tipped his head back and gave her a once-over. "I'd still have Jane during the week, but you'd be the one with a special assignment."

Anna's mind began making fast calculations.

"This is a piece of volcanic obsidian," he said, casually picking up a black paperweight. "It can be made so sharp its edge is measured in atoms. They use obsidian in eye surgery. I keep it on my desk to remind me how cutting-edge my brain needs to be, twenty-four seven. I have a good feeling," he said, putting it aside, "about your working for me."

"I see you're a man who is comfortable acting on instinct," she said quietly.

"Instinct is everything." Again his eyes flickered over her, and he smiled. "I might as well tell you I like the way you dress—not too showy, modest, just right."

She could feel her face flush. "Thank you."

"I want you to start this Saturday."

"This Saturday? I guess I could…"

"Good. I'll break the news to Jane. Come in Thursday morning at eight and we'll get started. I'll teach you the basics in a couple of days. The rest will be on-the-job training." Sharpe was out of his chair and holding the door open for her, all brisk business.

The man did not lack confidence, Anna thought to herself as she walked down the hallway and out of the gallery. Was he counting on her being sexually available? In her thirty-eight years she'd learned how to say no to men. Still, something about his confident manner was not unattractive. And the work he wanted her to do? He assured her she would not be at risk. She would only be his eyes and ears. The whole situation was turning out to be pleasantly ironic. She would get the chance to sell artwork painted by the father she never knew.

Almost home, Anna bumped her Subaru down into the *arroyo* and up the other side. The first thing she saw was the figure of Lant Wolverton, standing near the front door of her guesthouse. He seemed to be studying something on the adobe wall. She shook her head at the sight of him slouched there, thumbs hitched in his belt, broad-brimmed Stetson pushed back on his head as he studied whatever had caught his fascination. He must have heard her drive in but he gave no sign that he had. She coasted to a stop, turned off the ignition, and got out of the car.

Carrying her book and clean clothes, she was a few yards from him when Lant finally acknowledged her.

"Will you *look* at this," he drawled, jerking his head at what he'd been watching.

"I'm sorry, Lant, I've got to put these inside—maybe another time?"

"It'll be gone by then. You've got to see this."

From where she stood, Anna could see some sort of insect on the wall. In spite of her distrust of the man, she felt a twinge of grudging curiosity. She sighed. "What is it?" She edged forward a few steps.

"It's a hellfire bug. See it?"

The skinny black and red insect was unlike any Anna had ever seen. It had stopped crawling and seemed unaware of its human audience, concentrating instead on something important only to it. "I see it. I've got to go inside, Lant."

"Hold on," Lant said, his voice rising. "Now, see this cricket climbing up the wall?" One thumb was out of his belt and he was pointing at a large black cricket making its way up the wall toward where the hellfire bug was waiting. "Just watch now."

Anna sighed. Was she about to witness an insect tryst? Hardly likely, she thought, with two different species. "What kind of bug did you say it was?"

"Quiet now. Just watch."

The cricket had crawled to within six inches of the black and red insect but did not appear to see it. Or if it did, it appeared unconcerned. At the last moment the cricket veered off, seeming to sense something. The skinny insect instantly moved to intercept it. In seconds it had grasped the cricket's head in its clawed forelegs, cradling it. Anna was uneasy but fascinated. The black and red bug's scimitar-like mouthpart suddenly unfolded from its tucked-under-the-chin position, and sank into the cricket's head. The cricket shivered slightly, making no apparent effort at escape.

Lant cleared his throat. "That's an Assassin Bug. Sometimes optimistically called a Kissin' Bug. Right now he's injecting his venom into that cricket to paralyze it. It'll liquefy its insides." He chuckled softly. "In a minute he'll suck up that cricket's guts like root beer through a soda straw. 'Fraid old Jiminy's finished." Lant glanced at her. His right cheek was bulging with what must have been a plug of chewing tobacco. "Ain't nature something?"

Anna felt ill. "I never heard of such an insect."

"No? He shifted the tobacco plug to his other cheek. "There's Assassin Bugs all over the world. Different shapes, different sizes, different colors. There's one kind that looks like nothing more'n a piece of lint. Camouflages itself with bits of laundry dust and hides in beds. You might have seen one. Feeds mostly on bedbugs. The bite hurts like hell. Like getting stung by a hornet."

Anna turned away. Yes, she remembered once seeing a small piece of lint that seemed to move. She'd thought it was an optical illusion, a breath of air moving a speck of cotton. "I'm in a hurry, Lant. Thank you for your insect lesson."

Lant spat a stream of tobacco juice into the dust. "My pleasure. And one other thing." He re-hitched his thumb onto his belt. "I noticed you limped a little when you walked over just now. It wasn't you I saw came straggling out of the *barrancas* last night, was it?"

Anna didn't answer. She'd been right. He *had* been spying on her. She felt intruded-upon—and angry. She was paying for the guesthouse, and she was entitled to privacy. She would have to talk to Betsy to get him to leave her alone. The rental papers were in *her* name, not his.

Lant was scratching his chin. "I only mentioned it for your own good. I wouldn't want to see you get hurt out there."

"It wouldn't be the Native Americans who would hurt me, Lant."

"No?" He took off his Stetson and scratched the back of his head. "Couple years ago the archaeologists discovered some cooking sites of the old Anasazi Indians—about a thousand years old. They found human skulls. No skeletons, just the skulls. And you know what?"

Anna was silent, bracing herself for whatever Lant Wolverton was going to come up with.

"Those skulls had burn marks on their backs. Right about here," he said, rubbing the hat-pressed hairs on the back of his head. "They'd roasted 'em over hot coals, like hot dogs and marshmallows. Ate the brains."

She tried to conceal her revulsion. "If that's true, we can be glad it was a thousand years ago."

"Oh, it's true all right," Lant says, casually putting his hat back on. "As for a thousand years ago, well, there's rumors that even *these* days…"

"Lant," she said, shifting the hangers of clothes to her other arm. "I have a question. The other night I heard a strange noise and looked out my window. There was a car parked with its motor running just outside this guesthouse—a few yards from here. I had the feeling that whoever was in that car was watching me. Do you have any idea who that might have been?"

"A car?" He shrugged. "What'd it look like?"

"It was too dark to see the color, but it was low to the ground. I couldn't see who was inside. Do you know who that might have been?" she said, unable to keep anger from creeping into her tone.

"You talking about a low-rider?" He laughed. "That was probably Hector Montoya and his buddies—friends of mine. They stop over every once in a while, we have a few beers— that kinda thing." Lant shook his head. "Sometimes they get here a little early. They get bored, waiting, drive around a little. Nothing to worry about."

"They get here early and drive around? Why wouldn't you let them in?"

"'Cause they get here early."

"I don't understand. You wouldn't let your friends in when they arrive?"

"They're more like business associates than friends." A

note of irritation had crept into Lant's tone. "Anyhow, that other night it could be that Hector got curious about who's the present occupant of my guesthouse. Hard to know. But those boys are harmless—just out for a good time."

"I see," Anna said. "Lant, I pay my rent on time. I expect the courtesy of privacy. I would appreciate it if you would ask your friends not to loiter outside my guesthouse."

Lant's eyes narrowed. "Yes ma'am, I'll tell 'em."

"Thank-you."

"You know, you sure remind me of someone I used to know."

"I'm afraid I'm in a hurry." Clamping the Levi book under the arm holding her clothes, she fumbled her key into the door. She had no interest in learning whom she might remind Lant of—assuming there *was* somebody.

"She was someone that showed me you can never figure out a woman. Don't know why I even try any more."

Anna glanced back at him. His face betrayed something between exasperation and confusion.

Inside, after locking the door behind her, Anna murmured to herself, "Thank God I'm not Lant's therapist." Not that it would ever have occurred to Lant that he might need help, she knew. Fascination with a killer bug might have been understandable in an adolescent, but in a middle-aged man? Betsy had made it clear to her, when Anna signed the rental papers, that the main house was in *her* name and that she was allowing Lant to live in it only because an unoccupied house was slow to sell. Lant's pride, she guessed, was taking a beating at Betsy's calling the shots. He would have to be handled carefully, she reflected, as she hung her dry-cleaned clothes in the closet. It wasn't as if she hadn't dealt with difficult males—Anders and Sanderson, and a few hostile patients. Lant was a bother now because she was a woman alone. That, she'd learned, was a magnet for certain men.

By mid-August the children would be back. Tomorrow she'd call Betsy for lunch and explain her concerns. If Betsy couldn't help, then she and the children would move. It would be a shame, since the children loved their little guesthouse.

Chapter Ten

Anna tried not to limp up the steps to the Sharpe gallery on Thursday morning. She had dressed conservatively, with her emerald-green blouse and navy blue slacks. She was ready to begin learning the art gallery business. As she walked through the door she noticed that Jane Wilcox, sitting at her desk, was watching her.

"Well," Jane said, "if it isn't our in-house shrink." She rose and walked over. "What happened to your leg?"

Was Wilcox grinning? And what had Sharpe told her about the new employee? "Oh, I went for a hike and twisted my knee. Nothing to worry about."

"Donald may be displeased. He likes his salespeople to be fit."

"Then it's a good thing I'll only be apprenticing today. By Saturday my knee should be fine."

Jane looked Anna up and down. "I wonder if you know what you're getting yourself into."

"That sounds ominous," Anna replied, trying to parry with humor. Lingering by the table with its row of artist bio sheets, Anna gave her a friendly smile. She did feel guilty about Jane's reduced hours. "Am I meant to ask what it is I'm getting myself into?"

Jane continued to study her. "Perfectionism isn't the only thing you may find difficult about Donald."

"He has other qualities?"

"Maybe I ought to just let you see for yourself."

"Jane, I think I ought to tell you that I didn't ask him for weekend work at the gallery."

"Though you were happy to accept it."

Anna hesitated. "I wanted the work, but not at your expense."

"At whose expense did you think it would be? I was the only one here."

"I'm sorry."

"Anyway, I might have done the same thing in your place," Jane said, looking away.

"Thank you for that," Anna said. At least the woman was honest.

"So we understand each other. But again, I wonder if you realize what you've gotten yourself into. Donald can be a very difficult man to work for."

"So you've implied."

Jane sat down on the edge of her desk and crossed her arms. "He has his good days and his bad days. Right now he's having a bad day."

"What's happened?"

"Nothing, really. It's just his moods."

"Where is he?"

"Oh, he's in his office," Jane said, shrugging. "Just don't be surprised if on a day like today he forgets he even hired you."

Anna tried to think. Could Jane have told him something? But she knew nothing about her, beyond her interest in her father's paintings. "You say he's in his office?"

"Unless he has a secret back door."

"I guess I'll go and say hello." Anna smiled and walked past her. Further down the hallway, she knocked on Sharpe's office door and waited. She could hear Sharpe's voice. He was mumbling sporadically, as if he were on the phone. Her knee bothered her more when she stood than when she walked, and it was hurting now. She checked her watch. In a moment she heard the sound of a phone being slammed into its cradle.

"Yes?" his voice boomed from inside.

No mistaking the impatient tone. Anna carefully opened the door. A disheveled Donald Sharpe stared at her from behind his desk. His hair was mussed and his reading glasses had slipped partway down his nose.

"What do you want?"

Anna could feel her face flushing. "We talked yesterday—I'm Anna Croft."

"Who?"

"I'm the psychotherapist."

"I know who you are," he barked. "You're the shrink who liked the Kunstlers." He seemed to be staring through her, his mind elsewhere.

"This morning you were going to give me guidance for my work in the gallery."

'Well come on in." Sharpe kept staring at her. "What are you limping for?"

She felt her face redden. "I was out for a walk a few days ago. I slipped and fell. Nothing serious."

"I can't have someone working for me with a gimpy leg."

"It's really not that bad. You said I would start Saturday?"

"That's what I said before you messed up your leg."

"It will be fine by then," she said, barely containing her irritation. "And so, you were going to fill me in on my work at the gallery?"

"Better be fine," he mumbled. He motioned her over to the chair beside his desk. "Sit down."

Anna seated herself in the chair. Was his rudeness a ploy, a conscious bid to intimidate?

"Are you sure you're a shrink?"

Anna blinked. Back to square one, courtesy of Jane? "If you have any reason to doubt it, I can show you my Ohio license to practice."

"How would I know it's the real deal? Mail order outfits sell phony medical degrees for twenty bucks apiece."

Anna looked him straight in the eye. "Mr. Sharpe, when you hired me yesterday you told me that for you, instinct is everything. Does your instinct tell you that I am a person who would lie about my credentials?"

Sharpe took off his reading glasses and swung them back and forth. "I can't be too careful. You never know what's out there."

"Do you think one of the other galleries hired me to spy on you?"

"It's happened before. Anyway, you're here. So what else did we talk about?"

"We also talked about compensation. You mentioned fifteen dollars an hour in addition to a fifteen percent commission."

"Whoa! I said thirteen dollars plus fifteen on my *margin*." Sharpe locked his hands behind his head and studied her. "That's better than you'll get from any gallery anywhere." He began to swivel back and forth.

Anna guessed he was playing with her, testing her. "Mr. Sharpe, you offered me weekend work, and you specified fifteen dollars an hour. As for the fifteen percent commission on the margin, I would have to trust you on that."

"It works like this. If I sell a painting for ten thousand, the artist gets five, and you get fifteen percent of my five. Not a percent on the whole thing. Understand?"

"Well…"

"And you thought I said fifteen an hour? You weren't listening. I said thirteen." His eyes narrowed. "But I'll split the difference with you and make it fourteen."

Anna could have walked out. He was already backtracking on her compensation. How could she ever have known what the real margin was, anyway? Luckily she wasn't there for the money. Soon she hoped to meet her father. "One of us seems to be forgetful, but that's all right. Tell me what I'll need to know for the job."

Sharpe turned and grabbed what appeared to be a large coffee-table book from the credenza behind him. He dropped it face up on the table in front of her. "This is a book on American Southwest art. Memorize everything in it so you can drop artists' names when you pitch prospects. Important they figure you know what you're talking about. Bring it back on Saturday."

The book's cover depicted a painting of red desert hills swelling up against a distant blue mountain range. She glanced through a few pages and repeated to herself that she would be working for the man only as long as necessary. "I know some of this material already."

"Good. Now the rules…"

For ten minutes Sharpe rattled off a list of instructions on what to do and what not to do. "Talking *at* prospects instead of listening to what they say is the worst sales sin," he said, pointing his finger at her. "The first step is information-gathering. You get that by watching and questioning. Body language is first. When a prospect steps back for a macro view of a work, that's a positive and you talk up the artist. Listen for clues to the prospect's taste. Is the art supposed to fit a specific decor? Ask about that decor. All that will help you get a handle on their buying potential. If they're from out of town, ask where they're from. Are they urban or suburban? San Francisco or Fort Worth? All the details add up to a profile you can work from."

When Sharpe had finished, he stared at her as if to see how much had sunk in.

"Is all this," she couldn't resist asking, "only to gauge the prospect's capacity to buy art? Yesterday you spoke of my experience as a psychotherapist helping in ways beyond sales."

"Glad to see you're on your toes," he snapped. "But first you have to come across as a *bona fide* seller of art."

Anna stared at him. Donald Sharpe might have appeared clinically paranoid, but even if he was, he was likely reflecting the realities of a cutthroat art market. In any case it was best to humor him. "I understand. If I don't seem knowledgeable, any interlopers will suspect I'm a phony."

"Especially when you start asking questions."

"Of course."

He gave her a sardonic look. "You learn fast."

"A psychologist," she said, "learns to listen carefully to what the client says."

"You wouldn't try to shrink *me*, would you?" His tone was sarcastic.

"No, you're my employer, not one of my patients, Mr. Sharpe."

He shifted in his chair. "You sound pretty sure of yourself." He began playing with his glasses. "I haven't been sleeping well lately. Bad dreams. So I take pills. I feel groggy in the morning." He threw her a quick glance.

Anna nodded reassuringly.

Sharpe scratched viciously behind his ear. "I hate pills. I hate relying on anything. People included. They tend to fuck up."

Anna stopped nodding but maintained eye contact.

"Let's say you have a deal going with somebody and they screw you around. People always want to screw you around. Especially when they figure you trust them. They stab you in the back." He glared at Anna. "You know people like that?"

"Yes, in a manner of speaking. The key is how we tolerate the betrayal."

"I don't tolerate it well," Sharpe growled.

"That's understandable," she said. The man seemed to be carrying the scars of business combat and was having a bad day. Time to wind things up. "I imagine Jane will let me know the gallery's hours? The administrative details and so forth?"

"Yeah, she'll help you out. I'll be here for anything serious."

"Thank you," she said, rising from her chair.

"Just concern yourself with selling art and watching for jerks."

"Of course." She decided to hazard one question. "I was curious—do any of the artists ever come by? To see how their work looks, that sort of thing?"

"If they do it's usually after hours. Almost all my art's shipped in and out—or I pick it up." He looked at his watch. "Okay, that's it. Jane'll help with any other questions. I've got to get on the computer. Time is money."

"So, I'll begin work Saturday morning?"

Sharpe, already typing rapidly on his keyboard, frowned without looking up. "Payday's every other Friday. For you that'll be Saturdays."

Back at Jane's desk minutes later, Anna listened to her itemize the gallery routine—how to lock and unlock the doors, where the keys were kept, how the alarm system was armed and disarmed, the setting of the thermostat for the air-conditioning and heating systems, and various administrative details. She took Anna down the hallway past Sharpe's office, past the employee bathroom, to a small lunchroom with a table and chairs. A coffee machine, a microwave, and a tiny fridge sat on a counter. "When the gallery's empty you'll eat a quick lunch in here," Jane said. "But you always listen for customers coming in."

Anna was disappointed that the artists hardly ever came by. She had hoped that a painter living as close as the Taos High Road—her guidebook's map had shown its location— would occasionally check on how his work was displayed. Sneaking Kunstler's address out of Sharpe's computer files and knocking on her father's studio door one fine day—*that* she would do only if all else failed. She would have to be patient and gain Sharpe's trust. The opportunity would come.

"So, do you think you can remember all that?" Jane asked. "I see he gave you *The Book*. If you want to know why he picked that one, check the acknowledgements."

Anna opened to the acknowledgements page. Donald Sharpe's name headed the list. "I see he's well-connected," she murmured.

Jane nodded. "In a variety of ways."

Chapter Eleven

nna was searching the faces at "Cowgal's Corral" for Betsy. She tried to picture the compact woman with the bobbed chestnut-colored hair who'd had her sign the rental papers two months ago. Betsy had told her she would be wearing jeans and a leather vest over a yellow shirt, and would be sitting in a corner table. The room, bounded by split-rail fencing festooned with lariats and saddles, was noisy: it was a Friday, and the lunchtime crowd was boisterous. Someone waved and smiled from a far corner of the room.

"Place fills up fast," Betsy drawled as Anna took the chair opposite her. She smiled, her blue eyes probing. "I knew I'd recognize you, with that rust-colored hair of yours."

"My hair," Anna said, running her hand through her curls, "It's always been unruly." She glanced at Betsy's brush cut. "I see you don't have that problem." Anna had decided to be agreeable. She was here to complain about the man her landlady was divorcing—but Betsy, she realized, might have a residual loyalty to Lant.

"Yeah, it's easier this way." Betsy chuckled deep in her throat. "Listen, I'm having a Margarita. Want one? They make 'em great here."

Anna rarely drank during the day, but she decided to make an exception. "I haven't had a Margarita in years. I remember they salt the glass rims…"

"Sure do," Betsy said, flagging down their server and ordering the drinks.

Anna was disconcerted at *this* Betsy, very different from the serious, businesslike woman she'd met in her real estate office on that windy April day. She had seemed distant, probably distracted by the divorce. The new Betsy seemed energetic and pleased with herself. She seemed to have left distractions in the dust.

"So, how's Santa Fe treating you?"

"Actually, I've found a job."

"Really? Where?"

"The Sharpe Gallery on Gallery Road. Do you know it?"

"I know 'em all. Been in this town twenty-eight years, ever since I moved here from Kansas with my first husband." She shook her head. "Not that I want to put you off your new job, honey, but I know Donald. Be careful with him. Uses people up and spits 'em out."

"Well, I've guessed he's an operator."

"Nobody knows how he got the money to start up his gallery years ago." Betsy frowned. "How'd you pick him out of the couple hundred galleries in this town?"

"I was attracted to some of the work he shows."

"I don't know why you want into the gallery business, honey. Real estate's the place to be."

"Really?" But Anna's thoughts were on Sharpe. Was Betsy telling the truth? Was her father showing his work in a questionable gallery?

"So, how's the guesthouse? Like the new bathroom? I had that put in just before I left Lant. I figured I might move in there myself before I realized I could have a hell of a better time in town." Betsy's blue eyes seemed to be searching her for something.

"The bathroom's great." Anna fiddled with her fork and napkin. She glanced at the table next to them. A middle-aged woman in western clothes—leather vest, red scarf and black cowboy hat—was leaning forward, her attention on a prim young blonde in gray tights seated, in full lotus position, opposite her. "The guesthouse is fine, Betsy. But what I really need to talk to you about is Lant."

"Is he bothering you?"

"Well, yes."

Betsy grimaced. "Don't give him a second thought. Lant's a big baby—his bark's worse than his bite."

Anna needed to be careful. She didn't want to have Lant know she went to Betsy to complain about him. "It's nothing overt, but I do value my privacy. The last couple of times when I came home, he was at my front door. I'm not sure it was an accident. I don't know quite how to say this but..."

"Say it."

"Well, maybe it's me, but does his conversation normally take such dark turns?"

"Like what?"

"He warned me not to hike in the *barrancas* next door. He said the Ildefonsan Indians might attack me. He spoke of their cannibal Anasazi ancestors. Not that I believed every word."

"That's just Lant teasing. I suppose he scared you about the Black Death too?"

"Black Death?"

"Bubonic plague. It pops up in New Mexico every year or

so. People's cats or dogs pick it up from prairie dogs or rabbits and then they pass it on to their owners."

"Did you say Bubonic plague?"

"Don't worry. There're only a few cases a year, out in the
boonies, sometimes Eldorado, or up in Mora. So what else
did Lant tell you?"

Was Betsy trying to scare her even more than Lant had?
"Well, he has these visitors."

"What visitors?"

"Sometimes they park outside the guesthouse at night with
their motor running. It gives me the unpleasant feeling of
being watched."

Betsy ran a fingernail along a crack in the tabletop. "I'll
talk to him."

"I would appreciate it."

"Listen, sweetheart," Betsy said, reaching across to Anna's
hand, "Lant's nothing but a big kid. But he *is* a kid, which is
mostly why I left him. The only thing he really cares about
is his Ford pickup. My God, the thing must be ten years old,
but he loves it more'n he ever loved me. When I found him
he was living in a trailer, up to his eyeballs in debt with that
big shiny truck parked outside. I didn't see him as he was. All
I saw was a cowboy—you know, the romantic image." She
shook her head. "Then I got to know him."

"I know how that feels," Anna said, as the server arrived
with the Margaritas.

Betsy lifted her glass to Anna. "Here's to the men who wear
Stetsons—and here's to gettin' rid of 'em."

Anna sipped her tequila through the salt and welcomed
the sudden sourness. Sitting with Betsy reminded her of
lunches she used to have with girlfriends back in Columbus.

"I understand. I think I told you in April that I left my own husband, back in Ohio. I discovered he was having an affair."

"Men are cheaters from the day they're born, darlin'. It's in their DNA. They don't know what love is." She gazed at Anna thoughtfully. "But women do. Women know how to love, don't we?"

Anna took another sip of her Margarita. As her landlady, did Betsy feel obliged to act the big sister? Or was something else going on? Those probing stares—as if Betsy wanted an answer to something. "To tell you the truth, I'm not sure women know how to love either. In my years of practice I've seen many women choose the wrong men for the wrong reasons."

Betsy's face clouded. "You told me last April and I forgot. You're a shrink."

"Well, yes," Anna said, recalling how threatened some people were by therapists— as if a psychotherapist was a kind of voodoo priestess, casting spells.

"So you must have seen a lot of screwed-up women, raped by their fathers, messed up by husbands and boyfriends."

"I've seen some of that."

"That's why I picked Lant. Thought I'd be in the driver's seat. I was the one with the money. Thought he might even be grateful." Betsy's hand reached across and cupped Anna's. The fingers tightened. "Darlin', where it's a man you've got to be sure he loves you more'n you love him. Call it self-protection."

Anna nodded less in affirmation than in understanding. It was not the first time she'd heard a woman—it was usually the women—declare belief in such a formula. She almost always asked her patient which of the two came out ahead in such an arrangement—the one who won control, or the one who felt controlled. It was not difficult to see why Betsy's marriage failed.

"With a man you've got to watch out," Betsy growled. "At first it's exciting—you know, the challenge, the taming. But after a while everything gets edgy and old. You're tiptoeing around on eggshells or you're bored. With women, you don't have to worry. You can *dare* to love a woman." Her blue eyes were boring into Anna's. "I have to tell you—I find you very interesting, Anna Croft."

Anna sighed. She would have to deflect this. "And I think you are interesting too, Betsy. But given my hetero orientation I can't say I have personal knowledge of romantic relationships with women. Not that I feel inclined toward *any* relationship at present, with my divorce pending." She smiled affectionately to soften the rejection as she withdrew her hand, giving Betsy's a farewell pat.

Betsy grinned sheepishly. "As a therapist I thought you'd have learned by now that everyone goes both ways. Joan Baez used to say, 'double your pleasure.' I like women, I like men. Why do you think I married Lant?"

"I guess that would be a question only you could answer."

Betsy shrugged. "It's not complicated. I get in different moods for different strokes. Sometimes I want gorilla, and other times I want a little tenderness. I haven't yet come across a tender gorilla."

Nor have I, Anna thought. A certain self-involved professor in Columbus, Ohio was neither tender nor gorilla. He was merely remote, as Heather would discover, sooner or later. How many times had she asked herself why she fell for the detached, deliberate Sanderson? Was it the expectation that he would come around, with the right sort of love? That she would prove to herself that Anders' callous behavior with females was the exception? Or—she has begun wondering—did Sanderson's remoteness make him so emotionally undemanding that her own dysfunction remained safely concealed?

"So often," she finally said, "there is a third element."

Betsy grinned. "Oh yeah, tell me about it, darlin'."

Would Betsy grasp it? "For example, one's own exit strategy."

"Meaning?"

"The part of us that never committed to the marriage, the part we held back. Just in case."

"The bottom falls out?"

"The fear." Anna said, running her forefinger around the salty rim of her glass.

Betsy frowned. "I don't get it."

"Some people are so afraid a relationship won't work that they don't allow themselves to commit to it."

"You mean holding back?"

"It's a hedge that becomes self-fulfilling. Both genders do it." Had it been a mistake, she wondered, to bring the subject up? Betsy had probably never been attached to Lant. "It's sad, people avoiding hope and losing love," Anna said with a note of finality. She drained the rest of her Margarita. "But Betsy, my reason for getting together with you is my concern about Lant. You know him better than I do. I have two children."

Betsy wrinkled her nose. "I didn't leave him because I was afraid of him, if that's what you think."

"I didn't mean to imply that," Anna said carefully. "But frankly, there's something creepy about the way he's behaving. His being at my front door when I come home, his fascination with killer bugs and so on."

"That's just the kid in him." Betsy examined her empty

glass. "Although, come to think of it, Lant goaded me to kick the last tenant out. Said she was a pest."

"Perhaps she wasn't interested in what Lant had to offer. Maybe *he* was the pest."

Betsy stared past Anna. "As if it isn't hard enough to find tenants," she said under her breath. "The last couple years of our marriage, Lant was always off somewhere, I didn't know where. I'd stopped giving him money, but he was getting it somehow." She gave Anna a quick look. "Well, anyway, I'll talk to Lant—and tell him to mind his own business."

Anna leaned forward. "Please don't tell him I came to you and complained. It might trigger more misbehavior."

"Don't worry, I'll just tell him you and I had lunch, and then I'll give him my stone cold stare. I won't have to say a word. He'll get the message."

Chapter Twelve

By the middle of Saturday afternoon, Anna was embarrassed at several missteps she'd made with gallery prospects. Once, Sharpe had overheard her confuse the bios of two different artists. "You can't make sales if you don't know the artists," he'd snapped. "Learn them the way you learned your psychology. I mean *cold*."

At the moment she was setting up folding chairs for a four o'clock poetry reading. Sharpe held weekend cultural events periodically to boost traffic flow and give the gallery a highbrow edge. That morning, Sharpe had had her spend two hours in town asking storeowners to put event posters in their windows. Some were reluctant, though their windows showed similar posters. Was Betsy not alone in her opinion of Sharpe? Again, she wondered what David Kunstler thought of his dealer. Her father probably had few illusions. He would have to have been clever—but hardened too, she guessed—to have survived the Nazis.

"May I help you with these chairs?"

Anna turned to find the invited poet—a pale, dark-haired young woman dressed in an embroidered blue *dashiki*—giving her an engaging smile. Last fall, Penelope Wentworth had returned from doing humanitarian work in Africa. She had since published a slim volume of verse inspired by her experiences in Swaziland, and she was going to read from those pages. Such a virtuous soul must realize, Anna thought, that Sharpe was using her more to build gallery traffic and sales than to prompt anyone to send aid to African countries. On the other hand, Penelope might simply have wanted an audience for her verse.

"Why, thank you," Anna answered. "How close to the lectern shall we put the front row?"

Penelope had a firm idea of exactly where she wanted her audience. "Line up the first row *here*," she said, pointing to a spot four feet in front of the lectern. "I won't have a mike, and I want the back row to hear me. I don't want to have to *shout* my poetry."

"I understand," Anna said. The lady was on a mission.

By four o'clock the thirty chairs were filled. A few people were standing along the sides of the room and in back. Jane Wilcox had been pressed into ladling white wine into plastic cups at a table displaying stacks of the poet's books for sale. The gallery door and windows were open to catch the warm breeze. Donald Sharpe was leaning against the back wall, his arms folded, surveying the scene. Penelope approached the lectern with quick strides, her chestnut hair flowing onto the shoulders of her *dashiki*. She was clutching a copy of her verse.

After checking with the last row to be sure they could hear her, Penelope began her introduction in intense tones. "A little over a year ago ago—it seems longer than that—I decided that I needed to break out of the bell jar that is America." She paused for scattered applause. "Yes—shades of Sylvia Plath," she continued with a quiet smile. "She would have understood." Through the open windows came the roar of a car with a broken muffler making its way up Canyon Road. Rolling her eyes, Penelope waited patiently for the noise to pass. "I went to work for an NGO in Africa, to help those in need. I was to spend a year in Swaziland, soaking up Swazi culture, making every effort to shed the detritus of my American preconceptions."

Anna listened, smiling at her youthful fervor. Penelope couldn't have been more than twenty-one. How much detritus had she accumulated? Anna had her own thoughts on the psychological wellsprings that motivate idealism—everything from parental missteps that ignite rebellion, to a need to acquire the virtue of goodness.

"Before I read my poetry," Penelope continued, "I will tell you a story about a small Swazi boy I came upon, standing by the side of the road after a devastating hailstorm that had just passed. I was with two other workers from the group when we found him, huddled beside the road, seemingly oblivious to the violence of the storm. I insisted we stop. I got out of our Land Rover and ran up to him. He stared at me. In halting Swazi I asked him if he was all right. He gazed at the sky and said—it's so terribly difficult to translate—'Sky gods smile ice down in desert.'

"That was over a year ago, and I'm still moved. He was so beautiful, that splendid little black face with his huge eyes. The Swazi are so evolved, so integrated into the cosmos, while we Westerners are lost in our greed, our lust, our hatreds, and our wars." Penelope gazed out over the rows of faces, her pale cheeks now streaked with tears. "And then the little boy asked me where I came from. 'I'm from America,' I confessed. *'America?'* he answered, suddenly excited. 'That's where I could be basketball star and make much money. How can I go there?'"

Laughter rippled through the audience, and Penelope waited for silence. "I hope you grasp the tragedy," she said, her voice shaking. "This small boy, this child of the African Godhead, had already been inoculated with the American culture of *greed.*"

Anna heard the sound of Donald Sharpe clearing his throat. He was throwing Penelope a stern look, pantomiming the reading of her book.

Penelope took a deep breath. She opened her book with quivering hands and began reading. As she did so, a tall, older man slipped into the room. His gray hair was cut short. He was wearing a black shirt under a wrinkled white linen jacket, and khakis. He seemed to have little interest in the poetry reading. As he passed Anna on his way toward the rear of the room, he stared at her for a moment. His stare was so intense, the fiery eyes in his craggy face so bluntly questioning, that Anna smiled in self-defense. He moved on toward the rear of the room. After a few minutes he returned, paused again to look at her, almost as if he knew her, and was out the door before she could ask if she could be of help.

Forty minutes later, Penelope ended her reading with an impassioned burst of alliterative lines. At the applause she closed her eyes as if—Anna imagined—she was experiencing the warm spring African rain.

As the clapping died down and people began getting up to leave, Anna went to the front to help Penelope. "So good of you to visit," she said, "and share your poetry with us."

Penelope brushed stray hair out of her eyes. "We *must* try to shoulder the suffering of others. My way is through my verse."

"Certainly. How thoughtful of Mr. Sharpe to have invited you."

"Donald is very kind." Penelope said, blushing and glancing at where Sharpe still stood at the back of the room. "He is a very *spiritual* person."

"Spiritual?" Anna tried not to sound doubtful. "He hides it well, doesn't he?"

"He doesn't want anybody to know. He's very modest about his spirituality. It only comes out in a certain…physical presence. The Godhead shines through his corporeal person."

"Donald's corporeal person? I hadn't thought of him quite that way." Anna tried to recall any hint of Sharpe's spirituality during the brief time she had known him.

"My *what* person?" Sharpe had come up behind them.

"Donald," Anna said, "I think you have an admirer in Penelope."

"Really?" he said, grinning slyly. "Who knew?"

"He knows, all right," Penelope said, smiling reproachfully.

"So what *about* my person?" he said.

"You know very well," Penelope murmured. "I was going to tell Anna, but I've forgotten—are you a Tibetan or a Zen Buddhist?"

Sharpe scratched his head. "Tibetan. Without the demons."

Penelope frowned. "But how can you have Tibetan Buddhism without the demonology?"

Sharpe rolled his eyes. "Call it Reform Buddhism."

Anna noted that Penelope merely smiled. Did she see through his act? Did she care? Was she just too young?

A woman who had bought a copy of the poet's verse approached and asked the poet to sign it. Several more came up, and for a few minutes the poet talked to her admirers, signing copies while Sharpe looked on. The party rental people appeared. They began collecting and folding the chairs.

After fifteen minutes almost everybody had left. Jane was

off, washing the wine bowl in the little kitchen sink. Sharpe had just finished writing the rental people a check, when Anna approached him.

"Did you happen to see that older man come in while Penelope was reading?" she asked her boss.

"What?" Sharpe frowned. "That old guy? He only stayed a minute—obviously not a buyer."

"I noticed he went to the back of the room, to the Kunstler alcove."

"Kunstlers, Kunstlers. Anna, stop obsessing about the Kunstlers. He was just an old guy who wandered in and wandered out. He probably walks the streets. But you're doing the right thing—keeping your eye out for people who don't seem quite right. Now I…" Sharpe had just caught Penelope's attention and made a sign as if writing something. He quickly made his way down the hallway. The poet followed him.

Anna pondered the old man who was 'obviously no buyer.' He hadn't behaved like an art spy or an undercover cop. He walked the streets? A homeless person? Yet the old fellow hadn't tried to cadge a free cup or two of wine from Jane. No, he'd gone straight back to the Kunstlers—he knew exactly where they were hanging. Anna walked over to the *Wraiths* and studied them again. Last night she'd read the first fifty or so pages of Primo Levi's experience at Auschwitz. One warning from those pages haunted her…that in the Ka-Be Lager, the Auschwitz "infirmary," where interrogations took place, one's sense of self—*one's actual identity*—was in even greater danger than one's life. Might Kunstler's painted images of body parts be painful depictions of a personal disintegration he once feared for himself?

Minutes after Jane left to go home, a short, heavyset man

with a red-dyed comb-over walked in. On his arm was a blonde with the bland facial expression of a model. They made straight for a painting not far from where Anna was standing—a large desert landscape with a background of red hills, with a bleached-white cattle skull in its foreground. Within minutes the pair agreed that it would be perfect over the fireplace mantel of their vacation place in Aspen. "Who is Ivor Santizar?" the man asked Anna as he peered at the price. "What nationality is that?"

"I'm told he was a disciple of Georgia O'Keeffe," Anna answered. "According to the owner of our gallery, Mr. Santizar had emigrated here from the Carpathian Mountains in the late '40's, before he met Ms. O'Keeffe. A trove of his work was recently rediscovered in the home of a deceased Taos collector who knew him well."

"Is that all? The artist is from the Carpathian Mountains? No nationality?"

"He may have been Romanian, since much of that mountain range passes though that country," she said, recalling a long-ago geography class. "But again, the owner of our gallery says that he *was* a friend of O'Keeffe."

"Well, for $7500 I'm going to need more information on this Santizar. Is the gallery owner around? By the way, if I buy, I'll have to give you an out of state check."

"If you'll wait a moment, I'll check to see if the owner is here."

Anna hurried down the hall to Sharpe's office. The door was closed. She hesitated before knocking lightly. There was no response. It was her first potential sale and she was excited, even if it wasn't a Kunstler. She opened the office door a crack, then wider. She poked her head in. The office shades were drawn and it was dark. "Donald," she murmured, "someone wants to pay with an out of state…" Anna heard heavy breathing from the couch, smelled sweat and the musky scent of sex. A glimpse of bony white buttocks bouncing between splayed shins was enough. Anna quickly and silently closed the door. *Had Donald heard her?*

Anna, her face hot, returned to the red-dyed comb-over tourist with his bland-faced model. "If you'll just wait a few minutes," she said. "I'll have more information for you. The owner is unavailable just now."

"Unavailable?" the man answered, his voice rising. "I want to buy a $7500 painting and you tell me the owner's unavailable?"

"He's on an important phone call," Anna said, glancing helplessly in the direction of the hallway. "He asked if you'd be so kind as to wait."

Ten minutes passed, and Sharpe did not appear. "Business must be damn good these days," the heavyset, red-haired man fumed, as he and his companion walked out of the gallery.

Anna closed the door after them and nervously straightened the artist bio sheets on the table. Having to face Sharpe and Penelope was going to be unpleasant. They must have heard her voice. Should she simply leave, she wondered? Not yet, with Jane gone. She was surprised at the poet's attraction to Sharpe, her evident idealism bending to his crassness.

The gallery door suddenly opened. It was the old man again, tall and forbidding. His craggy face's fiery eyes scrutinized her.

Anna stepped back, startled.

"No, no," he croaked, shaking his head. "I won't hurt you," he said in a thick accent. "But tell me. What do you think of all this?" The sweep of his arm included the whole of the gallery's art.

"Well it depends," she murmured, trying to think. He didn't *seem* to be a homeless man. His clothes were clean, not ragged. There might have been a touch of mental disorganization, though nothing off-putting. "Some visitors like the landscapes, while others like the more difficult work. But if you were to ask me, I think I would…"

"Stop your pussyfooting." He frowned at her. "Do you know the Beethoven string quartets?"

Anna blinked. If he were dangerous, would he be talking about string quartets? "I…I know some of his piano music, the sonatas for instance, but the quartets…"

"When the B-flat Quartet premiered in Vienna, if you do not know, Beethoven did not attend. Why? Because he was by that time almost totally deaf." He stopped and coughed. "The seventh movement was the famous Grosse Fuga." He stared into her eyes as if searching for a glimmer of understanding. "Afterward, some who had heard the performance told him—or maybe handed him a note because of his deafness—that the serene fifth movement was adored and had to be repeated as an encore, such was the enthusiasm." The old man's eyes were wide and he was breathing heavily, nostrils flared, as if he could hear the soaring strings even now.

Anna was moved by his intensity. "That must have been gratifying for Beethoven."

"Gratifying!" The old man coughed again, almost shaking. "Beethoven was furious. He shouted…'the *Cavatina*, that delicacy. Why not the Fugue? Cattle! Asses.'"

Anna tried to make out the old fellow's meaning. "Well," she said, "Beethoven was famous for being a little cranky, wasn't he?"

"Bah! The Fugue, with its supreme counterpoint, its dark struggle—*that* was the masterpiece. The fourth and fifth movements were little Viennese pastries—sweet gems as far as they went, especially the *Cavatina*. So," he asked gruffly, waving at the painting nearest them, a desert landscape brightly colored with cactus flowers, "What do you see here on this wall?"

Anna did not know what to say. There was something almost violent about the man's intensity. She felt like a small child in a schoolroom, afraid of giving a wrong answer. "I guess I see a well-executed landscape, probably New Mexican."

"Exactly! A delicacy! A cream-puff!" He pointed now to the rear of the room, where *Fear* hung, centered, in the open alcove. "And what of that acrylic wash? Come closer!" They approached and stopped a few feet from the painting. Anna stole a glance at the old man beside her. His eyes seemed to bulge as he stared at the work. It was as if he was experiencing the terror of the subject sitting at the desk, as if he knew whose startled eyes they were, furtive behind their darkened lenses.

"This one does fascinate me," Anna answered truthfully. "The pain in the man's expression. I wonder if the artist himself might have suffered such terrible..."

"*Yes*, the artist," the old man's voice broke in, suddenly soft, almost tender. "This is his thorny...difficult...*Grosse Fuga* work."

Anna was struck by a thought. "Do you happen to know the artist? A David Kunstler?"

He gave her a sidelong glance. "I know *of* him," he muttered in his thick accent. Once again he was staring at her, as if trying to place her. "And who are you? You remind me of someone from long ago."

"My name is Anna," she said. "I've just begun working here."

"Anna," he murmured, as if tasting the name. "Thank-you, Anna," he said, nodding politely to her with a new, gentlemanly demeanor. "You have been very helpful."

"Have I?" she said, doubtfully. "I hope so." She suddenly did not want him to leave. "If you would like to know more about Mr. Kunstler," she said, stepping toward the desk, "here are some biography sheets with small reproductions of his work…"

But the old man was already past her, out the door, walking down the steps.

Anna stood there, holding the Kunstler bio sheet. The way he had stared at her, as if he knew her. That accent. Obsessed as he was with the Beethoven Quartet—and speaking of Viennese pastries. Her breath caught. She *did* have her mother's eyes, and her mother's facial features. Was it possible? But why would Sharpe say he didn't know him? Why would he disown one of his own artists?

Chapter Thirteen

A week after Anna's hike in the *barrancas* there had still been no rain. It was hot and dry. The last time a storm had passed through the area had been in April. The monsoon rains, she was told, wouldn't begin for at least a week or two. Santa Feans complained about their stressed fruit trees and flowerbeds. Anna thought of the lush greenery in the hills and valleys of Ohio that time of year.

Her knee hadn't stopped hurting, and so she had kept the Monday morning appointment at the hospital for the CT scan. The scan had gone quickly and professionally, in less than a half hour.

That afternoon, at Dr. Randler's office, she had to wait only a few minutes before the receptionist notified the nurse, who brought her in to see the doctor. He rose and greeted her with a smile. He offered her one of the two chairs facing his desk. It seemed to be his private office, different from the more clinical room the last time. "How is your knee now?" he asked cheerfully.

She was struck, as she was last week, by the intelligence in his quick brown eyes. "It's better," she murmured, "but I still have a touch of pain when I get up from a chair. Or when I have to step up or down."

He nodded and scribbled a few notes in his clipboard. Anna glanced around the office. Two framed medical degrees hung on the wall behind him, above a pair of text-filled bookcases. Near them was a reproduction of what looked like a Victorian painting. Anna could just make out the title—*The Doctor's Visit*. A young woman lay in bed, her face flushed with fever, her eyes closed. A doctor had just opened a medical case filled with old-fashioned capped bottles and metal instruments. Two concerned women peered at the patient from curtained shadows.

Anna watched Randler as he wrote. There was a boyish earnestness about him that reminded her of her brother. Thomas used to frown just that way as he concentrated on telling a story or anecdote. Dr. Peter Randler hadn't yet taken on the defensive distance so many older doctors adopted, jaded by years of difficult patients, failed surgeries, and corrosive lawsuits. He seemed fresh and unsullied, ready for the world. When he finally glanced up, she nodded toward *The Doctor's Visit*. "I like that picture," she said.

He glanced at it. "Medicine as it once was, when concern for the patient included such things as house calls. Technology is fine but it shouldn't replace a doctor's personal touch." He cocked his head. "But your knee—you're still taking Advil?"

"Yes, twice a day. It hurts somewhat when I put full weight on it. But for the most part it feels better." She did not want him to think she was a complainer.

"Your CT results from this morning just came in—we specialize in speed," he said with a chuckle. "Your medial collateral and anterior cruciate ligaments look fine. Whatever you did to your knee when you fell doesn't show up. Rest it a little, alternate a hot water bottle with ice, morning and evening, and you should be fine in a week or so." He rose and stepped over to a chart on the wall behind her. "You know, the knee is an interesting structure," he said.

She turned to look once again at the diagram of the knee joint. She watched Randler's pencil eraser trace the lobed ends of bones, which seemed as if they were held together by thick rubber bands. "These are the ligaments that hold your femur, your tibia and your patella in place. From the pain you experienced when I rotated your knee last week I suspect that one of your two cruciate ligaments—see the way they cross right here inside the joint—was stressed when you fell. You must have twisted the joint, though not enough to cause much damage." He smiled. "The knee is a little more complex than the simple hinge we imagine it to be."

Anna always found it interesting to glimpse the body's unseen scaffolding. What if damage sustained by *psychic* structures could be illuminated that way? How useful, if emotional trauma could be charted and color-coded. A diagnosis might read: *Note the layered stratification of your limbic system…this empty spot where there should be neurons is from your mother's death thirty years ago…while the fresh, aberrant bulge over here was caused by your husband's betrayal… and this small growing knob is the divorce you anticipate…*

Was that, in an abnormal sense, what her father did in his paintings and drawings, with his disjointed bones and skeletal bodies? Was he mapping the anatomy of human shock and despair with his torsos, vertebrae and skulls?

Anna was also aware of Randler's own anatomy as he stood less than three feet from her, moving his hand across the chart, elaborating on the physics of joint movement. Though he barely moved, his body seemed to possess an athletic energy—even grace—as he explained the compromises that nature had to accept in evolving such a design as the knee. She recalled the sensation of his hand on her knee on Tuesday, the feel of his fingers testing it at different points, as if he was exploring its susceptibilities.

She felt at ease with this man, sensing none of the queasiness that might have warned her off him. Yes, it was pleasant having him contemplate her body. Was she so eager for male attention? She certainly wasn't going to play the credulous female, awestruck at his revelations. She was a doctor in her own right.

"I occasionally envy the medical community's ability to map anatomical structures," she said. "We psychologists have to deduce patients' problems without benefit of CT scans. You MDs are lucky."

He gave her a surprised glance. "We fumble in the dark, too. These diagnostics are only tools. They leave plenty of room for guesswork. Medicine is still more art than science."

"I suppose." She appreciated his modesty. He hadn't been defensive at her implicit assertion of professional equality, as someone not long out of medical school might have been.

"So you're a clinical psychologist?"

"Actually a counseling psychologist—with a cognitive bias. I gave up my practice in Ohio last year when my husband and I parted company."

"Oh." His eyebrows rose. "I hope things are working out for you."

"Well, it's been a difficult year. I lost my stepfather not long after I left my husband in Ohio. I had to go to Italy for his burial."

"Italy?"

"When I was six we lived near Florence for a year when my stepfather was on sabbatical. Last fall he went to visit friends there and died."

"I'm sorry." Randler leaned against the wall, crossed his arms, and studied her. "So here you are, in your sadness, hiking the trackless New Mexico desert."

She laughed. "Not all sadness. I have two children—right now they're with my ex-husband for part of the summer." She noticed no reaction on his part at the mention of Katey and Tommy. "Right now I'm working in a gallery on Canyon Road."

He smiled. "It's not strictly Robert's Rules for a doctor to invite his patient out socially, but I could help acquaint a fellow professional with this so-called Land of Enchantment. Would you be interested in visiting one of the pueblos and watch a ceremonial dance?"

His eyes carried only a mild sparkle. He seemed to her safe, though not boringly safe. "Thank you, I would like that," she said. "It would be good to learn more about New Mexico."

When Anna left Dr. Randler's office fifteen minuts later, she felt a welcome, warm sensation inside her that she hadn't felt for many years.

Two days later, Dr. Peter Randler called to tell her that unfortunately there wouldn't be ceremonial dances scheduled in any of the surrounding pueblos for at least a few weeks. "So I wondered," he said, "would you care to join me for dinner this coming Friday at one of my favorite *tapas* restaurants?"

Anna detected his embarrassment at violating his "Robert's Rules." Did the situation bother her? He seemed a gentleman. And it had been a long time since an attractive man—not a New Age acolyte—had asked her to dinner. It would be good to get out socially. Why be a recluse, waiting for an opening to the world of David Kunstler?

"Dinner would be a pleasure, Peter—doctor to doctor," she said, teasingly.

For the occasion, Anna bought a flowing mid-calf skirt with a floral design, and a silver Concho belt. She had noticed that Santa Fe women dressed uniquely when going out evenings, combining elements of Spanish, Western, even New York ex-hippie. Nor could she resist a sheer Camelot-sleeve sienna blouse that complemented her slender figure and modest bust line. A pair of pendant amber earrings, and summer sandals, completed the elegant effect she was after.

———

"I have a confession to make," Peter Randler said, as they sat at a candle-lit corner table at *La Cochina* over glasses of Rioja. The waiter had just brought small dishes of shrimp—*camarones*—the first in a series of *tapas* appetizers.

Anna glanced at Peter over the top of her glass as she sipped the rich red wine. She hoped he wasn't going to confess love *this* quickly. As if she could trust so impulsive a declaration. But why worry about trust so early on? It had been so long since she'd flirted with a man. Love or infatuation or fling, it was time she loosened up a little. It didn't need to be real love—so elusive a thing anyway. "Well, now I'm curious. What could you feel obliged to confess to *me*?"

Peter grinned mischievously. "I'm afraid I have a weakness for older women."

Anna's heart sank. Was he gay? Peter? Not possible. Did he mean—in the French phrase—women *of a certain age*? But he couldn't mean *her*. For god's sake she was only thirty-eight. And he? Maybe five years younger? Did she count as *older*? She studied the faint film the wine left on the rim of her glass.

"How old are you, Peter, and how old do you think I am?"

His grin disappeared, and she realized he must have detected the injury in her tone.

"I'm thirty-one, and I was only…" he said, stumbling. "I wanted you to know I appreciate your not being a silly twenty-something I could never talk to."

"You haven't answered my question," she said, now more teasing than challenging. "How old do you think I am?"

He seemed genuinely abashed. "I saw it on the patient form you filled out. I told you it was a confession. I happen to be attracted to you. Is that so terrible?"

It was her turn to feel defensive. He was only being honest: she was seven years older, and he found that appealing. Was that the end of the world? But she hadn't imagined it that way. His youthful charm had made her feel younger herself—made her feel almost *his* age. She had of course known women—friends and patients—who had been proud of dating younger men. They'd bragged about it, wanted the world to know they attracted virile young stud muffins, as one of her patients called them.

"No, it's not terrible," she said. "But I hadn't thought of it the way you seem to." She was fibbing only slightly. She couldn't help a sigh. Much of the bloom was off the evening's rose. To have to explain…

"I'm sorry, Anna." He seemed to be studying the weave in the white linen tablecloth. "I see I've blurted the wrong thing when actually I was trying to explain how much I appreciate you. You're not just physically attractive, you're highly intelligent—a Doctor of Psychology for heaven's sake, a mother of two children, a woman who has lived in Italy." He took a quick gulp of his wine. "You're a woman of the *world*."

Anna sipped hers too. So this was the Peter hidden

within the confident, competent medical doctor. In college, she realized, he must have been immersed in his pre-med studies, up to his earlobes in subjects like organic chemistry. Then there had been the grind of med school, juggling textbooks and all-nighters, and finally the long days and nights of residency. No time to discover the world around him, certainly no time to decipher the subtle, often Byzantine ways men and women relate to each other. In Peter's eyes she was a woman who had advanced on life's path, had experienced marriage, motherhood and divorce, events he could probably only imagine. "I think I understand, Peter. But this worldly experience of mine—I hope not to disappoint you. I'm not as experienced or knowledgeable as you may think."

He seemed to appreciate her words. She drank more wine and ate her last two *camarones*. "So delicious, those shrimp," she murmured. "I wonder what's next."

"Anna, I'm old enough to know what I like."

"I'm sure you are. As well as *why* you like it," she said in a confiding tone.

Peter frowned. "I guess I'm not the kind to get obsessive about every little reason I might like something, or people for that matter, if that's what you mean. I'm too busy. I'm not even good at it."

He reminded her of a small animal searching its way through a maze it had stumbled into. Yes, she felt a slightly maternal feeling toward him, one mixed with—she had to admit it—a noticeable eroticism. It was an odd sensation, very different from her original attraction to Sanderson, whom she had worshipped from afar, always trying to close the distance, never succeeding, even in marriage. "Well," she said, "it's all the little reasons for behavior that I've always found fascinating. Which I suppose is one reason I became a therapist. But you're a medical doctor. You're involved in diagnostic work, as you said—physical, instead of psychic. *Your* obsessions are tibias and tendons and ligaments."

"You have a knack for putting things in context. Forgive my silly confession," he added, shaking his head. "I suspect it was more about my being so taken with you. It's not about age at all."

Anna could only smile.

Something caught Peter's eye. "I think I see our next course coming—I'm hungry."

So was she. The wine and *camarones* had stimulated her appetite. And Peter—there was something involving about him...*was* it his youth? Maybe it was time to stop analyzing and simply enjoy the food—the endless stream of *tapas*.

After dinner they walked from the restaurant toward where they'd parked their cars. The sun was setting, the heat of the day was dissipating, and a cool breeze had sprung up. As they walked, Peter took her hand.

"Anna, you've got a half hour drive back to Jacona. Are you going to be okay after all the wine?"

She smiled. Was he honestly concerned about her handling the alcohol on her drive home? Or was he fishing for a legitimate excuse for them to go over to his place? "Oh, I think I'll be all right, Peter," she said, hoping she didn't sound *too* confident.

"Well, all right—if you're sure. It's been a nice evening." He appeared in the dim light to be on the verge of saying or asking something else, but instead turned silent.

"Yes it has," she agreed, as they reached their cars. "I'd like to see you again, Peter."

"Why yes, yes. We'll have to, absolutely." He pulled her close and stole a quick kiss. "We'll have to, for sure."

She gave him a softer but longer kiss in return. "Thank you for a lovely evening," she murmured.

He took a step back and was silent as she turned and unlocked her car door. She got in, started the Subaru, and began backing up. She waved to him and he returned her wave.

"He's shy," she thought to herself, smiling, as she pulled away.

Chapter Fourteen

On July third, a monsoon storm finally unleashed its wild sheets of rain. For days Anna had noticed increasingly dark, threatening clouds surging up from the south. The sound now, as she sat beneath the guesthouse roof, was like a giant drum roll. Within minutes, Anna found brownish water trickling from her entry room ceiling, just missing the Wolvertons' piano. The water was colored, she realized, by the layer of insulating sod under the flat, tarred roof. Running into the dining area, she found rainwater dribbling onto her Italian trestle table. In her bedroom a long thin crack next to a *viga* beam was spitting water onto her oak *cassettone*. The two treasured pieces she'd inherited from Anders and her mother were in danger of being ruined.

Anna tried to move the *cassettone*, but it was far too heavy. She yanked open the drawers, pulled out her clothes, and threw them on the bed. She ran to the bathroom, pulled out the shower rod and slipped off the rings and the curtain. Taking the curtain and two bath towels, she hurried to the trestle table. Wiping its surface dry with a towel, she covered the table with the curtain. She then ran to the *cassettone* as water spattered her. She wiped it and spread the second towel over it. "Damn," she yelled. "Damn, damn, *damn*."

Anna grabbed her cell phone and punched in Betsy's work number. An assistant answered and told her that Betsy was at a real estate closing.

"Can you call her on her cell?" Anna gasped, exasperated. She could barely hear, with the rain pounding the roof.

"When she's at a closing she doesn't usually answer. But I can try."

"My furniture is being ruined by leaks in the roof!"

"As I said, I'll try. I have another call coming in. Can you hold?"

Anna held for two or three minutes as the drumming on the roof became deafening. She clicked off her phone.

Where, she wondered, was Ma-i? She found him crouched under her bed, peering out at her with saucer eyes. He'd been terrified that morning by firecrackers. New Mexicans had seemed to be celebrating the Fourth early. She hated to call Lant, but the rain wasn't letting up. He answered on the sixth ring.

"Bet you're calling about your roof."

"Yes, Lant, I am. And my valuable furniture is being damaged."

"Damaged?" he said slowly, as if turning the possibility over in his mind.

"*Damaged.* As in warped and water-stained."

"Now, don't get excited. Guess you want help. Let's see now," he mumbled. "Where'd I put that patching tar?"

Anna bit her tongue as seconds passed.

"I'll have to poke around in the shed and see if it's there."

"How long will that take, Lant?"

"'Course we'll have to wait for the rain to stop before I can do any patching."

"And what do I do in the meantime?" Anna had to shout

through the thundering on the roof. "The water is coming in *everywhere.*"

"That's the monsoons for you. That's the only time we ever get these leaks. Kind of lets us know where the roof needs fixing." He chuckled. "Lucky I set those bricks in sand. If I'd set 'em in concrete you'd be up to your knees in…"

"Lant, as my landlord I expect you to fix this leak. *Now,*" she shouted. "My clothes are soaked and probably stained. My antique dresser will be warped and ruined. I'm standing in a puddle right now."

"Whoa there. Okay, I'll be over…" He seemed to be talking to somebody with him. "Yeah, I'll be right over and fix things up. "

"A mop and bucket are what I need, Lant," she yelled. "And a tarpaulin—two if you have them. All I have are towels and a little sponge mop." But he had hung up. Had Lant been drinking? His speech had sounded a little slurred. These were the times she wished she weren't a woman alone. She might call Peter Randler, but what could he do? Abandon a dozen waiting patients?

Anna went and hid her clothes under the bed covers on the possibility that Lant *might* come. She had no desire to have him leering at her lingerie. Minutes passed, and she heard a knock. She ran to the entry and opened the door. Lant was standing there in the rain holding an armful of old rags. Water was streaming off the brim of his Stetson.

"These'll work. I use 'em to wipe down my truck," he explained loudly.

Anna picked up Ma-i and stared at the rags. They looked dirty and greasy. "You don't have any tarpaulins?"

"No ma'am."

There was no time to argue. "Well, hurry up and come in,"

she yelped. "We have to cover the dining room table—then the dresser in the bedroom. You'll have to help me move it." *And after that you could mop the floor...* she thought to herself.

"Let me take a look," he said, pushing past her. In moments he was back. "I laid what I had on top but I've got to go get Byron—that furniture's heavy," he yelled. "Be right back." He slammed the door behind him.

Anna hurried into the bedroom. Byron? Who was Byron? Lant alone was a handful. Water was splashing off the greasy rags Lant had piled onto the *cassettone*'s shower curtain and towels. She shook her head and stroked Ma-i. Where in God's name was Betsy? How long did a closing take?

By the time Lant returned with Byron, the downpour had slackened. Byron was a hulking figure with a face as feature-less as a fencepost. His nose, lips and ears seemed cemented on as an afterthought.

"Miss Croft, meet Byron," Lant said. "Byron and I, we're business partners. Between us, we've got some pretty big deals on the burner. Don't we, Byron?"

Byron stared dully at Anna, one corner of his mouth sag-ging open. He ambled over to the trestle table, a beer can clutched in his meaty right hand. "Cute li'l kitty you got here."

"Forget the cat, Byron. Can you see where it's leaking up there?" Lant yelled, pointing at the ceiling. "Now come on into Miss Croft's bedroom and look at the other leak."

"Don't need to yell," Byron growled sullenly. His voice sounded hollow, as if he were in a cave.

"Then go get up on the roof like I said and see if you can see where it's comin' in. Miss Croft's private possessions are gettin' all wet."

Byron stared at Lant. "Can't find a leak when it's comin' down like this."

"Dammit, Byron. Look at where it's coming down *here*, memorize it, then go on up like I said and see if you can find the crack."

"Comin' down too hard, Lant." Byron was scratching the back of his neck with his free hand. "You can't see a crack in all that rain hittin' up there." He took a gulp from his beer can.

Anna felt her face go hot. She realized that Byron was right. "Lant, as we stand here, my table and dresser are being ruined. The first thing I want you and Byron to do is move them out from under those leaks."

Lant stared at her wide-eyed. "Calm down, missy. No need to get all upset. Among his abilities, Byron here is a carpenter. If your dresser gets a little out of true, he'll fix it up as good as new."

Byron fixed Anna with his dead stare.

"Byron's a jack of all trades," Lant continued. "Why he's a plumber, an electrical contractor, an auto mechanic, and a horse doctor. On top of that he's a crack hunter. Maybe you heard him blasting away a little while ago down by the river."

Byron nodded and swung his beer can up to his mouth for another swig.

"I'm happy to hear that," Anna said with a roll of her eyes. "Now will you *please* move this table and then move my dresser?"

Lant and Byron ambled over and moved the trestle table several feet into the center of the room. Anna wiped it down, went to get the shower curtain, and draped it over the table. The men then followed her lead into the bedroom, where Byron suddenly stopped. "Who's that?" he said, pointing at the bed.

Lant stared at the bed. "Have you got company, Miss Croft?"

The clothes Anna had thrown under the covers inadvertently formed a hump, as if someone short and fat might be asleep there. "They're my clothes," she said dismissively. "Shall we continue?" She took a step toward the *cassettone*. The last thing she wanted was attention drawn to her bed. "Will you please move my dresser out to the middle of the room—right here." She pointed to a spot several feet in front of the kiva fireplace.

"Come on, Byron," Lant muttered. He squinted against the splashing as he bent down and reached under one end of the dresser. "You get the other end."

Byron didn't move. Instead he stared at the dresser, running his stubby fingers through his mussed wet hair.

"*Byron.* I can't scrunch down here all day. I'm gettin' wet."

Byron shifted his weight from one foot to the other. "Lant, that thing looks real heavy. I'm gonna need some candy."

Lant stood up and wiped the water out of his eyes. "Dammit, Byron, there's hardly any left."

"Well, I'm gonna need some. I can tell that thing's heavy just by lookin' at it."

Lant gave Anna a disgusted sidelong glance. "We'll be right back."

Ten minutes later Anna was about to march over to Lant's house, when they knocked on the door and tramped in. They were sniffling, as if their rain-blown trek of forty yards had given them instant colds. But there was now a spring to their step. The candy seemed to have put them in excellent spirits.

Lant and Byron picked up the heavy oak *cassettone* as if it were a balsa stage prop and set it down in front of the kiva fireplace. Grinning, they scanned the room for something else to do. Byron's face twitched as he scratched the back of his neck.

Anna wiped the chest down with one of the towels before eyeing the flooded floor. "What about all this water?" she said. "How long do you suppose it will take it to leak through these bricks of yours and dry up without a mop?"

Byron gaped at the flooded floor as if it had just materialized beneath his feet.

"Kind of depends," Lant mumbled. He dropped to his knees as if to study the bricks through the standing water. "See how I laid these, Miss Croft? Think it was easy? Took me weeks to lay these bricks. See how they butt right up against each other? The way you lay bricks is two to one, or one to two, however you want to call it. Then you pour the sand in between. Whole thing's got to be level—the sand's got to be flat as a pancake. I don't understand why the water isn't leaking through. I must have packed 'em too tight."

"When d'ja lay these bricks, Lant?" Byron asked, coming to peer over Lant's shoulder.

"Four years ago. Wanted to show Betsy what I could do. Not that she gave a damn about how hard it was. 'This one isn't straight, Lant,' and 'Lant, this floor looks like a roller coaster.' Damn wasted effort. Felt like taking a brick to her and planting her down here." He grinned up at Anna. "Just fooling."

"Why didn't ya?" Byron had straightened and was scratching furiously under his left armpit.

"Might have gotten caught. They'd have hanged me for it."

"Ain't no hangin' done in New Mexico no more."

"How do you know that, Byron?"

"Lethal injection—that's what they do."

Lant laughed. "A hotshot?"

They began laughing.

No, Anna reflected, the restorative candy was definitely

not chocolate. It had to be meth or cocaine, and nothing about it was funny, any more than her brother Thomas's dying with a blood-streaked syringe hanging from his arm was funny. Whatever Lant and Byron smoked or sniffed had them high as a kite. Lant was now working at the bricks with something. She stepped closer to see. He had wedged one long fingernail between two bricks, trying to loosen one by its edge. It was a dementedly hopeless endeavor.

"Lant?" she said sharply. "What are you doing?" He didn't seem to hear her. *"Lant?"*

He looked up at her, his eyes wandering.

"Lant, the rain is beginning to stop. Isn't this the opportunity you and Byron were waiting for, to go up on the roof and get ready to patch the leaks? You can tell from down here where it was coming in."

But Lant had torn off part of his fingernail. *"Damn,"* he muttered. "Will you look at this?" He was staring at his bleeding fingertip with odd detachment, as if it belonged to someone else.

"What'd you do there, Lant?" Byron asked.

Lant grinned at Anna. His face was creased with dirt and sweat, and his brown eyes were dilated. She was so close that she could see the tiny broken blood vessels on his nose and cheekbones. "Must be payback," he croaked, "for me joking about burying Betsy under here."

Byron laughed his hollow laugh. He wandered over to Anna's bed and sat down on it. Groping around under the bedcovers, he pulled out a cream-colored camisole. "Look what I just found," he giggled.

Lant staggered to his feet and stumbled toward Byron.

Anna felt dizzy. Things were spinning out of control. She had to get them out. She stepped over to the window. Outside, a bright mist was rising from the warming ground. "Did you hear that?" she shouted.

Lant, standing over Byron, turned to look. "What?"

Anna cocked her head. "A police siren," she lied. "I just heard a police siren."

Lant and Byron scrambled to the window and peered through the glass. "Don't hear anything," Lant muttered. He gave Anna a suspicious look.

"Naw," Byron muttered. "Don't hear nuthin'."

"I don't, either—*now*," Anna said, wide-eyed. "But I know I *did*. I can't believe neither of you heard it."

Lant and Byron looked at each other. "Well, Miss Croft," Lant said, "guess we're all done here."

"Yeah we're all done," Byron said, slogging toward the door.

In seconds they were out, slamming the door after them.

By evening the monsoon clouds had fled north. Anna waited until most of the water had seeped through the bricks before drying them with Lant's rags. She slid the dresser drawers back inside the *cassettone*. The two pieces of furniture, she decided, would remain where they were until the leaks were fixed. The roof repair might take weeks at the rate Lant worked.

At a little before seven o'clock, a car drove up. It was Betsy.

"Got your message," she sang as Anna walked out to meet her. "Didn't I tell you about our monsoons before you moved in here, sweetheart?"

Betsy, exiting her late-model silver Mercedes, was dressed in a white linen suit with a turquoise silk scarf at her throat, sunglasses pushed back on her head. "I had a closing on a three million dollar property at Las Campanas today," she chirped.

"Couldn't get away. When there's that much money on the line, sweetie, you've got to be there and watch like a hawk to make sure no hitches come along to gum up the works."

As she spoke, Betsy's cell phone began ringing crazily. She glanced at it, shut it off, and slipped it into her white leather satchel. "Now what seems to be the problem, Anna honey?"

Anna stared. This was not the Betsy of the Cowgals' Corral, with the broad western twang and the easy manner. This was the Betsy she first met, the driven real estate operator, impatient at being called away from important deals. Where to begin? The leak? The *cassettone*?

"Betsy, two weeks ago over dinner I told you that Lant worries me. Are you aware that your ex-husband is a drug-user?"

"Oh, they all use drugs, honey," Betsy said, pushing into the guesthouse ahead of Anna. "It's nothing to worry about. Either they're drunk or they're stoned, and in either case they've got their hand in your pants. Swat 'em away, sweetheart, like pesky flies."

Walking from room to room, they were now standing in Anna's bedroom, next to the *cassettone*. Betsy glanced around, frowning. "What seems to be the difficulty?"

Anna pointed at the ceiling. "Five hours ago, water was pouring from that crack onto this antique Italian dresser of mine. Lant and his friend had to move it, but it took a lot of convincing. I don't *normally* have it standing here in the middle of the room."

"Now dear," Betsy said, "you do sound upset."

"Upset, yes. This oak dresser is a family heirloom, and it was right under the leak. I couldn't reach you, and when I had to call Lant, he came over with Byron." Her voice was trembling. "Do you happen to know Byron?"

"That big galumph of a fellow?" Betsy had begun wandering around the room as if inspecting it.

"Exactly the one. I begged them to come and move the dresser. They were obviously under the influence of drugs. Don't you consider it risky to entrust the oversight of your guesthouse to your drug-addicted ex-husband?"

"Oh, but you don't *know* that he is addicted, sweetheart. That's just conjecture."

"Well, what isn't conjecture is Lant's attitude."

"What attitude, darlin'?"

"His attitude toward women. Like his hostility toward *you*, Betsy."

"You're imagining it, sweetheart. Lant and I have ironed out our differences."

"He clearly feels betrayed. I've seen his anger."

"In what way, darlin?'"

"Well, he let slip a violent fantasy."

"Like what, dear?"

"He spoke of killing you and burying you under this brick floor."

Betsy's eyes flared. "Honey-pie, you're gettin' carried away with all your shrinkery. You've got to understand Lant. He's your basic coward. All talk and no action. That's why he spends all his stupid helpless time cookin' up cold medicine… or so they say." She seemed to recover herself. "Of course I wouldn't know anything about that."

"About *what?*"

"Never mind. I'll speak to Lant. I have been after him to fix this roof for years. He's a shirker—I admit it. It's one of the reasons I left him." She paused dramatically. "I will see that he fixes it tomorrow, and moves your dresser back where it was." She gave Anna a broad smile and a gentle pat on the fanny. "We women have to watch out for each other, don't we?"

In a moment, Betsy was outside, walking toward her car.

Following her, Anna called out. "Betsy?"

"I have to run—stay in touch, my dear."

"Betsy? There's no point in moving my furniture back until the roof is fixed. And Betsy…!"

Betsy was climbing into her Mercedes, but she stopped to give Anna a little wave. "I'll take care of everything. And we'll get together again, darlin', before the summer's over—and before your children get home."

Anna walked back inside. Near the piano, she stopped to scoop up Ma-i. She had been about to tell Betsy that she was on the verge of moving out, of breaking her lease. She struck a piano key, held it, and listened to the tone die away. Again she heard firecrackers from the direction of the river. Such loud firecrackers, she thought to herself.

Chapter Fifteen

The next morning, with the dank scent of drying earth and brick still in her nostrils, Anna combed *The Santa Fe* classifieds for a new rental. Perhaps one in town, she was thinking, closer to work, though it would be more expensive. If Betsy refused to return her deposit and final month's rent, Anna would go to Small Claims Court and cite Lant's behavior for cause. Betsy's commission on yesterday's three million dollar closing, she calculated, would make her last month's rent seem small potatoes. It was not small potatoes to Anna. The barely one hundred thousand she inherited from Anders wasn't going to last long. What Anna hoped for was a place with enough space to include an office with which to resume her practice, if not in Santa Fe, then elsewhere in the area. Meanwhile, she had to leave the guesthouse before the children came home.

She went into the kitchen and poured herself a cup of coffee. She sat down at the trestle table with her steaming cup, a place mat, and the newspaper. Ma-i mewed for attention. She picked him up and settled him on her lap. Stroking the kitten had become close to an act of meditation. Her eyes wandered over the classified page, where she had circled half a dozen ads. Soon, though, her thoughts turned to the gallery.

Selling art had so far been an interesting education. She had studied the book on Southwest art and could now comment knowledgeably on Ellis, Parsons, Bakos, Bellows, Baumann and Nordfeldt, among others. She was learning to act more like a consultant than a salesperson at the gallery. Naturally, she steered likely prospects toward Kunstler's work. It was a major victory the day she sold *Wraiths #2*. She sold another of his to a New York investment banker after his wife (surprisingly) insisted, and a third to a reputable California artist on Saturday. Sharpe mentioned that they were among the only six Kunstlers sold so far that year. He'd hinted at adding weekdays to her schedule. Working five or even four days at the gallery would justify her relocating into town.

As she was re-examining the rentals she'd circled in the paper, the phone rang. It had been three days since she'd spoken to Katey and Tommy, and she was delighted.

"I found the patching tar," the voice drawled. "We're coming over to patch that leak. I've got a good idea where the water's coming in."

"Did Betsy call you?"

"Yep. Said you were upset. Can't have you being upset, can we?"

The sound of Lant's voice sickened her. But the monsoons would now be a daily event. The paper predicted it would pour every afternoon, that week and maybe the next. "I assume you won't have to come inside?"

"If you don't *want* us to." His tone was a mix of sarcasm and reproach.

"I'd rather you didn't."

"We can do it all up top. Our job is to make you feel safe," he said, more loudly than necessary.

"Thank you."

"'Except for that dresser bureau of yours. Can't move that from the outside."

"We'll just leave that where it is for the time being."

"Whatever you say." And he hung up.

The dresser could stay where it was, Anna thought. She'd be moving soon, anyway. Lant's tone had refueled her urge to flee. Picking up her pen, she had begun underlining the phone numbers of some of the ads she'd circled, when the phone rang again. It had to be Lant. Just let it ring? But it might be the children, she realized.

"Are you busy today?" It was Sharpe. His voice sounded flat and guarded. "If you are, you shouldn't be," he said. "It's July Fourth."

Anna hesitated. Why was he calling? "Well, I have a few things I need to do…"

"How would you like to meet David Kunstler?"

Anna's face went hot. "Kunstler?"

"This afternoon. I have to go up there and pick up some papers. He asked if I would bring you along. He wants to meet the young red-headed lady who's been selling his work."

"Red-headed lady?" The description rang like a bell for Anna. Kunstler knew she had red hair? *Then that was her father at the gallery.*

"That's what he said. So are you free this afternoon?" Sharpe sounded almost impatient. "Okay if I pick you up around one-thirty at your place?"

Anna's head spun. Was she ready for this? After all these years—was she *really* ready? "Yes. One-thirty. I'll be here."

By the time they set out in Sharpe's silver BMW station wagon for the Taos High Road, the sun was blazing. The Sangre de Cristo mountains shimmered in the distance. Unlike Ohio, the desert heat was a drying heat. Even with the monsoon rains it took only an hour for the humidity to vanish. Anna had put on her loose-fitting gray slacks and her expensive lime-green blouse, open at the throat. Such clothes made her feel elegant. She wanted nothing less, for what was to be one of the great meetings of her life.

As Sharpe drove through the barren desert between Nambé and Chimayó, Anna stared out the window. There were no piñon trees, little juniper, and not any chamisa that she could see. The car seemed to float on a river of heat as it wound over the road's rises and curves. Soon the waste-land disappeared, and they were passing through the leafy cottonwoods of Chimayó, whose Sanctuary, with its holy water, she planned one day to visit. Often called the Lourdes of the Southwest, the town was at the same time said to be a main heroin distribution center for Northern New Mex-ico. Apparently whole families in the area were addicted. With its lovely river, trees and gardens, Chimayó seemed to her so unlikely a place for the misery of drug addiction and crime. Anna couldn't help thinking, as always, of her brother, dying in Seattle.

"Kunstler is an old man who lives alone," Sharpe said, breaking the silence. "He's pretty cranky."

"Does he have anybody to take care of him?" An image of Anders living alone in his Tucson *casita* had crossed her mind again, with a twinge of guilt.

"A woman from the village cleans for him, but he's mostly solo. Couple of cats. He does his art—like Agnes Martin and Earl Stroh, Taos old guard, before they died. He knew them both."

"So, he's alone. Do you know if he ever married?"

"Not as far as I know." Sharpe maneuvered the BMW over

a dirt shortcut, cursing as the car hit a pothole. "Hard to imagine any woman tolerating him."

If Kunstler was the man she met at the gallery, he *had* seemed to her pretty outspoken—and crusty. How would he tolerate a daughter and grandchildren he'd never known? But was Sharpe one to be judgmental? What about his own wife? Jane had mentioned that he treated Belinda Sharpe badly.

"I've known some women," Anna said, "who manage to put up with difficult men."

Sharpe didn't answer, instead seemed focused on the road ahead. They were gaining altitude, once again winding through desert. Now Anna noticed occasional trees and roadside bushes, as the land began to drop off steeply on both sides of the road. But her mind was elsewhere. She was considering how to shape a question. "Kunstler never had children, I suppose?" she asked as casually as possible.

"None he knows of, I'm sure."

"You must know him well to be so sure."

"I know him very well." He glanced at her. "I might as well tell you. He was the one who stopped in at the poetry reading last month."

"I wondered. Why did you pretend not to know him?"

Sharpe shrugged. "David's always been paranoid about his privacy. Besides, you didn't need to know who he was."

Didn't need to know? *Who more than she?* "I *have* been selling his art, Donald. But why is he so paranoid, as you put it? Does he have something to hide?" Instantly, she regretted her words, thinking of the Nazi camps. Yes, that would be enough to disturb anyone's state of mind for a lifetime.

Sharpe frowned, ignoring her. "Listen, when we get there, I want you to keep quiet unless he asks you a direct question. Anything can set him off. If he goes into one of his funks it could be months before we get product again. Understand?"

"I understand." This would be a waiting game. With both Sharpe and her father.

"I'm only doing this to stroke him. Make him happy. He thinks you understand his stuff, otherwise you couldn't sell it."

"Do *you* think I understand his work?"

"I told you I had a gut instinct about you, didn't I?"

Anna again found herself staring out the car window as they began passing ramshackle houses, their pitched tin-roofs streaked with rust, their front yards littered with the hulks of ancient cars disintegrating under the hot sun. The skeletal vehicles reminded Anna of the wraiths Kunstler painted—abandoned and forlorn.

She began thinking of the way he had stared at her at the gallery. He'd said she reminded him of someone from long ago. He would have known she couldn't *be* Kate, but as people aged they could become confused. Past and present could overlap, as she knew from several of her patients. Her resemblance to her mother must have stirred old emotions in him. She squirmed as she sat there, clammy from anticipation and a kind of dread.

As they drove into the town of Truchas, Sharpe mentioned they'd reached an elevation of 8,000 feet. Just as they entered the village's roadside collection of old adobes and funky art galleries, they turned left. The sign read *High Road to Taos*, and the landscape began changing yet again. The storefronts and a few more galleries and houses were quickly left behind, replaced by grassy knolls and hills covered with pine and spruce forest. After a few miles the road dipped into a valley past a sign that read Ojo Sarco. Sharpe mumbled something about the name meaning "Dry Spring." Anna wondered why people would set up a community around a spring that no longer delivered water. A little farther, the twin bell towers of a huge old mud-adobe church loomed off to the right side of the road.

"Famous old church," Sharpe announced. "It's called Las Trampas. Spanish for 'The Traps.'"

"Traps?"

"They did a lot of trapping in the old days." Sharpe snickered, apparently at a private joke. Moments later, he turned left onto a rutted dirt road that twisted down past a cluster of stucco houses huddled together, the way cattle do in winter. The road then wound up into a forest of ponderosa pine, ending in a clearing where a strange building squatted beneath the tall trees. The whole structure—an old adobe building joined to a pea-green Quonset hut—resembled a beached sea monster with a squared-off head. Parked in front of the adobe section was an old GMC Suburban, the gray paint peeling from its broad hood.

"The Quonset hut is his studio," Sharpe said. "He added it onto the old adobe house some twenty years ago, once I began moving his work."

Anna couldn't help a sensation of dizziness, confronting her father's home and workplace, the precise geographic spot where he *lived*. She stared at the old house, at its low door and three visible windows, its white stucco cracked in places. She searched her mind for an outward expression of what lay within it, as if the weathered facade, like the decrepit truck, betrayed clues to David Kunstler's character. Everything seemed to announce that outward appearances did not matter to her father, that his only concern was his work.

Even a small tree beside the short path to the studio appeared neglected. By its few leaves she saw that it was a flowering crabapple. She'd had several at her house back in

Columbus. In spring the overflowing abundance of their pink blossoms had been a glorious reminder of life's renewal. This tree seemed out of place, here, at such extreme altitude, in her father's front yard. The little crabapple seemed to ask the same question—why had it put down roots here, of all places?

They got out of the car and walked up to the door. Sharpe turned the handle of a shaft-key. Anna heard the soft metallic tinkle of the interior bell. She studied the once-white paint that was flaking from the seams between the door's vertical planks.

A bolt was thrown on the other side, and the door squeaked inward. Yes, the tall, gray-haired man standing on the threshold in his blue denim shirt and gray work-trousers—this was the man she'd expected to see. His eyes burned out at her from his deeply lined face. The stare was so intense that Anna had to lower her eyes.

Chapter Sixteen

Kunstler seemed caught for a moment in some ancient reverie.

"Well, are you going to invite us in, David?" Sharpe snapped. "We're hot and thirsty."

"Yes, yes," Kunstler said, coming to himself. "Please come in."

The musty smell of the old adobe, mixed with the scent of cooking food, greeted Anna's nostrils as she crossed the threshold. Inside, it was dark and cool, the only sound the creak of their footsteps on the worn wood flooring. The room was dominated by a heavy old dining room table. Its six equally old straight-back chairs' leather seats and backs were mottled with age. Set against a wall was an ancient roll-top desk, covered with stacks of papers and books. Above it hung three icons portraying what Anna guessed might have been Russian saints from Tsarist times.

Kunstler led them through a hallway past the entrances to two tiny bedrooms, then to the kitchen, with its worn *saltillo* tile floor, yellowed walls, and wood cabinets above heavy stone counter tops. A partially covered terra-cotta pot on an old stove gave off a fragrance of tomato and garlic.

Leaving the kitchen, they passed through a door into the

large, well-lit space of the Quonset studio. The arc of its vault reminded Anna of the interior space of a church. Instead of incense, she detected the ambient smell of turpentine and tobacco smoke.

Kunstler, smiling stiffly, led Sharpe and Anna into the interior, to four chairs that surrounded a low wooden table, its surface bleached by time. "My first New Mexico acquisition," he explained, gesturing toward the table. "Spanish Colonial. I had the chairs made. Now," he said, rubbing his hands, "please sit down. I have prepared iced tea, with mint. Or white wine, if you prefer." He coughed nervously, watching them take their seats.

"Iced tea, David," Sharpe answered. "With lemon if you have it."

"I'll have that, too, thank-you," Anna said.

"Then I will have wine," Kunstler said, pronouncing his *w*'s as *v*'s in the German way. He walked quickly back into the kitchen.

Music was playing softly through what appeared to be two vertical black screens set up at the far end of the studio. The sound of a viola, a cello and two violins playing a string quartet lent an aura of civility to the utilitarian Quonset hut. The large space was pleasantly cool, helped, no doubt, by the tall ponderosa pines that shaded the roof. But Anna was imagining how difficult the large space would be to heat in winter.

The floor's surface of unfinished planks, with its array of spilled and spattered paint, had over the years come to resemble a giant, quirky, Jackson Pollock. Leaning against one long wall was a row of variously sized stretched canvases. In a far corner, under a large tarp, Anna could see the three sturdy black legs of what was obviously a grand piano. Piled on top of the tarp were a discarded easel, coffee cans filled with paintbrushes and several small wooden boxes brimming with paint tubes. Lounging contentedly beneath the piano on an old maroon rug lay two cats, one a large orange tabby, the other a black tuxedo with her white-tipped chin. Both cats stared at the visitors with casually inquisitive eyes.

Kunstler reappeared, carrying a large tray. He set it down on the table near a large stone ashtray. He then straightened up and rubbed his lower back. "Such a minor movement," he rasped, frowning, "to carry a tray." He studied the two glasses of iced tea, the short flute of white wine, a plate of almond cookies, a bowl of black olives, a sugar bowl, several lemon slices, napkins and three teaspoons. Apparently satisfied, he placed glasses of iced tea before Anna and Sharpe, and seated himself opposite Anna. He lifted his glass. "To those present," he toasted, "and to those absent."

Anna had always felt pleasure in ritual. That first sharing of drink and food with her father—even if David Kunstler had no idea she was his daughter—*that* deserved ritual. Who were those absent for him? Her senses were alert to every word and mannerism of the man, eager as she was to know and understand him. Kunstler kept glancing at her, his eyes betraying his own curiosity. Was he catching details, with his keen artist's eye, that recalled her mother? The slight arch of her eyebrows, the contour of her forehead, the hazel of her eyes—weren't those features giving her away? From her memory of her mother, and from the few photos she had of her, Anna knew that the resemblance must be almost uncanny.

"So, do you have the new work ready?" Sharpe asked Kunstler, after munching a cookie and gulping half his iced tea.

Kunstler frowned. "Donald, why don't we talk business later, if you don't mind." He picked his words carefully, their inflection noticeable as he bore down on the syllables. He had extracted a bright blue plastic pouch from his shirt pocket. To her surprise, Anna noticed *Gauloises Caporal* printed on its side. French rolling tobacco in the American West? He began filling a cigarette paper with pinches of the dark shreds. He paused to glance at Anna. "If you don't mind?"

She smiled. "Not at all. European cigarettes smell to me like pipe tobacco, which I also like."

"Shall I roll one for you?"

"Thank you, I don't smoke. But where do you find French tobacco here?"

"It might interest you, Anna, that some twenty years ago the manufacturer of Gauloises gambled that U.S. cowboys, who roll their cigarettes anyway, might want to roll their cigarettes with French tobacco. They even included rolling papers in the vacuum-packs they shipped to New Mexico. The gamble must not have paid off, since a few years later I could no longer find them in the stores. Fortunately, I had bought up a large supply. I have rationed them carefully." He laughed and ended up coughing. "You would think that my enthusiastic purchase might have convinced them that their marketing was on the right track." He licked the paper's gummed strip and sealed the cigarette. Leaning forward, he lit it with a wooden match he struck off the stone ashtray.

Sharpe shifted in his chair and checked his watch.

"What I don't understand, Donald," Kunstler said, after exhaling a cloud of smoke, "is how your new assistant has sold some of my best work in only a matter of weeks, when you yourself previously sold so little."

"I sold plenty of your art, David, just not the macabre stuff."

"Macabre?" Kunstler widened his eyes at Anna. "As bad as all that?" He laughed.

Sharpe shrugged. "You know I've sold tons of your work—the work that counts."

"*Work that counts?*" Kunstler repeated in a hushed tone. "Donald, the only work of mine that counts are the paintings this young lady so easily sells. The other is…is *poshlost*, as the Russians say." He gave Anna an ironic smile. "Vulgarity, triviality, banality."

Sharpe waved his hand as if to dismiss the subject. "The music you've got playing over there—how about turning it down?"

Kunstler gave Anna a sidelong glance. "How does one put up with a man who does not appreciate the string quartets of Franz Josef Haydn?"

Anna could see that the two men interacted as if their relationship over the years had become one of amused tolerance. She would be silent. It was enough that her newfound gift for sales seemed to have gotten things off to a good start with the men.

Kunstler leaned back in his chair and shook his head at Sharpe. "Donald, whenever you visit you ask me to turn the music down. You are as regular as a cuckoo clock. Do you have something against music?"

"I have something against *this* music. Ancient stuff. How about some jazz? Hip-hop? Classic rock?"

"Ah, yes." Kunstler turned to Anna. "Do you see why he does not appreciate my Grosse Fugue work? Tell me, Anna, do you prefer Beethoven's music or Donald's up-to-date Rock stuff?"

How could Anna ever have forgotten his speaking of the Grosse Fugue—that thorny passage in Beethoven's string quartet—when they first met in the gallery? But what did her father mean that some of his painting was trivial or banal?

Were they talking about the art she originally found on his web site? But Jane had said that that was his past work. His latest art was hardly banal. Unlike most of the other work in the gallery, it was difficult, even shocking. Were they playing with her? "I like Beethoven *and* the up-to-date music," she said, diplomatically. "But I have never heard Haydn's music so clearly—as if the musicians were in the room with us."

"Ah, you see? No wonder Anna sells my difficult work. She knows how to say the right thing. She wraps people around her little finger," Kunstler said, laughing. "Those two screens are actually loudspeakers," he said. "They transmit the music transparently, as if the musicians, as she says, are in the room." He began coughing from his cigarette smoke, and held up a hand as if refusing help. "But again…" he said, recovering. "only one who understands—no *feels*—my work can convince another to buy it. This requires a special quality." His eyes gleamed at Anna. "Tell me, where did you find her, Donald?"

"*Find* her?" Sharpe said, shaking his head. "She came into the gallery one day and I couldn't pull her away from your crazy work. That's how I found her."

Kunstler dragged deeply on his cigarette and exhaled. "Then we are fortunate." Turning to Anna, his eyes were abruptly peaceful. "And what do you see in my work, my child?"

My child. It didn't sound condescending from her father's lips. He said it as a church pastor might, but the words carried more personal freight than he could have imagined. "I can see…" she began, not wanting to sound corny, or pandering. "I can see the way your work conveys suffering. The human condition is what I see, reflected in your skeletal creatures and your half-people. You distort physical appearance to portray souls in torment. Anybody who has felt that torment, even a bit of it, will connect with your work."

Kunstler's eyes had never left her. "Half-people, yes," he said, smiling bitterly. "Once, a long time ago, I myself was a half-person. A *mischling*. I was called that because only half of me was acceptable. Do you by chance know any German?"

Anna shook her head.

"A *mischling* is a mongrel. To them, to the Aryans, I was a mixed-breed, a mongrel." He fixed Anna with a calm stare. "But now the geneticists tell us that we *homo sapiens* are all the same. Out of Africa, they tell us. So you see, one has only to wait long enough for the truth—for unexpected redemption."

"Wait long enough and we're all dead," Sharpe said carelessly.

Kunstler leaned forward and stubbed his cigarette out in the ashtray. "Anna, I can't be too hard on Donald. We are two sides of the same coin. I am the head and he is…" He laughed softly. "Well, I can't say he is the ass—maybe just my Eugen Meckler…my Mephistopheles."

Anna noticed Sharpe's face flush. Tired of being a spectator at a two-person drama with few plot clues, she decided to change the subject. "Mr. Kunstler, I see you have a piano over there." She pointed across the room. "My daughter Katey was taking piano lessons where we used to live. These days she is playing from Schumann's *Scenes from Childhood*."

"Really? Your Katey is playing from Schumann's *Kinderszenen*?"

Your granddaughter Katey is taking lessons…Anna thought to herself. "I'll have to find a teacher for her when she and her brother come back from visiting their father."

Kunstler seemed intrigued, even touched. "How wonderful that your Katey is playing such things."

"She's studying *Träumerei* just now."

"Ah yes, that gem from the *Kinderszenen*. It is called "Reverie" in English." He put his hand to his forehead. "Well, some time I would like to hear your Katey play Schumann's "Of Strange Lands and People.""

Anna nodded toward the piano. "And you? Do you ever play your piano, all covered up as it is?"

"Play the piano?" Kunstler glanced at the covered instrument. "Long ago. Now, never."

"And yet, there it is," Anna murmured, "almost begging to be played." Was she being flippant—too presumptuous? Of course she knew an outline of his history, but she wanted more, from his own mouth.

Kunstler stared across the room at the piano. "It was a gift from my great uncle, long ago. He gave it to me when I came to America, when he thought I might have ahead of me a concert career." Slowly, he shook his head. "So long ago."

"But you keep it," Anna persisted.

"It makes a fine shelf for my painting materials."

"I'll bet it needs tuning," she ventured.

"No doubt." Kunstler pulled out his pouch and began rolling a new cigarette. "So, this much I know—you are good at selling the Grosse Fugue work of an artist who is a stranger to you." He glanced at her. "What else do you do with your life?"

Anna decided to gamble. "I will tell you, if you tell me why you no longer play your piano."

"Another time," he said, turning away. "It is a long story."

"Another time," Sharpe said. "David's too busy painting to bother with playing a piano. It's okay for your little girl to plink away on Schumann or something, but not for a successful artist who's got work to do."

Anna watched Kunstler as Sharpe spoke, but his only reaction was to wrinkle the cigarette paper, spilling a few tobacco shreds onto his lap. The piano must remind her father of past pain, she guessed. She would ask again when the time came. And she would tell him about *her* life, but not with Donald present.

Over the next hour, after more iced tea and wine, Kunstler and Sharpe discussed the art market and the gallery's client list. Sharpe ticked off names on his fingers. At one point they seemed to speak in code of several of the artists Anna had studied for the gallery job—names like Bakos, Bellows and Ellis. But Sharpe and Kunstler used the names, it seemed to Anna, to define certain styles.

"Bellows is selling well, better than Ellis these days," Sharpe said, glancing up at the corrugated roof as Kunstler nodded imperceptibly. Yet the gallery had no work by Bellows or Ellis, at least that she knew of. Did Sharpe sell certain paintings on the side, by appointment, to select clients?

When Sharpe and Anna finally rose to leave, Kunstler disappeared and returned with a manila envelope. He handed it to Sharpe, who in turn gave him a letter-sized envelope.

At the door Kunstler coughed, cleared his throat, and coughed again. "Donald," he said at last, his face reddening, "I want Anna to come and sit for me."

Sharpe raised his eyebrows. "Portraiture? You?"

"Didn't Burlin? Didn't Henri and Gaspard? I need a model for my Grosse Fugue work," he said loudly, as if to forestall disagreement. "I can't work from imagination alone."

Sharpe turned to Anna. "Do you have time for this?"

Anna could barely breathe. "During the week I think I could…"

"By the way," Sharpe interrupted, "I'm going to need you at the gallery a few extra days a week."

"Then there shouldn't be a problem," she said. "That leaves me with two free days."

Kunstler glanced at Sharpe and handed Anna his card. "My phone number. I am almost always here. Call and we will schedule the time."

Anna accepted the card, running her finger over its sharp edges.

"You'll pay her?" Sharpe snapped.

"We will discuss that," Kunstler muttered. His eyes suddenly burned at Anna, as they did when they met at his front door. This time, though, he was smiling.

Chapter Seventeen

Anna felt a buzzing in her head all the way back to Santa Fe. David Kunstler wanted her to sit for him? She'd never sat for artists or photographers, or anyone else. She had known about artists having friends, even children, pose for them. And mistresses. She knew that Picasso and others had had their mistresses pose for them, nude and otherwise. Yet the Kunstler work she had seen didn't involve females reclining sensuously on divans. He painted partially clothed *skeletal* women, wraiths—as he put it—from the dark recesses of his mind, not erotic in any normal sense. She stared out the window. Normal? What was *normal*? The way Kunstler's eyes scorched her? Could she depend on his being too old to make a pass? Would she be forced to admit she was his daughter *before* such a sitting? She glanced over at Sharpe. He had been quiet since the visit, his eyes focused on the road ahead.

"You say Kunstler has a woman come and clean during the week?" she asked casually.

"That's what he says."

"And is that all she does—clean?"

"Maybe she cooks. Maybe a few other things."

She did not want to look at Sharpe. Was he smiling, reading

her mind? "I was only wondering how he takes care of himself in such a big place."

"No, you're wondering if he's an old goat—and if he's going to go after you."

"Well, as long as you've brought it up, *is* he an old goat?"

"I guess you'll have to find out for yourself." His voice was tinged with sarcasm. "Why are you even *thinking* of sitting for Kunstler? Tell him to go paint his cleaning woman."

What a reaction from Sharpe, she thought. Was he jealous? "You know I'm interested in Kunstler's work. I just want to see what sort of man would paint what he paints."

Sharpe laughed. "Curiosity killed the cat."

Anna checked him out of the corner of her eye. "At thirty-eight I can take care of myself."

"Maybe, maybe not. David likes to get his way. If he doesn't get it he can turn nasty." Sharpe's eyes remained riveted on the road ahead.

"He doesn't *seem* nasty. He only wants me to model for him."

"Tell him you have to work at the gallery—no time for modeling."

"That's not true, though."

"So what? It'll get you out of his clutches."

Anna watched as they passed a rusted flatbed truck loaded with blocks of red stone, its dual rear tires half-flattened by the weight. "But why assume the worst? He only wants a portrait. I seem to remind him of someone."

"Hah! He'll want your clothes off. Are you ready for that?"

"How do you know?"

"And believe me, that'll be just the beginning." He glanced at her. "But maybe that's what you want."

"It's not what I want," she said firmly. "I don't believe it's what he wants, either."

The sky was darkening overhead. A new mass of monsoon thunderheads was surging in, this time from the east. She imagined Kunstler in his Quonset studio, imagined the rain's deafening downpour on its metal roof. She pictured him at his easel, saw him frown, lay down his brush, walk over to a chair, sit down and begin rolling a cigarette. He smoked thoughtfully, she imagined, waiting for the noise to subside. At his age her father may have found refuge in life's memories as he smoked—at least the happy ones. What had he looked like thirty-nine years ago? How had he charmed her mother into adultery? Was it the intensity, that burning in his eyes?

By the time Sharpe braked in front of her guesthouse to let her out, the rain was hitting the car in slanting sheets. She began to open her door to make a run for it. "Thanks for taking me to meet Kunstler," she shouted against the noise of the deluge.

Sharpe gave her a brief, sardonic look. "I'll need you at the gallery tomorrow afternoon. We could have dinner afterwards. There's a new restaurant in town."

Anna stared at the dashboard. Refuse her employer's offer? Of course, *now* she could. She'd met her father—even had his card. He'd invited her to sit for him. She could get to know him with or without Sharpe. But would Donald be vindictive, and somehow hurt her father? Drop him as one of his artists on pretext? "I can work tomorrow afternoon, but I need to be back here by six," she lied. "My landlord's coming to repair the leak in my ceiling. I've got to be here when he does it. I don't trust him."

"But you trust Kunstler?"

She glanced at him out of the corner of her eye. "They're *very* different."

"Who did you say your landlord is?" Sharpe was drumming his fingers on the steering wheel.

"Lant Wolverton."

Sharpe seemed startled. "He lives around here?"

"Why, do you know him?"

"Once," he muttered. "Anyway, you and I'll have dinner another time. Next week, for instance." Everything about his attitude was demanding.

"Maybe," she said, reaching for the door handle.

He leaned toward her. *Was he going to try to kiss her?*

"Thanks, Donald," she blurted, pushing her door open and jumping out. As she dashed through the torrent, the chill rain felt purifying.

Unlocking her front door and hurrying into the kitchen, she tugged off her soaked green blouse and flung it across a chair. Ma-i was mewing loudly, chiding her the way he did when she'd been gone for hours. She spotted a handwritten note on the kitchen counter and snatched it up.

> *Roof fixed.*
> *Time for us to celebrate.*
> *Lant*

She balled the note up and tossed it at the garbage, missing. Ma-i chased the paper ball as if it were a new game. She picked up her blouse and hurried into the dining room, where leaking water was pooling on the bricks near the trestle table. Running into her bedroom, she saw water seeping from the earlier crack that ran across the ceiling, barely missing the *cassettone*. The floor was an inch deep in rainwater. "Idiots!"

she mumbled as she sloshed back to the bathroom and hung her blouse up to dry.

Moments later she was punching Betsy's number into her phone. A recording answered, asking her to leave a message. "Betsy," she said loudly into the phone, "it's Anna. It's raining hard, and my ceiling is *still* leaking. Lant left a note saying he fixed it, but obviously he didn't. I'm afraid I'll have to start looking for another rental."

Two hours later, Anna was in the kitchen, following a recipe for *posole* to divert her attention and quiet her nerves. The storm had passed, the sky was clearing, and the water had begun seeping away through the bricks. She had assembled the pork stew meat, chile pods, oregano and garlic, and had begun boiling the hominy kernels, when she heard a knock.

Opening the door, she found Lant slouching in the fading light. "Never call Betsy when you want something," he said, sounding tired. "When you do that she just gets cantankerous. I would have come over anyhow. I'd appreciate it if you'd call me in the first place."

Anna gives him an icy stare. "Why would I call you after you've shown me you can't fix my roof?"

Lant hitched his thumbs in his belt. "Sorry about the water in the back two rooms. Byron and I must have missed something. But I'll have another look at it if you don't mind."

Anna studied him. Something about Lant seemed changed. There was no mocking smile and his expression was downcast. Was it an act? "That's all right, the water is finally draining between the bricks. It's late, Lant, and I'm preparing my dinner."

Lant looked down at his boots. "You think I'm a brainless redneck, don't you?"

She sighed. "I don't know *what* to think about you."

He pushed his Stetson back on his head. "I'm a country boy, I'll grant you that. And I act stupid from time to time, especially when Byron's around. We act stupid together. But I'm not brainless. No one who fought in 'Nam and survived could be called brainless."

"I guess that might be true."

"Lucky maybe, but not brainless." Lant's eyes darted at her. "You got a minute? I'd like to talk if you don't mind."

The last thing she wanted to do was talk to Lant. What did he have up his sleeve? "Lant, I really am busy right now. Maybe another time."

"My platoon was wiped out in the Iron Triangle. Bravo Company, Second Platoon. Forty-six good men. I was the lone survivor."

"Lant, right now I really don't want to…"

"I took a round through the chest and my platoon sergeant got shot up and fell on top o' me. A PFC friend o' mine, name of Garcia, he got hit and he fell on top o' both of us. They were both dead and I thought I was too." Lant's voice seemed to crack.

Anna stared at him. The man seemed compelled to explain—or confess. It was a compulsion with which she was well acquainted. "Well, we can't just stand here. You can come in the kitchen while I make my *posole*."

Lant took off his hat and followed her inside. "Thank-you ma'am."

Anna closed the door and showed him a chair by the kitchen table. Keeping an eye on him as he sat just inside her field of vision, she poured oil into a deep pan for browning the pork. "Vietnam was a trying time for the country," she said in the awkward silence. "And I'm sure it was the same for you soldiers who fought there."

"Sometimes it's like I'm right there again—with the fear. Lying under my dead friend and the dead platoon sergeant, I could hear the NVA walking around, jabbering. And shooting. I could hear 'em finishing off our wounded. Pop. Pop. Pop. Like that." Lant had begun breathing heavily. "One of our guys screamed. I think it was the lieutenant. Pop. The screaming stopped. The NVA came closer and closer. I played dead and prayed."

Anna was by now caught up in Lant's story. It was the tone of his voice as much as the words. He was far away, in another time and place. She set the pork aside, lowered the flame under the hominy, which had begun to bubble, and sat down at the table opposite him.

"I'm lying there, and the blood from my friend Garcia and the sergeant is dripping all over me. I'm soaking in their blood and praying and praying and pretty soon one o' the NVA comes over and drags the sergeant and the PFC off of me to get a better look at me—whether I'm dead or not. I just acted like I felt. Dead. Guess I was pretty convincing with all that blood 'cause he kicked me hard and I didn't move. After a second he moved on. He didn't want to waste a round on a dead G.I."

"How long did you have to lie there like that?"

Lant glanced at her, seeming not to recognize her. "How long?" His chin dropped and he sagged in the chair. "The NVA sat around and cooked dinner over their fires. I could smell the smoke, and the stink o' their damn fish sauce. And I could hear 'em chattering—high-pitched excited chattering. Big victory for 'em. Wiped out an American Army platoon.

Forty-six good men." He stopped to look at her. "I lay there like that all night and all next day, even long after they were gone, with that hole in my chest. Figured I'd die any time. Couldn't understand why I wasn't dead. Kept drifting off and waking up and working my fingers against my leg to know it was no dream. I felt my fingers scratching an' scratching…"

As much as Anna distrusted and disliked Lant, she couldn't help being affected. The man seemed to be suffering even now. How much had the experience damaged him? Did he recite it to others when he wanted something? Was the story even true? She needed to test him. "Where and when did this happen, Lant?"

"March, '67. Binh Duong Province, near the village of Cu Chi. Hundreds o' tunnels underground where the VC ran their supply routes. Iron Triangle. Operation Cedar Falls. We were supposed to go in there and clean 'em out." Lant laughed bitterly. "They cleaned *us* out." He glanced at her. "Bet you weren't even born yet."

"How old were you?"

"Nineteen. Felt real old. Like I already knew everything there was to know. We'd clean out the slopes. Would've too. Except we picked the wrong fight at the wrong time. If it weren't for meddling politicians and the traitorous media." He shook his head. "Long time ago now. Many nights I'm still woken up by the groans o' my dying buddies like it was happening all over again. That and the pop…pop…pop… and I work my fingers against my leg like I did then, finding out if I'm dreaming." He stared at her as if at a stranger.

Anna looked away. Lant's description of the harrowing scene was too convincing to be made up. "I'm so sorry," she murmured. To avoid showing how much he'd moved her, she checked her watch, got up and went to the stove. She stirred the hominy and added salt. The silence in the kitchen was oppressive. "As a psychologist I have known many patients who have endured traumatic events. How do *you* manage the memory of such an experience, Lant?" she asked.

"I guess I never quite get over the fear that..." He cleared his throat. "That someone out there, any time, any place, could be just waiting to kill me. Behind a parked car, maybe. Behind a bush or a tree. Maybe bust into my house in the middle of the night. Comin' to get me."

"How do you manage such fear?" Anna asked as she turned to look at him.

"How? I got guns in pretty much every room in the house. In drawers, under beds, in closets, everywhere near at hand, so if someone surprises me, coming to get me, I'm ready, no weapon more'n six feet away." He smiled at her. "I know. You think I'm crazy don't you? Betsy sure does."

"This is not The Iron Triangle, Lant."

"Yes and no, ma'am. Yes and no. This isn't 'Nam. And yet," he said, frowning, "if there's someone out to get you, they only got to get to you *once* when you're sittin' there, maybe watching the TV or having a quiet beer. And if they drill you, there's your whole life gone in one second. I survived a VC round once, and I reckon I used up all my luck on that one. Don't want to find out if my luck's run out." Lant suddenly yanks open his shirt.

Anna averted her eyes, but not before she saw the quarter-size red scar inches to the right of his sternum. Slowly, she shook her head. She knew from experience that a sociopath will use sympathy as leverage to gain a person's confidence. Was he a sociopath? She didn't know the man well enough to say. He could be dangerous, with his guns and drugs, and her children would be home in a matter of weeks. "Lant," she said, "it's not for me to say, but if you're trying to avoid trouble I would stay away from the drug trade, if that's what you're doing."

Lant stared straight ahead. "Got into that when I came back stateside. Drugs cut the pain. Then…well…" He sighed.

Anna knew the sad fact of drug-addiction among veterans. "I understand that the Veterans' Administration provides counseling."

"Yeah, tried that down in Albuquerque, like a lot of other vets," he said, re-buttoning his shirt and rising stiffly from his chair. "Guess I better get going. I'll come take another look at that leak tomorrow. Sorry about that."

She felt an unexpected pang. "The *posole* won't be ready for another couple of hours, but if you'd like to come back…"

"Thank-you ma'am, but I need to be up early tomorrow. Got some business to tend to."

She caught his glance. "Good night then, Lant."

"Good night, ma'am."

Anna closed the door after him, locked it, and watched through the panes as he disappeared. He seemed so polite, she thought. Even contrite. Was it possible Lant had turned a corner? He'd never actually done anything hurtful—to her at least. But those drugs. And Byron. It was too dangerous. With Katey and Tommy coming so soon, she would have to be watchful. And ready to move out at a second's notice.

Chapter Eighteen

Anna couldn't see Kunstler's charcoal strokes on the other side of the easel, but she could hear the faint scratching on the canvas. She studied his face, the intent hawk-like features beneath the strands of thinning gray hair, the intense gleam in his eyes as he shifted his attention to her from the canvas and back again. It gave her a small thrill each time he studied her face—his pale blue eyes taking her in, assessing her, this man who seemed smitten with her yet who didn't seem to have guessed why that might be.

In his preliminary sketches for what was to be her full-face oil portrait, he had begun by commenting on the subtle curve of her cheekbones, the clarity of her complexion, even the Pre-Raphaelite red—as he called it—of her curls. He had spoken of her eyes' elusive hazel tint, the values shifting with the changing light. Anna wondered about such admiring comments. Was it possible he would use her features to resurrect the image of the Kate he'd known and loved so long ago?

She watched her father without averting her gaze as she sat, unmoving, in the olive-green upholstered chair. It was a luxurious chair, one he said he reserved for the models he rarely painted because long sittings required comfort. He had placed her before a pair of large windows set into the

Quonset wall. The late morning light that fell on her was diffuse, filtered by the branches of the Ponderosas shading the studio.

But the Pre-Raphaelite color of her hair? Anna was struck at his comparing her to those Victorian ladies with their flowing russet tresses. She remembered a reproduction of Rossetti's Pia de' Tolomei that hung above Anders' desk in his Tucson *casita*—she of the long auburn hair and the doomed stare. Curious, Anna had researched and found that the 13th Century Sienese noblewoman's husband had had her murdered for adultery. Had Anders' hanging of Pia's portrait on his study's wall been a gesture of solidarity with Pia's husband—the cuckolds' revenge? Or was it a sign of regret—even penance—for his part in the death of Kate, her mother?

"Are you still comfortable?" They were the first words Kunstler had spoken in what seemed almost an hour. He spoke absent-mindedly, breaking the silence as if suddenly aware that he was not alone, that his subject lived and breathed.

"More than I thought I might be." She laughed inwardly at her words' private meaning. In truth she felt a little stiff in the joints. "Do your other models complain?"

He kept his eyes on his work. "The few I've had? Not often."

"I was just thinking of the way you described my hair."

"Yes?"

"You described my complexion and my curls as Pre-Raphaelite. I've been wondering how such luxuriance could find a place in your Grosse Fugue art."

He looked up. "I don't always paint bones, you know."

"Well, your comment reminded me of a picture of Pia de' Tolomei that my stepfather used to have in his study."

"Rossetti's?"

"Yes. Pia's hair was so flowing and beautiful. Mine's shorter, with curls."

Kunstler was silent for a moment. "Do you dislike my describing you as Pre-Raphaelite because of Pia's tragic end?"

"No, not that. I don't mind being compared to Pia. She was just one of many women who have suffered throughout history. Of course a few who deserve punishment escape it," she said, thinking of Heather.

"True of men too, I suppose," he said. "Who do you know who might deserve to suffer?"

"Oh, no one in particular. People get away with things. Adultery and so on."

"Adultery," he mused. "Were we put on this planet to judge others?"

"Not to judge." She would not be on this earth, Anna knew, if no spouse ever strayed.

He cocked his head and examined her. "Yes, of course your hair is shorter than Rossetti's *Pia*. I was speaking really of the *color* of your hair, with its flickering highlights. I suppose I should say you resemble a Madonna by Piero della Francesca, with your ivory skin and your fine curls floating above your head like a nimbus."

Nimbus? A divinity's halo? Were old feelings for her mother behind such words? His German accent was misleading. It made his words sound analytical, she thought, like a scientist, not someone caught up in the emotion of nostalgia. "I confess I don't know Piero's work."

"Piero was a great painter, one of the greatest of the Renaissance."

"Well, I appreciate your compliment. I'm not sure I deserve it."

"Deserve? Of course you do." He stared at her. "I have

to tell you—you do remind me of someone I once knew. It's your upper face. And your eyes."

Anna could almost hear her heart beating. "Really?" She was struck by the change in his expression, his austere manner dissolving into confusion and admiration. "Was it someone you knew well?"

"Not as well as I wished. She was like someone you reach out for, but cannot quite touch."

"Did you try? Did you try to touch her?"

"Yes," he said, averting his eyes, "I did. But not in ways—other ways—I had always hoped to touch a woman—and be touched by her."

"Was she married?" Anna dared. She was immediately ashamed. She *knew* her mother was married.

"Why do you ask?"

"It sounds as if you adored her. Much like the Provençal poets."

"Yes, those poets. They adored married women from a distance," he said, smiling faintly. "She wasn't at first, but later...." He shook his head. "Here, let us continue."

As Kunstler resumed sketching, Anna tried to imagine her mother's fling—if that was what it could be called—with this man. *But not in...other ways.* Was their attraction one-sided? Had she dallied with him, only to drop him? Had it been a long, drawn-out, off-and-on affair, with pain on both sides, begun when they studied at the Conservatory? That much she'd guessed—that they'd met, both studying music. Perhaps Kunstler had been too demanding, too needy beneath his stern persona. Had she returned to him later, for a last taste of something Anders could not supply?

"So, why did you begin working for Sharpe?" Kunstler asked.

Anna was caught off-guard. How to explain? "I was visiting Santa Fe and found myself in his gallery. I thought it might be interesting to sell art." Not an outright lie, at least.

"What did you do before that?"

"I am a psychologist. I had a practice in Ohio."

"You're a shrink?" His accent gave the word a harsh, metallic ring, as if the word were spelled *schrinck!* "I must be careful what I tell you from now on," he said, giving her a mischievous wink. "So what happened to your practice?" Kunstler worked on, but most of his attention seemed on their conversation.

"I temporarily dropped it when I left my husband."

"And why did you leave him, if I may ask?"

Was there a hint of disapproval—was he asking why women leave men? "I discovered he was having an affair with one of my patients."

"Ah. And how did he meet one of your patients?"

"She was a student of his—they were having an affair before I ever met her. She came to my office one day and begged me to take her on. Of course I knew nothing about her affair with my husband. In retrospect I realized she wanted to spy on me."

Kunstler was silent, working. "You said the other day that your children were visiting their father in Ohio. And that your daughter Katey plays the piano."

Anna was pleased. He might be old, but his memory was good. "Yes—you remembered."

"It is difficult for a child to lose a parent, even temporarily. But permanently, through divorce, or death, that is a serious matter."

Did she hear a catch in his throat? What about *his* parents—her grandparents? "I've read your biographical sheet, the one they have at the gallery. It doesn't mention your parents."

"I lost mine when I was young," he said quietly. "My father at the Battle of Stalingrad in Russia, and my mother in the camps during the war." He coughed. "Anyway, so you left your husband, and you came to New Mexico."

"First to Tucson."

"And you grew up where?"

"In North Carolina. My stepfather was a professor at a university there."

Kunstler said nothing for a minute, just sketched onto the canvas. "I knew someone from Georgia once. She grew up in Atlanta."

Anna flinched. "Really?"

"Yes."

She waited for more. But he was silent, working. "Was she a good friend?" she asked, feeling deceitful.

"She had your eyes." He was gazing past the canvas at her. "You even have the shape of her face. The upper half. I noticed it when I first met you."

Anna laughed nervously. "I think my looks are pretty commonplace. I resemble lots of women."

"That is not true. Not commonplace." He was quiet again, working. "What did you say your last name was?"

Anna froze. Not Croft. Certainly not Summers, her mother's name. Her married name? "Blackwell," she said. "Anna Blackwell."

"Anna Blackwell," he murmured. "And so do you like working for Mr. Sharpe?"

Anna was relieved, yet disappointed at the shift in subject. But she would avoid discussing Donald. "Oh, art is a pleasant diversion from psychotherapy. I must say I enjoy selling *your* art."

Kunstler's leathery features screwed up into a wry smile. "A real achievement to sell my stuff, I'm sure. Naturally, there is your commission."

"It's not just that."

"What then? It must be difficult to sell Grosse Fugue work."

"I *like* a challenge," she laughed.

"You like hard work? You must have some German blood in you."

"I think I do. But now it's my turn to ask. What brought *you* to New Mexico?"

"Me? It was after my art studies in Europe. Other artists had spoken of the incredible light in Santa Fe. Something to do with the altitude."

"The light?"

"Like a lion devouring the shadows, a friend once said. Light is everything to a painter. And then there is the New Mexico landscape. You can see the bones of Mother Earth, stripped of her skin and flesh."

"Much like your own work?"

"*Inspiring* my work."

They were silent for a while, until he announced it was time to rest. "It has been over an hour and a half," he said. "Would you like a cup of tea, or coffee?"

Anna sighed and stretched. Finding out about this man who had no idea he was sketching his own daughter made time go quickly. "A cup of coffee, thank-you."

Kunstler lifted the canvas from the easel and set it against the wall under a window.

Minutes later they were at the table, drinking coffee. One of the cats, the orange tabby, jumped up on her lap, and she stroked it.

"I have a cat too—a kitten named Ma-i."

"Cats are self-possessed and disciplined. Good examples for people."

"But they can be affectionate, too. And smart."

He nodded. "Smarter than some people. Craftier than dogs. That one's name is Johannes—'Little Johnny' in German. Named after Brahms."

Anna was curious about another name—that of a person. "When Donald was here the last time, you compared him to someone named Meckler. I didn't understand. Should I know the name?"

Kunstler gazed into his coffee cup for a long time, so long that she wondered if he had heard her question. "No one has a monopoly," he finally muttered, "on the devil's business." He glanced up at her. "You said you read my bio at the gallery."

"Yes."

"Well, then you know that as a child I was sent to the German camps…along with my mother " His eyes seemed to convey anger, fear and shame, all at once.

"Yes, I read that."

"Eugen Meckler was an SS officer. He was adjutant to the Commandant of the camp my mother and I were sent to. That was in November of 1944," he said, his voice sounding half an octave lower. "The camp was Ravensbrück. When Himmler decided in 1938 that there should be a special camp in which to eliminate the daughters, wives and children of undesirables, he decided on the lovely forests and vacation lakes of Northern Germany. Ravensbrück was out of the way, but conveniently near the rail hub of Furstenberg."

Anna listened silently. Her father had to be treading frightening territory, certainly for him, and now for her.

"Meckler was a disturbed man. I got to know him

well—too well. He took me under his wing, as he liked to say, once I was separated from my mother the moment we arrived at the camp." He put his coffee cup down, pulled out his tobacco pouch and rolling papers, and stared at them. "My mother's last words to anyone within hearing as they dragged her away from me were, 'My little David is a piano prodigy.' She shouted that again and again, like a mantra. *'My little David is a piano prodigy,'* she kept shouting in German, until I could no longer hear her. She must have thought that telling the SS guards that I was a prodigy would save me, which was ridiculous on the face of it—those psychopaths. But it turned out that my poor mother had guessed right. She understood the German psyche—at least the psyche of the *educated* German."

Anna watched Kunstler slowly roll his cigarette, lick and seal it, then light it from the flare of a wooden match. She found herself growing nervous at the dispassion with which her father spoke. "Did you ever," she asked, "were you eventually reunited with your mother?"

"My mother was Jewish. My father was an Aryan, but an Aryan tainted in Nazi eyes by his incomprehensible marriage to a Jewess—that was the term they used. My beloved mother was marvelous and tough, and a brilliant pianist and teacher." He paused, evidently to control himself. "My father was in the Wehrmacht—the Army—like most healthy German men his age. I suspect it was the disgrace of his marriage in the eyes of the Nazis that prompted his being ordered to the Eastern Front."

Kunstler took a deep drag and exhaled, watching the plume of blue smoke. "Hitler made sure few Germans understood what a catastrophe befell General Paulus and the German 6th Army at Stalingrad. 'A victory in the making,' Goebbels shrieked over the radio as hundreds of thousands died that winter. My father was killed, or froze to death, we were never told which. Only that Papa had died for the glory of the Reich. With Papa gone, I've always suspected that the delay before they came for my mother and me was because *her* father had been a decorated veteran of the First War." He shook his head. "But you never knew the truth about such things."

As he talked, Anna was aware of a brooding quality, his full lips pushed out, his eyes inexpressibly sad. She was beginning to see part of what might have attracted her mother to her father so long ago, this man who had lived and suffered so much.

"Obersturmführer Eugen Meckler happened to be within earshot of my mother's imploring words that day at the selections at Ravensbrück, and he was evidently intrigued. So, he thought—a piano prodigy. There were not such good hi-fis in those years of the war in Germany. They were mostly of the wind-up variety—especially in military quarters. Meckler was lucky. He happened to have a small Bechstein in his quarters, a piano he'd confiscated from some unlucky musician of the wrong racial or political persuasion. It was an opportunity he could not let pass. He had an SS guard bring me to his quarters that evening, where he put me to the test: did I have unusual talent, or was my mother lying in an effort to save me?"

Anna watched her father's aged features and tried to imagine the small, terrified boy, torn from his mother, being led by a menacing, uniformed guard to the officer's quarters. How did anyone's sanity survive such psychic scarring?

Kunstler had smoked only half his cigarette. He leaned forward, and with a quick darting movement, put it out in the stone ashtray. He sagged back in his chair. "Perhaps I will tell you more about Herr Meckler at our next session." He turned his eyes on her. "Why am I telling you this anyway? I never talk about my experiences." Slowly, he rubbed his chin. "What is it about you, my Anna, that I should talk to you of such things?"

Chapter Nineteen

Mid-morning Saturday, Anna watched Sharpe transfer a dozen paintings and packages from his BMW station wagon to a storeroom in his office. His stringy salt and pepper hair was pulled into a ponytail. Sweat was running down his forehead, and his glasses were sliding down his nose. It was already hot for a July morning. Anna had left Jane inside to attend to a male couple taking forever to decide whether a Southwest landscape or a Pueblo scene would best adorn their New York condo.

As she held the gallery's back door open for Sharpe, Anna noticed that only two of the canvases he was digging out of his trunk were signed—two Grosse Fugue works, which stood out oddly from the Southwest landscapes, Native American portraits and adobe villages. Why, she wondered, were the Kunstlers the only ones signed?

"Watch it!" Sharpe growled as he brushed by her with the last of the canvases. "That's it—we're finished. Lock the door behind me and bring the key."

Anna obliged, double-locking the reinforced steel door to the parking area after re-entering the building. She wasn't prepared for Sharpe's being in such a sour mood, with his shouting and cursing. How could her father stand doing business with him? Certainly an artist wanted his work shown, to make a living, but there were other galleries in town. No need to have such a cranky dealer.

"Have a nice sitting on Thursday?" Sharpe snapped, moments later, when she brought him the key. He was wiping his glasses on his shirt.

"I thought it went well," she said, surprised. How could Sharpe know that she *did* decide to sit for him? Did her father tell him?

"So, did he hit on you?" he said, watching her out of the corner of his eye.

"Not at all, Donald. He was a perfect gentleman."

"Glad to hear it. You're probably not his type."

"Well, he wanted to paint my portrait."

"You should see some of the types he paints."

"Types?" Anna tried to ignore Sharpe's innuendo. "Donald, if you dislike Kunstler, why do you show his work?"

"Business is business."

"But you yourself said his work was hard to sell. You called it morbid."

Sharpe shook his head, as if there was no use wasting his time if she didn't understand. "I have work," he said, putting on his glasses. "Go help Jane sell those guys."

Stung by his condescension, Anna felt an impulse to challenge him. She could ask him why so many of the new paintings were unsigned. But he'd only brush her off as being too naive to be told his business secrets. Better to calm down, she realized, and keep her eyes and ears open.

She joined Jane, who was trying to mediate a noisy row between two New York men who couldn't agree on which of two paintings to buy. The shorter, pudgier of the pair seemed especially provoked by his bearded partner.

"You know absolutely nothing about art, Harold," the pudgy one said, tossing his head.

"I know more than enough to have an opinion, *George*."

"*I* was the art major, Harold."

"Yes, with your C minus average."

"Better than no art courses at all. Besides, *I'm* the one *paying*."

"You *always* say that when you want your way."

Anna guessed that the drama had little to do with art. Harold was feeling diminished in front of Jane, and he was trying to show that he counted—that he *had* an opinion, especially since George had the art degree and the power of the purse. They both needed to be reassured, their feathers smoothed, the focus of discussion returned to the paintings.

"It happens," Anna said, addressing George, "that you gentlemen have chosen two examples of our artists' best work. "Moon Over Black Mesa" and "Ruins of Pecos Pueblo" happen to be among my favorites. For one thing, the Black Mesa subject is just a couple of miles from my house near Jacona. The artist has captured the extinct volcano, with its ancient mystery and its night moon glow, held sacred by the Pueblo Indians. This Pecos painting," she said, turning to Harold, "depicts the unique ruins of the old pueblo whose inhabitants pointed Coronado eastward toward the mythical Cities of Gold. How can you choose?" she said, shaking her head. "Both paintings sing the sweet flute songs of the Southwest Indians. They belong together. When you bring them back to New York you will have two windows into the beauty of our High Desert—not to mention two shrewd investments." She smiled at George, and Harold in turn.

Harold and George appeared almost relieved at Anna's interruption. She knew she had laid it on a bit thickly. But she was drawing their attention away from each other and toward the bright side of their purchase. Ten minutes later the couple decided to make peace and buy both paintings. Anna couldn't help smiling. Was she, in spite of herself, beginning to develop a little of that coyote cunning?

Jane later offered Anna half her commission on the sale, but Anna smiled and shook her head. "Maybe some day you can do me a favor."

By one o'clock, the gallery was empty. Sharpe had gone out for lunch and Anna joined Jane, who was at the front desk going over paperwork. "Jane," she said, "when Donald was unloading paintings this morning, I noticed most of the work was unsigned. I asked him about it and he said that not all artists sign their work. Yet everything showing in the gallery is signed."

Jane shrugged. "He would be right about O'Keeffe—she hardly ever signed her work. But Donald once let slip that a few of our painters are Mexicans. He said some are illiterate and can't sign their names."

"Really? The bio sheets don't mention any of our artists being from Mexico."

"One of Donald's little secrets. I'm sure he has his reasons. Anyway, he signs their names afterwards."

Anna frowned. "Why would the Mexican work have been in the same load as the Kunstlers? I doubt this morning's run included Mexico," she said, sarcastically.

Jane laughed. "Like a shop owner picking up piecework from local housewives? No, Donald owns two large self-storage units. He stores his paintings there and picks them up when he needs them."

"I hadn't thought of that," Anna murmured.

"But what amazes me is the money he seems to make,"

Jane said, glancing at the art on the walls. "His Seven-Series BMW, for instance—worth at least seventy thousand. And his house on Old Santa Fe Trail? Probably worth over two million. How many paintings do you think he'd have to sell?"

"I have no idea. Maybe the car's leased."

"Maybe. But there aren't that many 6,000 square foot rental homes in Santa Fe. He'd have to have a hundred percent turnover of his inventory every other week. Close to forty pieces every fourteen days."

"How many does he actually sell?"

"Every two weeks? Maybe twelve, if he's lucky. And he splits half the sale with the artist."

"Does his wife have money?"

"Not from what I hear."

"What else could it be? An inheritance?"

Jane shook her head. "Not likely, after that hardscrabble upbringing of his. Knowing Donald, it could be anything. His computer might tell the story, but it's got a security lock, and he never gives out the password."

"Quite a mystery, then."

"Every painting has a serial number on the back. Which could mean anything, I suppose. But I hardly ever see those paintings on these walls. After he signs them they just disappear. Which makes you wonder why he even brings them here...unless it has to do with his computer filing. He photographs everything with a digital camera before he stores them."

"That's just record-keeping," Anna said.

"But why so secretive?"

"I don't know Donald well, but isn't secretiveness in his nature?"

Twenty minutes later, Anna was eating a sushi roll in the lunchroom as she listened for the bell that announced visitors. She was mulling over her conversation with Jane. If much of the work was done by illiterate Mexican artists, she reasoned, Sharpe must buy up the paintings for very little. Was the art market so opaque that he could get by with work that compared to Canyon Road art? The paintings that Sharpe unloaded that morning appeared well executed. Did her father have any notion of Donald's business practices?

Anna glanced up as a figure suddenly darkened the doorway. Black Stetson, greasy scarf, jeans, scuffed boots. She almost dropped her sushi roll. "Lant!"

"I told Betsy I needed to return something to you," he said, grinning. "She told me where I'd find you."

"What did you need to return?"

"Not what I told Betsy." He stared at his boots. "I just wanted to say thank-you."

"For what?"

"For listening to me about my time in 'Nam. You understand me like no one else in this town does." He began cracking his knuckles. "I can see you care for me. And the thing is," he said, staring at the floor, "I care for *you*."

Anna couldn't believe her ears. "Lant, I appreciate your coming by, but this is my workplace."

"Oh, I know. I don't intend to take up your time. I was just in town and decided to drop by and say hello. Make sure you're okay," he said, nodding significantly.

"Make sure I'm okay? Why wouldn't I be?"

"Well…" Lant began, leaning backward and glancing up and down the hallway, "seeing as how you're working for the likes of Donald Sharpe."

Anna stared at him. "Excuse me?"

"If you don't know, I reckon it's not my place to be saying things. But when Betsy told me where you were working, I said to myself, Lant, either that Anna's got a whole lot more savvy in her than I gave her credit for, or the poor lady's going to find herself in some nasty trouble."

"What?"

"Considering who you're working for."

Anna took a deep breath. What, she wondered, would Lant know about Sharpe? "Lant," she said, measuring her words, "I appreciate your concern for my welfare, but this isn't the place and it really isn't the time. What about my roof? Have you fixed my roof?"

Lant's head snapped to the right and his smile disappeared. Anna heard a voice and footsteps coming down the hallway.

"I thought I told you I never wanted to see you here." It was Sharpe. Their faces were suddenly inches apart.

"Just stoppin' in to see a friend," Lant muttered between his teeth.

"Get out of here."

Lant grinned at Anna. "Be talking to you, then?"

Anna nodded slightly.

"Good-bye, Lant," Sharpe growled.

Anna listened to the sound of Lant's boots clumping back up the hallway. The gallery front door slammed.

"Nice friends you keep," Sharpe said, glowering at her.

"As I told you when you dropped me off at my place, he's my landlord. I didn't invite him here. But you've said you know him yourself."

Sharpe turned away. "We had business dealings a long time ago."

Anna blinked. "Business dealings with Lant Wolverton?"

"You finished lunch? I want you out there with Jane. I'll be in my office," he said, turning on his heel.

Anna got up, washed her plate and cup, and set them to dry. On her way back to join Jane, she passed Sharpe's office. Through the closed door she could hear the rapid clicking of his computer keyboard. What sort of business, she wondered, could he have had with Lant? As for Lant's "caring" for her—that was unnerving. She would have to step up finding a new place to live. The children would be home soon.

Telling Jane she needed to stretch her legs for a moment, Anna went outside and scrolled through the phone numbers on her cell phone. She couldn't face the possibility of Lant's dropping by to see her tonight. Would the good Dr. Peter Randler be home on a Saturday? He had phoned several times. In fact, hadn't he left a message a few days ago, asking if she'd be free this very evening, and she hadn't gotten back to him? Why had she hesitated? Had her divorce made her man-shy? Was she exhibiting the approach-avoidance behavior she had seen in some of her Ohio patients? As if she were a hungry lab rat approaching the cheese, sniffing it, and running away for fear of the random electric shock?

"Hi!" she said, when Peter answered. "It's Anna. Forgive me for not getting back to you about tonight."

"I was beginning to wonder if you were okay."

"Actually, I've been busy. Work can become endless. But I *am* free tonight if you are."

"Great—I didn't make any plans. Shall I pick you up at seven? We could have dinner at Candido's. It's not far, and they have great *guacamole*. They make it right in front of you."

Anna laughed. "That sounds wonderful."

"See you at seven, then."

She switched off her cell phone and put it in her purse. Was it a twinge of guilt she felt? Peter *was* young, but he was nice, and attractive. Not that she had forgotten his crack about liking older women. It was possible that Lant might decide to come knocking, but either she would be away at Candido's, or Peter's car would be in front of the guesthouse. Was she using Peter? She preferred to think of it as *needing* him.

Chapter Twenty

The waiter at Candido's rolled his serving cart up to their table, and Anna hungrily watched him scoop out the avocado and squeeze lime juice into the mixture that would become the restaurant's trademark guacamole. She felt elegant in the little black silk dress she so rarely wore, and smiled appreciatively across the table at Peter. He was handsome in his navy blue blazer and maroon-striped shirt, open at the throat. He had just asked her, with a twinkle in his eye, if she was still taking dangerous hikes in the desert. She was in the act of inventing a humorous answer when her cell phone bleated. "Can't imagine who could be calling," she said, giving Peter an apologetic smile. She dug the phone out of her bag and saw Sanderson's name on the cell's window.

"Mommy, Tommy and I…" It was Katey, choking back tears. "Mommy, we want to come home *now*."

"What's the matter, dear," Anna said, rising from the table. She walked out of the room to where it would be quieter.

"Daddy and Heather went out tonight. They left us with this baby-sitter who is really *mean*."

"What did she do, sweetie?'

"She hit Tommy's hand really *hard* with a spoon when he wouldn't eat his peas, and now he's crying really loud."

Katey stopped to sniffle. "I yelled at her not to hit Tommy and she slapped me in the face *hard*. Mommy, we want to come home, *now*."

"She didn't hit you in the eye or anything, did she?"

"No, but my face still stings."

"Katey, please tell the baby-sitter I want to speak to her."

"Mommy," Katey whispered, "she's downstairs in the kitchen and she doesn't know I'm calling you. If she finds out she'll get really *mad*. She might slap me again."

"Honey, please tell her your *mother* is on the phone, and I want a word with her."

"All right, Mommy."

The long silence across fifteen hundred miles was broken only by the light chatter of nearby patrons and the clink of glasses. Anna tried to imagine the scene in Ohio. Tommy could be rebellious, especially with vegetables, but hitting him was out of bounds. And slapping Katey? That was too much.

"Mommy, she won't come to the phone. She says whoever you are, you didn't hire her. Daddy and Heather did. She said your mother ought to mind her own business."

Anna felt the anger rise into her throat. "Katey," she said, as calmly as possible, "I'm sorry the baby-sitter hit you. I'll give you a big kiss when you come home in a few weeks. Sweetie, will you please tell your father to call me just as soon as he gets home? I will have to discuss this with him. Meanwhile, dear, obey the baby-sitter for the time being. She has gone against our rules about hitting, and I will discuss this with your father."

"Okay, Mommy."

"Tell Tommy I love him and of course I love you, honey."

"Thank-you Mommy."

Anna felt helpless as she clicked her cell phone off. She

would ask for the children to be home sooner, but she would be at work on weekends and wouldn't be able to leave Katey and Tommy home—not with Lant and Byron around. She would *have* to find a new place tomorrow, she realized, maybe in the Sunday classifieds. With luck she'd be able to make a decision about her father and wind things up at the gallery within a few weeks.

When she returned to the table, Peter gave her an inquiring look.

"My children in Ohio," she said. "Problems with a nasty baby-sitter."

"Here, have some," he said, handing her a blue-corn chip laden with the newly prepared guacamole. "This and the margarita should cheer you up."

He had indeed ordered cocktails while she was away. "A timely fix," she said. She hadn't felt much like eating after talking to Katey. Heather was obviously resentful of her lover's children by his former wife. That attitude might have been communicated to the sitter. Was Sanderson so clueless that he couldn't look out for his own children? What could she do now? Nothing.

The rich taste of avocado mixed with garlic, chile and onion flooded her palate. Slowly, she put her her anger and frustration aside. Perhaps Epicurus did know a thing or two about the healing effects of pleasure. The children acted up occasionally, but surely they weren't in real danger in Sanderson's house.

"Here's to the medicinal power of cocktails," Peter said, raising his glass to her.

Anna smiled and tasted her margarita. It was like an electric shock. What a strong sense taste is, she decided. Peter was right. "Did you ever see *Babette's Feast*?"

He shook his head. "Can't say I did."

"It's about a woman who was once a famous chef in Paris. She wins a lottery, then spends her whole winnings on a single gourmet feast she prepares for a cult of ascetics who live on the coast of Denmark."

"Must have been quite a feast. Did the ascetics enjoy it?" Peter asked, sipping more Margarita.

"At first, no. But they came around. It's a fable, really."

"Teaching us what?"

"Teaching the healing power of the senses."

"I'll drink to that," he said, smiling.

Anna sipped thoughtfully. She didn't want to encourage him too much—such a fine line between keeping her head and losing control. Pleasure and control, she reminded herself, were uncomfortable bedmates.

By the time Peter drove her home she was feeling giddy from the two margaritas and a final Bailey's. Not that she had forgotten the children, or that Sanderson might call, but she'd been having a good time, and that was something. Peter seemed a gentle man, not interested in manipulating her. He had the smile, confident and engaging, of a man at ease with himself. His brown eyes were alive with humor and intelligence, his lips full and sensuous. He would be difficult to resist.

By the time they pulled up in front of her guesthouse the sun had dropped behind the Jemez Mountains. It was a summer night in the high desert, dark except for a cold slice of moon. There was enough light for Anna to see that there was no sign of Lant. Peter switched off the engine and made no move to do anything more. Anna was sure she knew what he was waiting for. Would she be too much the prude not to invite him in? How harmful, she thought, could a kiss or two be?

"Would you like to come in for a cup of tea or something?" She found herself surprisingly breathless.

"I would like that very much." He said the words easily.

The kitten greeted them as they went in. She locked the door, picked him up, and caressed him. "Poor Ma-i," she whispered. "Alone all day without me."

She put the kitten down and checked his food bowl. It was almost empty.

"Who plays this?" Peter asked, nodding toward the piano.

"My daughter does, but the piano belongs to the owners. Let me give the kitten some food, then I'll heat water for the tea."

Anna quickly filled Ma-i's bowl and ran some water into the kettle."Would you prefer black tea or peppermint?" she asked as she set the kettle on the stove and turned on the burner. She was calculating that it had been almost three years since she'd had sex—banal as it had been—with Sanderson.

Suddenly she could hear Peter's breathing close behind her. She turned, and before she could say a word he pulled her into his arms and began kissing her. She hadn't expected this quite so quickly from her quiet doctor. She made a weak effort to pull away, but that seemed only to encourage him to kiss her more roughly, and it was that roughness—that force of passion—that undid what remained of her will to resist. Her arms were around his neck and she was kissing him back with the surprising force of her own pent-up desire. Her knees were going weak. She had the presence of mind to turn off the burner before she and Peter stumbled through the dining room, the children's room, and into her bedroom.

As she fell backward onto her bed she was struck by the bravado with which she had staged each step of her own seduction. But no—had she really done this? Consciously? The idea gave her an exultant sense of her own allure, of her power. He was trying to push her short black dress above her waist and she found herself lifting her hips to help him. In seconds he had buried his face between her legs and was kissing her damp underwear. His lust seemed wild, like an animal's. She was aware of a rippling sensation in her belly as he pulled her panties, slick with wet, down one leg and then, as she obliged, the other. Now she was free, and could feel the smooth sheet under her damp bottom. Again his face was between her spreading legs, his tongue at work. And now, with nothing to stop wave after wave of sensation, she soared on a hot spout of orgasm.

After a hiatus of movement she managed—as if swimming from depths to the surface—to sit upright. She pulled her dress over her head, unclasped her bra, and fell back naked on the bed. As she lay there she heard the click of his belt buckle and the sounds of his clothes being torn off. Suddenly his mouth was on her breasts, everywhere sucking, his tongue flicking her nipples. The whimpering she heard—was it coming from *her* throat? He turned slightly, and she felt his hard penis against her thigh. She reached down to feel it, feel its smooth hardness. In moments it was inside her, plunging. All thought of who this man was or what he might have thought was swept away in a wash of sensation as she lifted herself to meet him, again and again.

Was it hours or only minutes later that a man was calling, trying to wake her, summoning her from a distance amid the sound of a brutal *thumping*? She'd been dreaming she was in a coffin, somebody marching over its lid, stomping heavily from one end to the other, over and over.

"Anna! Anna—are you awake? Somebody's on the roof."

"What roof?" she murmured, still dreaming.

"Anna?"

"What?" She woke with a start, and opened her eyes in darkness. Someone *was* up there, overhead, walking around. In the stillness, the footsteps above boomed like a giant's. But why…who?

"Who would be up there in the middle of the night?" It was Peter's voice, beside her.

"It must be Lant, damn him," she mumbled. Her own voice sounded hoarse to her, like a stranger's.

"Who's Lant?"

"He's my crazy landlord. I complained about a leak when the monsoons came. He's been trying to fix it ever since." But she understood why Lant was up there. He was telling her he knew there was a man down there—with a woman he considered *his*.

"Well, I have half a mind to tell your landlord off. It's almost midnight. No time to be looking for roof leaks."

"Midnight?" Two in the morning in Ohio? *Sanderson was supposed to call.*

"Yes—just checked my watch."

The last thing Anna wanted was a confrontation. If Peter tried to be the white knight, Lant could be high on drugs, even armed. "We'd better leave Lant alone," she whispered, fearful her voice might be loud enough to be heard above. "Anyway, I'll be moving out of here soon."

"I thought you just moved in."

"Peter, he's a traumatized Vietnam veteran. He has guns all over his house. He could be dangerous."

"Well, in that case I'm not going to leave you here alone with him."

As if on cue the footsteps stopped. Anna listened into the silence. Far off, in the direction of the *barrancas*, she heard a chorus of high-pitched yips. The coyotes must be on a rabbit's scent, she thought. The small creature had to be listening and running, listening and running...

She stared up at the ceiling—was Lant gone, or just waiting? There was no way to know. "Let's not worry about him," she said, sleepily. "The door's locked."

Chapter Twenty-One

Peter had gone back to sleep, but Anna had been unable to. Instead, she'd been listening to his dream-mumblings and to the beating of her own heart. Her anger at Sanderson's not phoning was still fresh. Beyond that, Lant's raucous stomping overhead had cast an obnoxious pall over what ought have been the finale of a lovely evening. She hadn't realized just how much Peter's presence would antagonize him. She should have.

Peter's gentle, rhythmic snoring had now begun to irritate her. He could hardly have protected her if Lant had become more difficult. The sex had been good, a reminder of how exciting it could be to have a man she desired want her. Still, how attracted had she been to Peter, really, now that the margaritas had worn off? Would this amount to anything more, she mused, than a random toss in the hay?

But something else was keeping her awake—something old, familiar and unpleasant. Trying to identify it was like reaching into the back of a dark closet for a lost shoe, as if her fingers might close on a spider or a rat. Weren't the footfalls on the roof a grim reminder of what men would do? Again, she stared at the dark shape next to her, made barely visible by the sliver of moonlight shining through the window. For a brief moment she had imagined the sleeping hulk next to her was *Sanderson* of all people. That must have been why she was suddenly feeling sick to her stomach. She slipped out of bed and hurried barefoot to the bathroom, barely closing the door and making it to the toilet where she vomited up the lovely Candido's dinner.

Back in bed, Anna turned onto her side, her back to Peter and his sleep noises. What a relief it was for her to have vomited Sanderson up and into a toilet! Because that was what it had been, she knew. Anna took a deep breath and felt a trickle. Was it Peter's sperm? There would have been no bleeding this time of the month. No matter—they were her sheets to wash, not his.

Her mind wandered. She had tried to avoid sex with Sanderson those last two years. Even before Heather appeared, the idea of it had left her numb. So his turning to Heather was not all his fault? She had to grudgingly accept it. Yet what of the simple phone call she'd just asked of Sanderson? Was he, in his passive-aggressive fashion, forcing her to worry about her children? Did he exult in having his ex-wife stew?

Was it similar disappointments in men, she wondered, that sometimes turned women like Betsy to women for love? Which reminded her, she would have to call Betsy for lunch tomorrow, Sunday or not. A table at Lucinda's, just down the street from the gallery—that would be a convenient setting for the breaking of her lease.

Hours later, the bedroom was faintly illuminated with early morning light. Anna slipped out of bed, careful not to wake Peter. She dressed quietly and quickly, yearning for a walk in the morning freshness. Perhaps she would find a large rock by the river. She could sit and watch the water slide by. An hour later, sitting on the rock, she remembered to call Betsy.

Walking over to Lucinda's from the gallery at noon, Anna was surprised by her own lightness of spirit. Sunday tourists were winding their way up Canyon Road in the bright sunshine. Did they feel the relief that she did? She laughed at herself. In spite of everything, had last night's lovemaking been a balm? Or had it been the morning walk to the river, to watch the water flow smooothly over the pebbled sand?

"What a nice surprise," Betsy said, grinning, minutes later, "to have you call so nice and early this mornin'."

"I wish I could say I was calling out of friendship," Anna said as she took a seat at the table. "It's Lant again. I had a date spend the night last night and your ex-husband decided that midnight was a good time to come stomping around on my roof."

"He's such a child," Betsy said, nonchalantly pouring dressing on her chipotle and shrimp salad. "I suppose it's about time I told you what this is about," Betsy drawled. "I can't get over how much you look like the woman Lant and his brother Sam fought over—the same one Sam finally married. Almost the spitting image."

Anna stared at the tiny puddles of oily, ochre-colored dressing on Betsy's salad. *"What?"*

"It's partly your red hair. For Lant it must be like wavin' a red flag in front of a bull."

Anna glared at her. "This is something you've realized all along?"

Betsy sneaked a mischievous glance across the table as she squeezed a quarter lemon into her iced tea. "I can't say it *completely* occurred to me," she said. "It sort of crept up on me after you first walked into my office back in April. But after you took the rental I thought your resembling Sallie Ann might actually settle Lant down. Put him back on the straight and narrow. He'd respect you since you'd remind him of a girl he'd been crazy about."

Anna rearranged her silverware. She felt a new anger welling up inside her. Was Betsy making this up? But why would she do that? "You might have told me," she said, trying to stay cool. "I might not have behaved differently, but at least I would have known. No wonder he's around all the time."

"I can see that with twenty-twenty hindsight, dear, but things could've gone either way, don't you think?"

"What do you mean?"

"I'm not God—I can't see the future. Who knows, darlin', you might have thought Lant was cute."

Anna resisted rolling her eyes. "You said you were attracted to me. Why would you try to set me up with your ex-husband?"

Betsy scanned the room as if searching for an answer. "Don't know, baby."

"Betsy, I make a living as a psychotherapist. Knowing this would have helped me understand the basis for his behavior. I have children, you know."

Betsy gave her another sneaky look. "Guess I was afraid you might not want to rent the guesthouse."

"Well, that's a frank admission."

Betsy sighed. "It's true, I fell for you from the beginnin', darlin'. Couldn't help it. Thought we might get to know each other over time. Maybe more than that."

"No wonder Lant's been weird. His trying to scare me at first, then his craziness with the leak, then trying to impress me with the experience of his Vietnam near-death."

"Sorry, sweetie."

"No wonder he didn't want to fix the leak. He just wanted more chances to come and pretend to fix it. And the grudging hostility—it's the kind you *might* expect from a man who's been spurned by a woman."

Betsy stared at her plate. "Honey, I do understand."

"What were you thinking, Betsy? A man damaged by his war experience, then a Sallie Ann look-alike moves into his guesthouse?"

"So he told you about fighting in 'Nam? His being the last survivor in his platoon, the North Vietnamese shootin' his buddies?"

"I'd have had to be made of stone not to be affected."

Betsy shook her head. "That wasn't the only thing that messed him up. As I said, when he got back from 'Nam he discovered his brother Sam had bought up a bunch of oil and gas leases, made a ton of money and got Sallie Ann to marry him. Well, that was the last straw. Lant went crazy for a while. All he could think about was makin' more money than his big brother. Beatin' him out. They say he went and did some unsavory deals with that guy you work for. You know, gettin' seed capital for his future."

"Donald Sharpe?" she blurted.

"Then he went and nevertheless married me, I guess, for my cash flow 'cause I had a good job. Kind of sad, isn't it? Lant always idolized his big brother, but couldn't match him. Then he lost out on the only woman he ever really loved. Which of course was not the woman you're lookin' at right now."

Anna could only stare at Betsy. "Please tell me again what you just said? Lant did unsavory deals with Sharpe?"

"That's what people said, darlin'. A good many years ago. It's supposedly how Sharpe got the money to open his gallery."

"How do you know this, Betsy?"

"Those were the rumors, sweetheart."

Whatever Betsy's motives, Anna felt pity for this woman whose blue eyes were tearing up. "You think Lant married you because you had a good job?"

"Men do things like that to women," Betsy murmured. "You had your marriage fall apart, too. You know."

"Yes," Anna said quietly.

"Anyway," Betsy said, smiling, "I've got a solution for you."

"Solution for what?"

"A place to stay. I just bought a condo next to where I live, on upper East Palace. Closing's the last day of this month. It's a nice two bedroom, big enough for you and your children. I could rent it to you for the same price as the guesthouse. We could look at it this afternoon."

Anna wondered what in the world she had to say to this woman. "Betsy, that's thoughtful. You do understand, I hope, that whatever problems I've had with men, I'm not attracted to women?"

"All I'm tryin' to do is help you out, darlin'. At least take a look at it."

Anna sighed. She knew it wasn't smart to burn bridges, especially if she found herself in a bind in two weeks. "Let me think about it."

———

Driving into town Monday morning with the paper's marked-up rental section, Anna asked herself if Betsy knew what she was talking about. The thought that Lant and Sharpe might have done criminal deals, even decades ago, was disturbing enough. But what did that say about her aging father? Had he known about Donald's past, if what Betsy said was true? At least she would be doing more sittings for him, she hoped, before the children came home. She would have chances to question him.

The first and second rentals she saw in town turned out to be small, depressing second floor apartments in buildings that would be thought shabby if not for their adobe style. The third, a guesthouse on a dirt road off Old Las Vegas Highway, was more promising, though more costly. The owner was an elderly woman, her white hair drawn into a bun, who got herself around with a walker. Mrs. Mabel Lopez was a life-long resident whose ancestors, she made clear to Anna, had settled in Northern New Mexico in the 1700's.

Looking Anna up and down, Mrs. Lopez mumbled to herself in Spanish for a few seconds. "Well," she said, turning to English, "now that you're here, you'll want to see it."

"I had hoped to," Anna answered, half-smiling.

"You can't be too careful about tenants these days."

Using her walker, Mrs. Lopez made her way down the path to the rental unit.

Anna followed, reminding herself that landlords, too, must be vetted.

The rental unit turned out to be the size of the Wolvertons' guesthouse, but half again as expensive. It didn't have the charm of adobe, but it had a pitched tin roof that appeared leak-proof. It sat on a rise among fruit trees, with a view of the far-off Jemez Mountains to the west.

"You say you have two children?" Mrs. Lopez said, as she unlocked the door. "This isn't even a thousand square feet. It has two small bedrooms. How will you manage that?" she asked, leaning on her walker, frowning doubtfully.

"They're small children, Mrs. Lopez. Katey is eight and

Tommy is five. I'll put the children in one bedroom in their double bunk bed and I'll sleep in the other."

Mrs. Lopez seemed to ponder the concept as she led Anna inside. "Well, with that large a family you'll need to keep my little guesthouse clean."

"Oh yes."

"If you can't," she said, her voice rising, "I'll have to ask you to hire someone to clean it."

Indeed, the rental unit was neat and clean, with the charm of wood floors and wood wainscoting. "Don't worry, Mrs. Lopez. I'm very tidy, and so are my children."

"You'd be the *first...*" Mrs. Lopez mumbled, turning away.

"No, I mean it," Anna said earnestly, thinking that Mrs. Lopez might be picky, but she was many notches above Lant. And the location among the fruit trees was appealing.

"I suppose you have a job?"

"At a fine art gallery."

"Well, you'll have to give me a month's rent right now if you want me to hold it for you."

Anna hadn't checked the schools, but she assumed those in town must be good. She now knew Santa Fe to be a well-heeled, highly educated community. At least she would have two weeks to change her mind. She ferreted her checkbook out of her handbag, scribbled out the check, tore it off and handed it to the old lady. "You'll see I wrote my cell phone number."

Mrs. Lopez held it to the sunlight, tilted her head back and squinted at it. "All right, then. No pets, I hope?"

Anna smiled. "Only a kitten. Tiny and well behaved."

"Well," the old lady grumbled, turning away, "as long as there aren't any dogs."

Anna decided she wouldn't mention renting a piano for

Katey. She'd seen a place for one though, against the wall between the dining and living areas. By the time Mrs. Lopez saw what good tenants she and the children were, she wouldn't mind.

As she followed Mrs. Lopez up the path, Anna's cell rang. Peter's name showed in her phone's window.

"Hi, Peter. Can I call you back later?"

"Sure, no problem."

Anna clicked her phone off. Oddly, she couldn't think of a thing to say to this man she had slept with forty-eight hours earlier.

Chapter Twenty-Two

By mid-morning Tuesday it was already hot. The forecast, Anna had heard, was for a day in the high nineties, with little chance of cooling monsoon rains.

Sitting at her kitchen table, Anna examined her checklist. She had arranged for the phone to be disconnected and the gas and electric to be transferred to the Wolverton name. A local mover was to pick up the furniture. The things in storage would stay where they were. By mid-August everything would be in place. Tommy and Katey would need certainty and stability after their time with Sanderson and Heather. She had visited the Acequia Madre elementary school after meeting with Mrs. Lopez, and it seemed fine.

She would tell Betsy that she wouldn't be accepting the offer of her condo. Betsy would of course tell Lant that the tenant was leaving. He probably wouldn't react well, but it couldn't be helped. Long ago she'd learned not to allow herself to be taken virtual hostage by her patients, or anyone else.

She crossed off the final items on her checklist, and was getting up to make lunch, when her landline phone rang.

"Anna, it's Sanderson."

Her heart raced. "Yes, Sanderson. I've been wondering when you might call."

"I'm telephoning about the unfortunate conversation you had with the children over the weekend."

"Unfortunate?" Anna stifled a spike of anger. "I discovered that your sitter was abusing our children. Katey found it necessary to call me. Why has it taken you so long to get back to me?"

"I've been busy. You must remember that the world does not revolve around you."

"I've learned how busy you can be, Sanderson, with things that differ markedly from your work. So, are you objecting to my questioning your sitter's abuse of our children? How could you think of hiring such a person?"

"Anna, I'm not going to take the bait on this one. You're spoiling for a fight and I'm not going to engage. The sitter was perfectly responsible and the children were getting out of hand. They needed to be disciplined, that's all."

"Really? When the children act out, you just slap them down? Those are not the rules you and I raised them by."

"Well, the difference is that the children are not behaving as they once did."

"And why do you suppose that might be? Could it have something to do with how upset children become when their parents divorce? That they feel responsible, even guilty about the divorce, as I explained to you last winter?"

"Yes, yes, yes. You and your psychobabble. And the divorce is all my fault of course."

"Was *I* the one who had the affair? Did *I* refuse to go for marriage counseling?"

"We've been through this many times, Anna. Let's get back to the point. The children have been acting like spoiled brats and I will not accept it. Nor will Heather. She has done her very best, but as you know, having been her therapist, she is young and is still learning how to be a parent."

Anna took a deep breath. "Sanderson, why do you suppose Heather came and *asked* to be my patient?"

"Because she hoped and trusted that you could help her."

"No, Sanderson. She wanted to get to know me to figure out how best to pry you away from me. The better to fabricate things I supposedly said, to drive a wedge between us. Worse, you *knew* she was seeing me as a patient *even as you were bedding her.*"

"You're raving now, Anna. And you, a psychotherapist. The poor girl…"

"Poor girl! Heather would have been a major figure at the court of Caligula. Can't you see that she would love nothing better than *not* to have Katey and Tommy around her neck?"

"Anna, you're a paranoiac, pure and simple. And I won't discuss this further except to tell you that I'm sending the children back earlier than I expected. While they're with you over the coming year I suggest you teach them how to behave themselves. Did you *advise* them to misbehave so that it would make things more difficult for Heather?"

Anna barely kept herself from throwing the phone against the wall. "Exactly when will the children be coming home?"

"Home? Wherever it is you've touched down just now is not their home. The home the children *had* disappeared when you left me."

This was too much. "And who left whom? Who wandered, Sanderson? Which married man with children was it who took up with a girl young enough to be his daughter?"

"And what wife was it who was a block of ice in bed?"

"Enough of this. When are you sending the children?"

"The first of August."

"Two weeks early. Good. Send me the flight number, date and time of arrival at the Albuquerque Airport ASAP," she said coolly. She dropped the phone into its cradle and took a deep breath. August first, instead of mid-month? *The day after moving day?* She reached down, lifted Ma-i onto her lap, and stroked him to ease the throbbing in her head. She had to gather herself, try to regain a semblance of equilibrium. In two hours she would be in her father's studio.

———

Sitting in Kunstler's upholstered chair as he worked on her portrait, Anna resolved to keep up her questioning. There was less and less time to decide whether or not to reveal who she was. She had to listen for character clues.

"I've been meaning to ask you…there is a portrait, *Fear*, that hangs in the gallery. I've been wondering who he might have been. Was he a friend of yours?"

"*Fear*?" he answered vaguely, seated at his easel, deep in his work.

"Yes. Before I met you I thought he might be you. But I can see he's not."

"No, he's not me." He glanced up at her. "And yet he is."

"Really? What do you mean?"

He sighed and placed his brush in the easel's tray. "Imagine a man sitting at his desk, working. He hears the sudden pounding of knuckles on his front door. What goes through his head? Do his entrails cramp as he guesses it is the Gestapo? Or if he happens to be a Muscovite in 1935, does his brain chill as he realizes that Stalin's Cheka has come for him?"

"Did something like that happen to you? Like that?"

"I'm really speaking of *anyone* assaulted by the totalitarian…*die Gewalt*…by brute force, whether by the political Right or the Left. Both systems insist on molding everyone's thought to their prescriptions. Totalitarianism of *thought* is still totalitarianism. This *Fear* is a metaphor for anyone forced to conform to forces that may eventually knock on his door in the middle of the night."

"All right, but…"

"Of course you are speaking of my personal case." He turned to stare out the window. "Some time after my father was gone, my mother received a notice to report to Gestapo headquarters. She was terrified and claimed to be sick. So they came for us in the night. Less resistance from sleepy victims, you know."

"How awful for you," Anna whispered.

"That was only the beginning." He shrugged his shoulders in a distracted way, as if he was describing an experience told to him by a long-ago friend. He picked up his brush and examined it. He set back to work at the canvas.

She listened to her father's breathing as he worked. He occasionally coughed once or twice. Thoughts of her father's motivation to work flew through her head. Was her father caught in a closed loop, futilely painting Grosse Fugue art as if to change a certain time in his life when things went terribly wrong? Did he find it therapeutic? She cleared her throat. "Do you paint these pictures because it helps you?"

Kunstler said nothing, only painted, glancing at her from time to time, occasionally sighting her between two fingers, as if to measure her.

"Out of curiosity, when did you begin showing at the Sharpe gallery?" she asked, cautiously.

"The gallery?" he answered after half a minute. "Maybe twenty…no, twenty-two years ago."

"Did you know Sharpe before that?"

"Only by the gallery name."

"May I ask how you happened to meet him?"

He stopped and glanced at her. "Such questions!"

"Sorry. I'm just curious."

"If you must know, he came by during a studio tour. I had a little place in town in those days. He asked if he might show my work in his gallery. I readily accepted."

"Were you doing your same Grosse Fugue work then?"

Kunstler gave her a suspicious look. "No, different. Now, may we continue?"

"I only wondered if you've always painted these subjects," Anna said, hoping that her father didn't know Sharpe in those days, if it was really true that Sharpe and Lant were up to their criminality then. For a few minutes she watched him work. She felt a wave of pity for this man. So incredible that he survived. "Last time you were going to tell me about this man, Eugen Meckler. You said he'd meant to make you prove you were a piano prodigy."

Her father continued to work as if he hadn't heard her. "Yes," he said finally. "The Bechstein. The little parlor piano with the sweet tone. Meckler tried to play it himself, but he was clumsy and had no talent. Still, he thought he knew how to judge the playing of others."

"I guess I don't quite understand how he had a piano in a military barracks."

"Anna, my dear, we are not talking about a fast-moving, mechanized Wehrmacht division. He was an officer carrying out garrison duty at a prison camp with a special mission. For such officers of the SS, carrying out so sacred a duty as the elimination of the enemies of the Third Reich," he said sarcastically, "such privileges were warmly granted. You must remember, he was second in command. He lived in no barracks. He had found somebody's summer cottage and requisitioned it for his quarters."

Anna tried to imagine a world in which such a man in such a system could exist. "A murderer having a piano at an extermination camp seems especially awful to me."

Her father glanced over at her. "Lucky for me he had it or I would not be here," he said, examining his canvas. "Among the many faces of evil are those that appear kind—even sensitive—with occasional smiles that ingratiate when necessary. Meckler had that sort of face."

"But these exterminations. I've always wondered. Didn't any Germans notice and object?"

"Some knew, of course. But the German people were told that these camps were only for internment before transfer to other countries. No further details were given. In the Third Reich it did not pay to be curious. Hitler was careful. The masses might accept the idea of a Judenfrei Germany, but when it came to gassings and belching chimneys and piles of corpses down the street, that was another matter. That is why, with one exception, there were no extermination camps in Germany—only concentration camps. There, the political and racial undesirables were merely starved, beaten or tortured." Kunstler smiled grimly. "If typhus didn't finish them off, they could always be individually shot or hanged."

For Anna, Kunstler's words hung in the air like acrid smoke. "How horrible," she managed. "But where *were* the extermination camps?"

"Virtually all in Poland."

"To conceal them?"

"Also to accommodate the masses of Jews and others being transported from further East—from Silesia, the Ukraine..."

"But in all that horror, the piano. I don't understand the piano."

"Yes, the piano," he said, staring at her. "For that you must understand what music is to Germans. Even in the First War it is said that from miles away you could hear the lusty German marching songs over the tramp of their boots." He shook his head. "At one or two of Hitler's camps, they even had Jewish string quartets playing Mozart."

"I see," she said, shaking her head. "And so Meckler's having a piano in his quarters was not considered out of place. In fact it was thought *appropriate*?"

"Yes, appropriate. Music with which to relax after a hard day's work." Her father was silent for a moment, gazing at his canvas. "When Obersturmführer Eugen Meckler sat me down at his piano, child that I was, he stepped back and folded his arms. Like this," he said, crossing his arms. "'Play something from Schumann's *Kinderszenen*,' he commanded, staring at me, his eyes like a dead mackerel's. He wanted children's pieces? What did this black-uniformed character have to do with *Scenes from Childhood*? I sat there on that round-seated wooden piano stool with my hands shaking. Could I produce any music at all, much less music that could save my life? The row of white ivory keys rippled in waves before my eyes. I was hallucinating. They would not stand still. How could I play keys that moved? With all my willpower I commanded them to stop moving. Finally, they obeyed." He raised his hands into the air and examined them, as if noticing them for the first time.

"A nightmare," she whispered. "My own Katey plays pieces from *Kinderszenen*."

"So you told me. Anyway, my fingers were stiff as wood. Meckler had no sheet music. I had to play from memory.

I hadn't practiced for weeks—the time it took for us to be rounded up and quarantined, the time it took the trains to transport us with long delays from our city's railway station to Berlin, then to Furstenberg, then on to Ravensbrück. I was weak with hunger and thirst. And terror."

He became silent, staring off into space. "Over and over I see the desperate expression on my mother's face as they dragged me from her. I told myself that I must make her proud of me—that I would be able to hold my head high when I next saw her."

"How could you play *anything* under such circumstances?"

"A good question. When I was at the piano, Meckler's Luger hung from his belt in its leather case at the level of my eyes. On that first day in the camp as we were pulled off the train I had seen an old man try to run. How he got in among the women and children I have no idea. I heard a shot and saw the old fellow fall. He was still moving when an SS officer ran up and shot him in the back of the head at close range with his Luger. Either I would make Meckler's piano sing or that would happen to me. That is what I told myself. And so I began to play. Or rather some part of me I had not been acquainted with began to play. I remember watching my fingers play *Träumerei* as if they belonged to someone else. How sensitive, I thought. I was outside, gazing in, a stranger to myself. Years later at the Conservatory I tried to find that lost self to fulfill my mother's dream for me of a concert career. But it seemed I had left him behind at Ravensbrück."

"Never to be revived?"

"At the Conservatory they called it performance anxiety. But whatever it was I had lost, remained with Meckler and his Bechstein. A naive self-assurance? My life? Who knows what? Except that Meckler had made promises."

"Promises?"

"When I looked up at him after playing *Träumerei* that first time, those dead mackerel eyes were wet with tears. It was a sight I cannot forget."

"That evil man—weeping?"

"I did not know what to think. Only that if Obersturm-führer Meckler could cry, I might be saved. If an SS officer could weep, then there was hope."

Anna slowly let out her breath. "And what were those promises?"

"He said '*Mischling* Kunstler, your Yid mother was not lying. As long as you play like that I will let you live.' He sat down on a chair, took off his cap, and began to twirl it around and around on his finger. 'I will make you an offer,' he said. 'Each time, you bring me to tears I will save one child.'"

Anna felt her own eyes well up. "This man blackmailed you, a small child, into believing your playing could save the children?"

"It was a little game he invented. Who would know? Who would care? As I said, Germans adore their music. Hitler wept when he listened to Wagner." Her father's grin seemed almost a grimace.

"He made you his secret confidant," she murmured.

"With that gun on his hip."

"And together you would save the children. That is, as long as *you* didn't let *him* down. Such a weight on your little shoulders."

"Of course he lied to me. As far as I know he never saved any children. It was part of his game." Kunstler got up and began to walk in small circles beyond the canvas. "Anna my dear, you may be shocked when I tell you that during the weeks after that, gradually, amidst my terror, I found myself experiencing something like deep *affection* for that dreadful man."

"No, it is not shocking," she said softly. "That phenomenon has been studied. We now know that stress-induced reaction to captivity as the Stockholm Syndrome." And it might be difficult, she thought sadly, for her father to find in himself the trust to *love*, as a father would love a daughter. "But David, I believe you can overcome these things. I can help you. If you can bring yourself to play your piano again, with me as your audience—there might be a healing. You might find your lost self again."

"My lost self?" he suddenly shouted. "*der liebe Gott*, Kate, you *always say that*, but you don't understand the difficulty—you don't *know*!"

Anna was stunned. "Do you know what you just called me?"

He glared at her. "What are you talking about?"

"You called me 'Kate.'"

"I did not. I don't know any Kate."

"Never? You never knew a Kate?"

Her father turned away. "You are playing with me, young woman."

"Why would I play with you, David?" That was it. When she called him by his first name, it evoked a time when he studied piano—*possibly with her mother at the Manhattan Conservatory.*

"You...*that voice.*" He narrowed his eyes, studying her as if trying to decipher a hieroglyphic. "Who are you? A girl I might drink wine with, smiling into each other's eyes?" He is speaking rapidly, the German accentuation noticeable. "Your fresh face is so smooth—it makes me young," he said, shaking his head.

She gasped—was it time to tell him? Tell him that she was the daughter he never knew? That she was the child, so many years ago, of his and Kate Summers' passion? "I think the time has come…"

"No, I'm not finished." He sat down and picked up his brush. "Another half hour."

"But…"

"Only one thing I will ask of you." He was staring his hawk stare. "My Grosse Fugue work…"

"Yes?"

"You know my torsos and femurs and skulls, the metal screws and bolts and nails. Everything except what people call one's soul. I have known people without souls—smooth and strange, like stones on the moon, satanic, subhuman. But you remind me of a different beauty I once knew. The beauty in wine and laughter, in adoring glances."

"What do you want?" Anna asked, her voice trembling.

"I want…" he began. "I have drawn your face." His voice is clear and forceful. "Now I need a figure study. I need to paint the light that falls on your arms, your legs, the flesh tones and curves of your belly, your breasts, all that tells the story of your life. The unique principle that moves you." He smiled. "Please don't worry. You won't be the first I've painted, nor will you be the last."

Anna felt her face go hot. "You…you think I have such a good figure?" The silly words were out of her mouth before she could stop them.

He raised his eyebrows and laughed. "Good? Bad? What do these words mean?"

It was as she'd feared. She'd thought she would know what to say if the time came, when he would request that. But she was not prepared. A few minutes earlier she had been ready.

Not now. Why? She sat up and squared her shoulders. "I'm sorry, David. You'll have to give me time to think about that."

Kunstler tilted his head and pondered her for a minute. "Perhaps we need to become better acquainted. Why don't you come up into the mountains next week and hunt mushrooms with me. The late summer *steinpilz* season is almost here. You know *steinpilz*? Americans call them boletes and Italians call them *porcini*. My parents and I hunted them in the mountains in Germany this time of year. The taste of these mushrooms sautéed in garlic and olive oil is marvelous." He smiled. "But it is hot in here, and you, young lady, must be tired from sitting. David, be a good host and fix her a glass of iced tea," he said, rising and making a slight bow. "I will be right back."

Anna heard him inside, moving around in the kitchen. Not for the first time she glanced at the line of canvases, set facing the Quonset walls. Were any of these figure studies? What sorts of poses did he expect of his nude models? Walking over, she stooped and tipped back the nearest one and peered at it. She did the same with another. Then another. They were not figure studies. They were not even Grosse Fugue work. They were paintings of the wishy-washy variety he'd said he despised. She tipped back several more. There were desert landscapes, portraits of Indians in feathered headdresses, renditions of sun-flecked pueblo villages, all unsigned, in various styles. One even resembled a Diego Mezada—the artist whose work Sharpe told her would go into the permanent collection of the New Mexico Museum of Art. Worth fifty thousand, Donald had said. She let them fall back. What on earth was her father doing with these paintings? Were they old ones he hadn't gotten around to getting rid of?

Chapter Twenty-Three

Wednesday at noon, Anna was sitting in the gallery snack room eating a turkey sandwich and sipping a bottle of iced tea. She was there because Sharpe had added Wednesdays to her schedule. Not that the gallery had more traffic than usual that day of the week. The request seemed to have more to do with Donald's increased possessiveness now that she was sitting for Kunstler. As she bit into her turkey on rye, she again puzzled over the canvases in her father's studio. What would have possessed him to be painting scenes he'd criticized as kitsch? Had Sharpe demanded it? Had *all* the art Donald unloaded from his car the previous weekend been Kunstler's work?

Of course there was the other problem—how to avoid taking her clothes off for her father. Anders might have suggested such a thing had he been an artist. Were all old men *goats*, in Sharpe's distressing phrase? Had her resemblance to her mother been behind David's suggestion? As far as he knew, she was just a woman who reminded him of an old love.

Yet there was one aspect about the whole thing she found intriguing. It was almost as if some part of her wanted to catch a glimpse of her father's long ago passion for her mother. In her therapy practice she had come upon a number of cases of what could be called the Electra Complex, one of Carl Jung's contributions to analytical psychology. It was the love a female patient might have had—or still have—for her father, in competition with her mother. Anna hadn't been an uninterested observer in such cases. She had taken note, if only because she couldn't help wondering, at times, how things might have been had she grown up with her real father. Would she have adored him as the ancient Greek Sophocles character Electra adored her father, Agamemnon? And would *he* have adored *her*? Although it had been out of the question for her with Anders, she was open to the possibility of loving David, but in a traditional, daughterly way. Should such a love come to be, she would appreciate the irony of its occurring not in some ancient Greek city like Athens, but in the remote High Desert of New Mexico.

Flushed and disconcerted at such thoughts, Anna crumpled the wrapper from her sandwich and tossed it and the iced tea bottle into the waste bin. She got up and walked down the hall, passing Donald's office. His door was half-open and she saw he was not at his desk. She noticed sheets of paper lying on the floor between the credenza and the shredder. Had he meant to destroy these papers? She went in and kneeled down to look at them. The top sheet bore the words *BILL of LADING* in large type. The others seemed to be copies of shipping documents for works of art sent from an Albuquerque company to an import/export concern in Mexico City. Other bills of lading seemed to involve art shipped in the other direction—from Mexico City to Albuquerque. The itemized weight of the art shipment returning from Mexico was nearly 200 pounds, more than three times the weight of the shipment going *down* there. Had Jane been serious that illiterate Mexican painters produced much of the gallery's art? But what work would Donald have been sending to the Mexico City address? A last sheet of paper seemed to list art dealers in Europe and Asia, with their addresses. Did any of this relate to her father's work?

"Well, what have we here?" Sharpe demanded from where he was standing in the doorway.

Startled, Anna dropped the papers. She'd heard no tone from the gallery front door—she realized he must have come in through the back. "I saw these on the floor," she blurted as she picked up several papers and got to her feet. "I wondered whether they were meant to be shredded." She stepped over and handed them to him.

Sharpe glanced through the papers. "What do you think these are?" he asked, studying her face.

"Just…some sort of shipping documents?"

"Well, they're nothing. Just some pro forma business ideas I had."

Act casual and clueless, Anna told herself. "That's what I thought. If they were going to be shredded, I didn't think they were important."

"Exactly," Sharpe said, smiling. "And what would a shrink need to know about the gallery business anyway?"

Anna felt her face flush. "Not much, I suppose."

"You're good at sales, Anna," he said, "and that's enough. A successful gallery needs good people. Lunchtime over?"

"Yes, all finished."

"You can leave now." He stepped over and began feeding the papers into the shredder.

Entering the hallway, her heart was beating fast. She was embarrassed he'd caught her snooping, angry too at his condescension. Yet the papers had piqued her fears about what part her father might have been playing in Sharpe's business ventures. Those canvases of Southwest scenes in his studio—was Sharpe blackmailing him into painting pictures he claimed to despise? Was the work being copied in Mexico and sold overseas? Was her father being cheated of his share of the income from secret sales? What did her father know? She might have a chance to find out during their mushroom hunt next Tuesday.

Anna got home late that afternoon. She took a bowl of leftover *posole* out of the refrigerator, ladled it into a pan, and put it on the stove to heat. She now had barely a week and a half before she would pick up the children at the airport. There was so little time. Everything had to be ready for their arrival.

After fifteen minutes of unfolding, assembling and taping cardboard cartons for the packing up, she stopped to eat the *posole*. As she did, she heard the *pop, pop* of firecrackers in the direction of the river. It was well past the Fourth. Such an obsession with explosives had always puzzled her. Was it boys setting them off, or men who behaved like boys?

Her cell phone rang. Peter's name flashed on the tiny screen. He had called several times since Saturday. She had listened to his messages asking her to call back, something she hadn't done. Was it embarrassment she felt at having yielded to him so easily that night?

"Peter, how are you?"

"Anna, you had me thinking you'd left town."

"No, I'm here."

"You didn't get my messages?"

She detected a hint of hurt in his voice. "I did, but I've been so busy. Sanderson called—he's sending the children back early. I've had to speed up finding a new rental. Then there's been the packing—an extra day at the gallery, and so on."

"Saturday night was very special for me. I hope it was for you too."

"Yes, Peter. Dinner was wonderful, and…"

"I didn't mean just dinner. I was sorry to miss you in the morning. Did you go for a walk? Your car was still there."

"Oh, I just needed to get some air. I love walking by the river in the morning. I guess it was a little antisocial of me."

"I looked for a note."

"I'm sorry. So, how is everything?"

"Okay, except that I miss you."

Yes, she thought, Peter must have fallen for her. But the physicality of the sex with him had roused *her* sleeping demons—along with Sanderson goblins. "But everything's all right?" she said, at a loss for anything else to say.

"Almost not. Driving back to Santa Fe Sunday morning, some cowboy in a pickup ran me off the road. I saw him coming up fast in my rear view mirror and assumed he was just in a hurry to pass. But when he pulled alongside he swung his wheel and I had to stand on my brakes to avoid a collision. Then he stayed even with me. He kept staring over at me as if he knew me. I pulled into the breakdown lane and he went on by. I never did get his license number."

Anna felt a chill. "He was a stranger?"

"Total stranger. Must have been drunk or crazy. You never know who you're dealing with in a situation like that."

She was almost afraid to ask. "Did you notice the pickup's color?"

"White. Shiny white. Do you know anybody who drives a white pickup?"

"It's a pretty common color, white."

"Guy probably had a fight with his wife. Or lost his pay-check at the casino up the road. Took it out on the first guy who came along."

There were many white pickups, Anna told herself. But Lant *had* stomped around on her roof—and, if he had a flash-light, probably got a good look at Peter's car. Did he really consider her his Sallie Ann to lose—again? A shiver went up her spine. "At least you weren't hurt," she said. "It's a good thing you ignored him."

"No kidding. I didn't want to make him any crazier than he already was."

Moments later, Anna said goodbye and clicked off her phone. She had agreed to have dinner with Peter after she'd settled into the new house. He was young, but a good person, really. An innocent. After hearing about his incident with the pickup, she was suddenly beginning to feel responsible for him.

She resumed packing, the children's toys first. Though it was only a few minutes after five, the sky was darkening. She cursed softly as the first heavy drops fell on the roof. She had hoped the monsoon season might be over. She turned on the lights.

Over the next hour the rain fell sporadically—and the roof didn't leak. She had finished most of the packing when she heard a knock on the door. Going to see, she found Lant and Byron grinning at her from the other side of the door's glass panes. "Yes?" she said, opening the door a few inches.

"Betsy tells me you're going to be leaving us," Lant drawled. "I wanted to come by to tell you how sorry I am."

Anna noticed they were pale, sweating and twitchy. If they'd been drinking, their faces would have been flushed.

"Thank-you, Lant, but I'm very busy right now."

"Anyway I need to see if there's any more leaks after the rain," he said, pushing the door open and brushing past her.

"Lant, *excuse me*!" she shouted.

"Look, Byron, she's got another couple of weeks an' she's already packin'. Our Miss Croft can't wait to leave us."

Byron stumbled into the kitchen, a beer can wedged in his right hand. He gaped at the cardboard boxes. "I hate packin'," he mumbled, "you gotta make everthing fit."

"Byron, you're just a lazy good for nothing," Lant said, scratching his neck. "Now I just know you don't want to leave us, Miss Croft. You need to be *un*packing, not packing. I've got some candy that'll light you right up and change your mind. Got it right here," he said, reaching into his shirt pocket. "Byron and I want to keep you happy so you can stick around. Don't we, Byron?"

"That's right," Byron mumbled, blinking at Anna.

Anna fixed Lant with her sternest stare. How could she defuse this situation? Could she resurrect some part of him that would want to impress a Sallie Ann—at least before she had to phone 911? "Lant," she said, "when you told me about your Vietnam experience I thought I saw a man who was different from my first impression. I saw a soldier who had survived a tragedy and come through it stronger. I thought I saw a Lant I could respect. What has happened to that man?"

Lant's eyes carried a strange glint. "I was lying. What I told you never happened. I made it all up."

"Not according to Betsy. If you'd made it up she would have said so."

"What does Betsy know?"

"And you showed me that bullet scar in your chest."

"Got that another time," he said, grinning. "What are you talking to Betsy for anyhow?"

"It was through Betsy that I rented this guesthouse, Lant." But Anna sensed she was on treacherous ground. *Damned drugs,* she thought to herself.

Lant hitched his thumbs onto his belt. "You don't know Betsy like I do. She gets excited when I start talking about candy. She just *loves* a good snort." He was eyeing Anna as if for her reaction. "Betsy can't do without me."

"Lant, I don't know anything about your candy, and I don't want to," Anna said, crossing her arms. Betsy was turning out to be stranger than she'd imagined. Was Lant really her drug connection? Was that why it took her so long to end the marriage? She might at least have waited before telling him their tenant was leaving. Was this payback for not signing up for her next-door condo?

"Byron," Lant said, "Miss Croft seems fidgety. Do you suppose our target practice down by the river might have gotten on her nerves?"

"Wouldn't o' wanted that to happen," Byron said, staring blankly at her.

Anna felt a queasy sensation in her stomach. Shots? Not firecrackers?

"Me an' Byron had a bet on who's the better shot—him with his Smith an' Wesson Model 29, or me with my Colt Python."

"I'm going to have to ask you both to leave," Anna demanded. "Right now."

"Now that just isn't polite, Miss Croft. We came here to bid you farewell—and see about that leak. Betsy thinks we didn't even *try* to fix it. That's the impression she got—like I'm some kind of lazy low-life. Reckon I got to make good on my promises. Ain't that right, Byron?"

Byron grunted, took a swig of beer and wiped his mouth with his sleeve.

"Byron here can split a dime edgewise at 50 feet with his Model 29." Lant frowned for emphasis. "That's what we were doing this afternoon down by the river. Came across an old mangy three-legged mutt. All skin 'n' bones. Byron blew her to kingdom come."

Anna caught her breath. Did they shoot that poor emaciated dog? The one that had run away the afternoon she hiked in the *barrancas*? Is that what they were telling her? Anger and outrage welled up, choking her, crowding out her fear. "You two *big men* killed a poor, lame, defenseless dog?" She could barely control the shaking of her voice. "That must have taken real guts."

"Guts don't come into it," Byron drawled. "Killin' animals ain't like killin' people." He was staring hard at Anna. "There's laws against killin' people. Ain't no laws 'gainst killin' mangy old dogs."

"I advised him not to," Lant said, shaking his head sadly. "We were shooting tin cans, and the dog busted out from behind the bushes all of a sudden, must've been scared by the firing. Before I could stop Byron, well, he just..." But now he was smiling.

Anna walked over to where her cell phone lay on the trestle table. "I'm going to call the police if you don't leave."

Lant squinted at her. "Now hold your horses. We were only joking. He didn't really kill an old dog, did you, Byron?"

Byron grinned. "Naw, I didn't shoot no old dog."

"It was just the tin cans we were shooting," Lant said, 'for target practice. See, when you got a business of your own you can't afford to let your aim get rusty. Got to be your own bodyguard. Someone could come along, try and grab your customers. Or they could kill you, straight off. It's a jungle out there, Miss Croft. A real certified jungle. Ain't that right, Byron?"

Byron stared at Anna and nodded.

So, *this* was the face of evil, Anna realized. The same evil that fed drugs to her brother and killed him. It was a brand of evil that seized people and changed them. Evil was what her father had faced as a little boy at Ravensbrück. It was the face of an SS storm trooper grabbing a baby from a mother to kill it right in front of her. If you could kill a starving dog for pleasure, mightn't you kill people? She took a deep breath. "Do you think that because I rent your guesthouse I am at your mercy? You will now leave before I call the police and have you arrested for trespass!"

Lant's eyes flared so furiously that Anna took a step back.

"Ordering me out of my own house?" he hissed through clenched teeth. "Like Betsy's goin' to do to me? Don't mess with Lant Wolverton," he whispered. "No, don't you ever." He glowered at her for a moment. "I've got a key and you ain't gone yet. Come on, Byron, it's time we left Miss Croft for the time being."

Anna quickly locked the door after them. She found Ma-i crouched under the bed in her bedroom. She took him in her arms, sat on her bed and stroked him. He wasn't purring, instead he was staring up at her, wide-eyed. In the stress of the moment she hadn't noticed the onset of a violent head-ache. She put Ma-i down and pressed her fingers against her temples. Finally, her heart slowed its crazed beating.

Minutes later she phoned the motel where she'd stayed in April after flying in to sign Betsy's rental papers. Finding they had a room available, she grabbed her suitcase and began throwing things into it. Clothes, shoes, bathroom

articles, all went into it before she snapped it shut. She listened at the kitchen door, but could hear only the sporadic
patter of raindrops on the roof. She ran out, stowed the suitcase in the Subaru, then came back for Ma-i and his litter
box. Moments later she was gunning her car's engine to get
out of there.

Chapter Twenty-Four

Anna woke to Ma-i's soft mew next to her ear. She knew the kitten must have climbed up the side of the bedspread to watch for her eyelids' first flicker. The room was hot and stuffy, and the air had a stale, smoky smell. It was not her bed, nor was it her bedroom. She remembered. She was in a room in the Western Saddles motel. She was there because she was running from Lant. Her stomach twisted as she relived last night's fear.

She got up, set Ma-i on the floor, and made her way to the bathroom. Sitting on the john, she tried to think. Yes, she'd had patients who were hostile during the therapeutic process. Aggravated hostility could feel like a stream of toxic chemicals. She'd never lost sight of the possibility of threats to her personal safety. But Lant was not a patient who had come to her for therapy. He was unstable, operating without restraint, often under the influence of drugs. It was most likely he who had run Peter off the road. He could have killed him. Would he come after her like that?

Anna flushed the toilet and stepped into the shower. In moments the cool water was sluicing down her body. It was bracing and refreshing, clearing her mind. She had to determine how much danger she was in. Had Lant and Byron really been the ones who were shooting over by the river? If so, had they really killed that poor dog, or was it just talk? And what if the dog was still alive, only wounded? She could take it to a vet. She was going to have to drive back to Jacona. She needed to find out.

Climbing out of her car at the Wolverton guesthouse, she saw no sign of Lant or Byron. She let herself in at the kitchen door. Glancing around, she went and checked the other rooms. Packing boxes were strewn where she had left them. Everything appeared untouched, a small surprise given the aura of threat she'd left behind. The brightness of the sun shining through the windows seemed to mock her terror of fourteen hours ago. She pulled on her rubberized Bean boots and slipped outside. The neighbor's two chestnut horses neighed softly and stared at her from the far side of the fence. As always, they seemed to ignore the black and white magpies perched on their backs. She heard the hiss of an occasional car passing unseen on the tarmac by the river. There was no sign of Lant. Was he sleeping off his drug binge?

Anna locked the door behind her and made her way around the back of the guesthouse, across the tarmac, to the arroyo. Though the rain had seemed light yesterday afternoon, it must have been heavy in the mountains. The runoff had transformed the riverbed into a swollen torrent, even flooding up onto the tarmac in places. A car slowed as it approached. Anna waited for it to pass, then made her way west along the bank of the river. Bits of clothing were snagged on cottonwood roots that reached out from the banks like human arms. On the far side, a muskrat popped its head out and disappeared. The sunlight lit up a red plastic gasoline container dancing its way downstream. Skirting the large puddles, Anna continued to hike along the riverbank.

After three or four minutes something caught her eye. Hooked from the current by a blown-down cottonwood branch, it looked at first like an old bunched-up rug. As she approached it, Anna made out a jaw line and teeth. Half the head, to her horror, seemed missing. The body, half out of the water, was weirdly twisted and matted with dark splotches. Those splotches, she now saw, were patches of dried blood. Gray fur along the ridge of the dead animal's back rippled in the morning breeze. It was the three-legged dog, but hardly recognizable.

Anna sat down on a fallen tree and tried to keep from throwing up. She was shivering. Thank God the children were far away in Ohio and couldn't see this, she thought. What pleasure could anyone find in killing a starving dog? The poor animal must once have been abused, considering the way it ran from her. On scraps of *what*, along the river-bed, had it eked out a living?

Slowly Anna rose. Where could she find a shovel? She would not let the poor thing lie there, carrion for coyotes and buzzards.

An hour later, Anna's back and shoulder muscles ached. She was sitting in the guesthouse with the phone book on her lap. It was open to the blue government pages. Her hands were red from gripping the little *kiva* fireplace shovel she'd used to dig the grave. She had bent the shovel's slender shaft digging through the packed wet sand. Just let Lant or Betsy complain, she muttered to herself. She picked up the phone and punched in the numbers.

"Pojoaque Valley state police, Sergeant Garcia speaking."

The male voice had the lilting inflection of many of the local Hispanic residents.

Anna panicked for a millisecond. Exactly what would she say? "I want to report threatening behavior."

"Excuse me, ma'am?" His tone was polite. In the background she could hear the on-and-off blat of a police radio.

"I have reason to believe that my life may be in danger." Had she really used those words?

There was a pause. "I'm going to begin recording what you say now, ma'am—let me just turn this on." For a moment she could hear only the police radio. "There, now, please give me your name and location and the nature of the threat."

"My name is Anna Croft. I rent a guesthouse in Jacona. There are two men…"

"Yes ma'am?"

She stared at the brick floor under her feet. "I consider these two men to be a threat to my safety."

"In what way, ma'am? Have they assaulted you?"

Assault? As opposed to battery? How does she explain the nature of Lant's and Byron's threat? "Not exactly assaulted. But they have guns and they boasted of shooting a dog by the river nearby."

"Shot a dog? Well that's certainly illegal. Did you see them shoot it?"

"I didn't actually see them shoot it, but they bragged about it and I went out and found the dog's remains."

"But you didn't actually witness the shooting?"

"No, not actually witnessed it."

"I see. Well, ma'am, if the dog's owner wants to press charges—I take it you're not the owner?"

"It was a homeless three-legged dog," she said, a litle louder than necessary. "There *was* no owner."

"Yes, ma'am. But now you mentioned a threat to *yourself*."

"Yes, to myself." She took a deep breath. "One of the men said, *don't mess with me,* in a very threatening manner."

"To you or to the dog, ma'am?"

"To *me*!" She felt the heat of frustration welling up. "They were bragging about their guns, about shooting the dog, and they're on drugs they call candy and…"

"Candy, ma'am? You said candy? I'm having trouble hearing you with my police radio going behind me."

"They're on *drugs,*" she yelled, stamping the bricks, hurting her foot.

"Calm down, ma'am, calm down. Now please describe the nature of the threat as exactly as you can. Did one of them point his gun at you?"

"No. It wasn't a threat like that. It was more of an *implied* threat."

"An *implied* threat, ma'am?"

"As if they were going to *get* me."

"*Get* you, ma'am?" In the background the police radio went on a ranting jag.

"Yes, get me, as in *do me harm.*" She was nearly shouting. "I don't know how I can be any clearer."

"Ma'am, I can take the men's names but until a crime is actually committed, or they actually threaten to harm you, there's nothing we can do about it. We can't just go out and arrest someone on suspicion of a threat."

Anna tried to control herself. "So you have to wait until I'm dead, is that it?"

"I can take their names, ma'am. Go ahead and give me their names, so if there's further trouble we have a reference."

Anna took a deep breath. "Lant Wolverton is one."

"Yes, ma'am…Lant Wolverton. Does that end in an 'e-n' or an 'o-n?'"

"An 'o-n'."

"And how do you happen to be acquainted with Mr. Wolverton?"

"I rent a guesthouse from him and his ex-wife."

"I see. We're talking about a tenant landlord dispute?"

"Not as such. I mean, there's a leak in the ceiling but…"

"A leak?" Anna heard the police sergeant mutter something to someone. "I understand, ma'am," the sergeant said, as if everything had become clear. "And the other man? The one who isn't your landlord?"

"All I know is, his first name is Byron."

"Byron? All right, I'm writing that down, and it has also been recorded. Is there anything else?"

"So what will you do now?"

"As I said before, ma'am, we can't arrest these men just on suspicion. Especially in light of it's being a dispute between a tenant and a landlord over the roof leaking. Of course if they were to assault you, or attack you in any way, call the 911 number and we'll be over there pronto."

"It is not over a tenant landlord dispute!" she shouted.

"Yes, ma'am," he said politely, "but I have another call coming in."

"He's a stalker!"

"Yes, ma'am. If Mr. Wolverton gives you trouble, or stalks you, be sure to give us a call. Have a good day, ma'am."

———

"I'd like to buy a can of pepper spray," Anna said to the paunchy, balding, middle-aged man behind the counter of the sporting goods store. It was the first time she had ever entered such a store. Racks of hunting rifles and shotguns covered much of the floor space, row on row. The display cases were filled with a bewildering variety of guns and knives in all shapes and sizes. The walls were hung with an array of military matte-black assault rifles and automatic pistols. Why, she wondered, did they have to be *black*, as if they weren't menacing enough?

"Actually, ma'am, the pepper spray we sell doesn't come in cans."

Anna noticed that the man said this in a matter-of-fact way, minus the sneer she might have expected from a gun dealer approached by a clueless female. He ran a business, after all, she reflected. She was a potential customer.

"A can would be pretty bulky in a lady's purse," he said. "No, we sell the First Defense Model MK-6C, right here." He turned and reached behind him, producing a cylindrical piece of yellow plastic about four inches long. "This little fellow will slip into and out of your purse in the twinkling of an eye. As you see, it's really just a pistol grip with a trigger on top. It even has this little plastic clip that you can slip on your belt."

Anna stared at the device dubiously. "How does it work?"

"Well, let's say a strange dog jumped out at you…"

"I'm not going to use it against a *dog*."

The man appeared startled at the force of her reaction. "Sorry," he said. "I was just using that as an example. Whatever the threat…let's say you pulled the Model MK-6C out in self defense." He was hunched over, his elbows on the display case. "See this writing on the curved part? You want that going into the palm of your hand. Then you hold it just like you would a pistol, with your forefinger in this groove, here, in front. You point it at the threat, push this little flipper up, and then press down on the red button. Simple as that."

"How far does it shoot the spray?"

"It'll shoot up to ten feet but the closer you are, the greater the effect. Of course you don't want to let the threat get *too* close." He squinted at her. "Just what kind of threat do you have in mind?"

How could she phrase this without seeming a hysteric? "I...two men happen to be threatening me."

"In a *life*-threatening kind of way?" he asked, mildly.

"I think so," she said, looking away. How was she to explain her intuition about Lant?

"So you think these men could do you serious harm?" he asked, putting the First Defense Model MK-6C pepper spray back on the shelf behind him.

"I'm afraid so," she said, feeling small and vulnerable.

"If your life is in danger you may need something more than pepper spray, ma'am. You're not the first woman to come in here afraid for her life. Trying to deal with prowlers, jealous boyfriends, homicidal crazies. Just the other day a woman had a flat tire in a parking lot in town. She was trying to change it and asked two nearby men for help. One of them grabbed her socket wrench and hit her over the head with it, putting her in the hospital. Just for her purse. Can you imagine that? There're some real animals out there. Getting sprayed with pepper spray could just make them mad as hell."

He had produced a small flat box. He set it on the display case and opened it. Inside was something resembling a black plastic squirt gun. "This is what you need, ma'am."

Anna stared at it, thinking it couldn't be real. Was it meant to scare somebody? "What is it?" she asked.

"This is a Kel-Tec P-3AT semi-automatic," he said as he removed it from the box and laid it down gently on the glass before her. "Its magazine holds five .380 caliber rounds. When you count one in the chamber, you've got a total of six rounds at your service. It's very popular with the ladies because of its stopping power and its small size. It's light—its frame is made of ultra-modern polymers—and it fits right in the palm of your hand. Here…"

Anna shrank back. "No, I don't want a gun. I think the pepper spray will be fine."

He sighed. "If you weren't scared, ma'am, you wouldn't have worked up the courage to come in here. It's not like I sell ladies' shoes. Depending on who these guys are, you must figure your life is in danger. I have to ask you what you think your life is worth."

Anna's mind flashed back to Lant's snarling, twisted face…*I got a key an' you ain't gone yet.*

"What with all the drug problems in the area these days," he continued, "the police have their hands full. They can't defend everybody. Now, this same semi-automatic comes in .25 and .32 caliber, but I have to recommend the .380 for stopping power. You don't want a bad guy to keep coming at you after you've fired a couple of small caliber rounds into him—particularly if he's high on drugs. Might just turn him into a maniac," he said, shaking his head.

Anna's stomach turned at the thought of Lant and Byron *coming at her*. Reluctantly, she half-reached for the pistol. He gently placed it in her hand. It felt to her so small and light. She found it hard to believe that it would do anybody harm. "Are you sure this is a real gun?" she asked.

"It surely is," he said, smiling. "It even comes in this attractive black pouch that looks like it might hold jewelry." He handed her the compact woven case. He plucked the manual out of the box and turned the pages. "It says here… *The small grip size and light trigger pull make the P-3AT ideal for female shooters.*" He returned the manual to the box. "I should add it's reasonably priced. Only two hundred forty dollars plus tax."

"I wouldn't have to be licensed to own a gun?"

"No ma'am—not in New Mexico, or in most Western states. Of course we'll have to run a background check but that won't take more than a few minutes. Shouldn't be a problem. You don't exactly look like an escaped felon," he added with a grin.

Something about the feel of the gun in her hand was giving her the creeps. Not that she'd never shot one before. Back in North Carolina, when she was in college, she'd dated a guy who owned a .45 automatic. He'd dared her to fire it one afternoon when they were hiking in the mountains. When he laughed at her for being scared, she had to show him she wasn't chicken. To her surprise she managed quite well—even hit the tin can twice. But carrying a pistol around in her purse wasn't the same. Not to speak of actually using it on another human being. She handed it back to the dealer in such a hurry that she almost dropped it. "No, I couldn't," she said. "I just couldn't."

He put the gun in the box but didn't close it. "From what you tell me, I take it you're not married?" he asked, quietly.

Anna shook her head.

"And no children, I suppose?"

Anna hesitated. "I do, but they're away."

"Permanently?"

"No, they'll be back," she murmured.

"Soon?"

"Soon," she whispered.

"Are they young?"

"Yes, young," she said, reluctantly.

The man hung his head as if saddened. "And if something happened to you, would your children be taken care of?"

He'd guessed she was single, divorced or otherwise. She didn't answer, imagining Sanderson's and Heather's grim, put-upon expressions as they met the weeping Katey and Tommy at the Port Columbus International Airport. *Her children put on the plane in Albuquerque by whom?*

"You know," the man said, as his eyes roamed the store, "a mother bear will fight to the death for her cubs when threatened."

She listened for more, but that was all he said as he closed the lid of the box holding the KelTec .380 semi-automatic pistol.

Was she making a mistake? But the image of the dog's bullet-smashed body was too fresh. Only people like Lant and Byron used guns. "I couldn't shoot someone," Anna said. She thanked him, turned, and walked out of the store.

Chapter Twenty-Five

Early Saturday morning in the motel, Anna was doing her best to put on her makeup for a day at the gallery. Her clothes and shoes, retrieved the day before, were heaped along the room's walls in plastic bags. Ma-i was unsettled, and staying close. Anna hoped the motel wouldn't complain about the litter box. She hadn't been able to cook, of course, but at least the plug-in tabletop appliance had made her a cup of instant coffee.

The last two nights gave her a sense of what it was to be a fugitive. Was Lant already on her trail? At least she wasn't carrying a loaded gun around in her handbag. Should she have bought the pepper spray? How would he react, she wondered, if she were to spray him with it? Would he go berserk and attack her, as the gunstore man warned? Would she be able to get away in time? She has been pulling aside a corner of her window's curtain every so often to check the traffic on Cerrillos Road. She's counted over a dozen white pickups.

Half an hour later, parking behind the gallery next to a gray panel delivery truck, Anna sighed. She'd arrived at a place of safety, away from Lant.

Juan and Diego, the driver and his assistant, were using

hand trucks to transfer crates through the gallery's back door. Sharpe was there, pacing back and forth. He looked unusually nervous. Was she mistaking his jitteriness for her own? Hurrying inside to join Jane, Anna passed the crates stacked at the entrance to Donald's office. There were more than usual, even for a Saturday.

After Juan and Diego left, and shortly before opening time, Anna could hear the squeal of the crates being wrenched open in Sharpe's office. The expected customers, carrying their briefcases and valises, would soon begin showing up. Anna had been told by Sharpe to usher them into his office immediately—they would have first crack at the newly arrived work.

When the front door opened, there turned out to be seven of them. Three looked like aging hippies, with their faded denims and graying ponytails. Jane had told Anna about the hippie trust-funders in Santa Fe, ones you wouldn't have guessed had money. The others appeared to be cowboys, dressed up in brand-new denims, bolo ties and fancy boots, as if they were in town to party all weekend. Anna would never have imagined by their appearance that any of these were art collectors. But she was learning that Santa Fe was an unusual city.

By eleven-thirty the last of the collectors had come and gone. Anna had seen only two leave with paintings. Had Sharpe had meager success? Or had the others been given time to either make up their minds, or come up with the money? Operating a gallery must require patience, she thought, a trait she would not have counted among Donald's virtues.

But when Anna stopped by his office to mention that she was leaving for lunch, she found her boss to be a happy man. It seemed that most of the art had been sold for delivery.

"It's been a good day, Anna," Sharpe said, leaning back in

his chair, hands clasped behind his head. A hammer and a pry bar lay on the credenza behind him. Splintered boards were piled between the credenza and the door to his storage room.

"Jane said she'd watch the floor, and I thought I'd get something to eat."

"Take your time," he murmured. "There's no rush."

"I'm glad this morning's sales went well. But did you hurt yourself?" she said, noticing blood on one of his fingers.

"Nothing to worry about," he said, shrugging. "Yes, it was a good morning. As always, it's a matter of knowing your customers."

"I guess it helps to know your business, too." She noticed a faint scent in the air, one that she couldn't quite place.

"Pre-sold and ready to buy. Even a shrink would know the pull of get-it-before-it's-gone." He laughed. "Have a seat and relax, Anna."

She reluctantly took a seat on the couch. Such conviviality. She understood. He was in an expansive mood, brimming with success. The world was a beautiful place.

"Want me to tell you why I hired you, Anna?"

"You hoped I could tell the buyers from the browsers. And spot the criminals, you said."

"No, why I hired *you*," he said, lifting his boots and crossing them on his desktop. "You come across as a care-giver— someone concerned with people's well-being. Like the way you asked about my cut finger. You have class. You don't give the impression you've had to shift and scratch for a living."

"Well, I'm not a street person if that's what you mean." That smell—she realized it was baby powder. She used to sprinkle it on Katey's and Tommy's behinds to stop chafing and diaper rash—that is, until she became aware of the health warnings.

"Exactly. Your brain isn't hampered with street smarts—on the lookout for your next dollar. Your kind of intelligence operates on a higher plane. Street people are *suspicious* people. They have to be to survive. But customers can sense when someone's streetwise. It makes *them* suspicious. Know what I mean?"

"I think so." Sharpe, she realized, was congratulating himself for his wit in hiring her. It was his expansive mood speaking.

"I want my gallery personnel to operate on the same superior level as my artwork. When I first saw you, I thought, *yes.*"

"Well, that's very flattering. But may I ask you a question?"

"Go for it."

She pointed at the pile of splintered crates. "If you'd had Juan and Diego open these crates, wouldn't you have avoided cutting your hand?"

"It's not their job," he said, averting his eyes.

"But I'm sure you could hire someone…"

"No. Unlike you, I'm naturally suspicious of who that *someone* might be. My private sales are my private sales. Nobody else's business." He cocked his head. "Which again is why I hired *you.* I can trust you." He stared at her. "Because of who you are."

"That's kind of you to say," she replied warily.

"See?" he said, pointing at her. "That's what I mean. 'That's kind of you to say.' So polite, so educated."

"Not to change the subject," Anna said carefully, "and forgive my curiosity, but it looks like some of that splintered wood was the paintings' frames. Weren't the paintings packed carefully?"

"Not only that but you notice details," he said, eyeing her. "Damn Mexicans. They send the art up here with these flimsy frames. Clumsy shipping does the rest. And customs. They split frames, checking everything. Always suspicious." Sharpe slid his boots off the desktop and leaned forward in his chair. "So how's the modeling going? Kunstler attacked you yet?"

"No, and I really don't expect him to. He's been a gentleman."

"Just wait," he said, flashing a sardonic smile. "He's setting you up."

"I certainly hope not." Was now the time to mention the Southwest art she found in his studio? "One thing I've noticed is how eclectic his work is."

"What do you mean?"

"Well, he doesn't paint only the surreal work that's difficult to sell."

Sharpe's face went blank. "Really?"

"The last time I was there I noticed he also paints realist scenes. Pueblo villages, American Indians, desert landscapes, like most of the art on our gallery walls."

His eyes flashed at her. "He used to paint things like that. He probably does that to amuse himself. Or he's selling it on the side. That would piss me off—excuse the expression."

"How would he sell it? Where?"

"You never know. Maybe over the Internet, bypassing me. Thanks for mentioning it—I'll look into it." He stared at her over his reading glasses. "Now I've got work to do." Clearly they had no further business. Anna got up to leave. Again, there was that whiff of baby powder. She glanced back at Sharpe. His hands were shuffling the papers on his desk, but his eyes were following her. Had she created trouble for her father? But the wishy-washy art, as her father called it, couldn't have been news to Sharpe. The way he looked at her. He'd known about it already.

Anna decided to walk a couple of blocks to a place she knew for lunch. The restaurant was in one of Santa Fe's older buildings. Its dark, wood-paneled interior promised relief from the mid-day heat. A guitarist played there many evenings, though there would be no serenades for the Saturday lunch crowd.

A bearded, dark-haired waiter showed her to a table by the wall. She ordered a shrimp salad with chipotle sauce, and iced tea. As her eyes adjusted to the darkness, Anna noticed that Juan and Diego were sitting several tables away. They didn't seem to have seen her. The two truck drivers were talking and laughing over a pitcher of beer and chips and salsa.

As she watched, a waitress brought them what looked like plates of enchiladas and tostadas. Balding, heavyset Juan and skinny Diego bantered with their blonde teenage server for a minute. They seemed to be kicking up their heels like twenty year-olds instead of men in their forties. After the server left, Anna noticed Juan pass something to Diego, who then left the table. When he returned, Diego sat down and handed Juan something, and *he* left the table.

By the time her salad and iced tea arrived, Anna was ravenous, having had only her motel coffee that morning. Between mouthfuls she noticed Juan and Diego were again chatting up their blonde server, whispering jokes and making her laugh. The girl enjoyed the attention, or at least pretended to, perhaps hoping for a good tip. Suddenly Anna's eyes met Diego's. He smiled at her. For a few minutes he whispered to Juan. Finally he got up and came over to her table.

"Nice restaurant, no?" he said.

She nodded, embarrassed. "Yes."

"We see you eat alone. We would be happy for you to join us." His voice was soft, Spanish-accented, and slightly slurred, probably from the beer. He seemed to be making an effort to be polite—and sober.

Anna considered the offer. She had never had an opportunity to talk to the two. Diego seemed friendly. Might he drop hints about goings-on at the gallery? "Just for a moment. I have to be back at the gallery in fifteen minutes."

Anna asked her waitress to bring her food, as she followed Diego to their table. Juan rose and pulled out a chair for her. Anna, self-conscious, took her place between them.

"We are sad," Juan said, as he and Diego reseated themselves. "We see a lovely lady eating by herself with no one to talk to. I will ask the waiter for a glass for you?"

"Thank-you, but as I told Diego, I have to go back to work in a few minutes." She glanced at each in turn. "Those were a lot of crates this morning. Have you been delivering Mr. Sharpe's paintings for a long time?"

"For over four years," Diego said, importantly.

"All the way up from Mexico?"

The two men looked at each other. "Oh no," Juan said. "We drive only from Albuquerque. Do we look like Mexicans?"

"No, no," she said, aware of many New Mexican Hispanics' opinions of Mexicans. "I just thought that since the artwork is painted in Mexico…"

"Yes," Diego said after a glance at Juan. "Some Mexicans are fine artists. They are poor. These paintings help feed their families."

"But you drive from Albuquerque?"

"From Albuquerque, yes."

"And that's where you live?"

The two men looked at each other. "We live sometimes in Albuquerque and other times where our work takes us."

"Ah. So you move around."

"Yes," Diego said. "We move around. No place to call home. Is a very hard life." They laughed for no apparent reason, as if they had been suppressing it, but couldn't stop themselves.

"Why are you laughing?" she asked, smiling.

Diego shrugged. "We are very happy. Always happy after important delivery." He drained his glass and filled it again from the pitcher.

Anna noticed Juan staring at his *compadre*. "More important than usual?" she asked.

"*Muy importante*," Diego blurted, muffling a belch with his hand.

Juan said something under his breath in Spanish to his partner.

"So Donald Sharpe is a good customer?" she asked. "You take good care of him?"

"Very good customer. We take good care of him."

"And he must take good care of you, I hope?"

"Ver-r-y good care of us," Diego said, rolling his eyes. He leaned forward and extracted a large wad of bills from his back pocket. "You see?" he said, grinning.

Juan growled something again in Spanish, and Diego quickly pocketed the money.

Anna had seen that the bills were hundreds. This, she thought, for a delivery of crates? "I noticed there was damage to the paintings," she said, shaking her head. "Mr. Sharpe had to throw away much wood from the broken frames. Was he very upset?"

The two men looked at each other. "No damage," Juan said curtly.

"No, no damage," Diego agreed.

"That's strange. He had a pile of broken frames in his office. He said it was from damage from the shipping. Could he be mistaken?"

"He *muy* mistaken," Juan said. "If anything was broken inside it was from way it was packed."

"He maybe broke them himself," Diego added, shrugging.

Again Juan muttered something to Diego in Spanish. "Mr. Sharpe signed papers—everything okay."

"Yes, everything okay," Diego agreed. He drained his glass and asked her if she was ready for some beer.

She checked her watch. "I'm going to be late. Thank you, gentlemen. It was kind of you to invite me to join you. Perhaps I'll see you next Saturday?" She couldn't read the expressions on their faces. They rose unsteadily as she got up. She placed fifteen dollars on her check and left. At the door she glanced back. Juan and Diego were watching her. She smiled back at them and walked out into the scorching midday heat. Hadn't she read somewhere that baby powder can be used to cut drugs?

Chapter Twenty-Six

Early Tuesday morning Anna was in the motel's front room having a coffee and corn muffin when a plump, dark-haired woman at the desk motioned her over.

"A cowboy was here last night wanting to know which room you were staying in," she said, confidentially. "He said he wanted to say hello. Oscar, our night clerk, tried the phone in your room but there was no answer. Oscar refused to give the man your room number. That's Western Saddles policy. He told the man he could leave his name, but the man wouldn't. He just said he would be back."

Anna's stomach turned. "What did he look like?"

"Oscar said only that he was a cowboy."

"Cowboy?"

"A *vaquero*, you know." The woman gave Anna a curious look. "He told Oscar he had something for you. Oscar said he could leave it and we'd see you got it. I guess he wanted to give it to you in person."

Anna stared at the woman. "I went out for a bite to eat. I couldn't have been gone longer than forty minutes." So Lant had found her. How did he miss seeing her last night, either when she left or came back? "Please thank Oscar for me. I have no relatives or friends in Santa Fe who would come calling, and I definitely do not want my room number given out."

The young woman shook her head. "Don't worry. We won't. We have many women who come here to get away from men."

"Thank you for understanding," Anna said. It did feel strange to be classified among women who run to motels to escape violent husbands—or stalkers.

Anna returned to her coffee and muffin. She tried to chew, but was conscious only of a vise-like sensation in her stomach. She glanced at the people milling around the coffee and muffin table—mostly tourists and out-of-town salespeople. What now? What would the police believe? She had to relax. Soon she would be away, up in the mountains with her father—the father she had yet to fully understand, for her and her children's sake. When she called Katey and Tommy last night, they sounded thrilled to be coming home.

Twenty minutes later, Anna was in her room, lacing up her hiking boots. Her knee seemed almost healed, a good thing since it was sure to be stressed in the mountains. Finished, she armed herself with her backpack, a bottle of drinking water, a paring knife, and a rolled-up canvas shopping bag. Having given the woman who cleaned her room a ten-dollar tip not to let Ma-i out, Anna left her room and locked the door behind her.

Outside, she scanned the vehicles in the parking area—no white pickup in sight. Lant wouldn't be up this early, she told herself. He'd be sleeping off whatever whiskey or drugs he'd had last night. She walked quickly toward the parking lot's northwest corner. She soon spotted the old gray Suburban parked next to a utility pole. Drawing closer, she made out the features of her father's face through the sun's reflection on the windshield.

As Kunstler's ancient Suburban labored up the winding two-lane road into the Sangre de Cristo Mountains, the air gradually cooled. Anna's anxiety about Lant was already fading. Her father was clearly elated. He cheerfully cautioned that it was early in the season and they might not find any *steinpilz*, but that it would be a fine excursion anyway. He pronounced the word as if the *s* was a *sh*, his weathered features alive in a way she hadn't yet seen. He rambled on about mushroom hunting with his parents as a child in Germany before the war, about the excitement of those early mornings, getting ready for the search. His mother, he said, flushed from the work, would scurry about, boiling eggs, and packing bread, sausage and chocolate, making sure nothing would be forgotten for their picnic lunch. He described the family's dachshund, Willi, leaping around, sensing departure. He recalled his father emptying his two canteens, ready to be filled with sparkling water from a hillside spring they would pass on the way.

With a smile Kunstler told of his father driving the family's black 1933 Auto Union Wanderer, of which he had been so proud. As they'd drawn near the mountainside where generations of Kunstlers had harvested the mushrooms, David's father would peer into the rear-view mirror, on the lookout for mushroom spies. If anyone appeared to be following them, his Papa would motor right past their spot, as if the family was merely out for a drive in the country. Then he would double back and park in a hidden place behind bushes. Then out they would scramble, up the mountainside, to their secret *steinpilz* spot.

As Kunstler talked, describing those lost years in vivid

detail, Anna gazed at the aspens and evergreens covering the steep mountainsides, reminding herself that he was describing her own grandparents. It hardly seemed possible. The world of his childhood—his family, Willi—it was all of a lost age, a different planet, before a war that erased whole cities, millions of lives, entire ways of thinking about mankind.

Eventually her father stopped the Suburban—he called it his *Vorstadt,* the German word for "Suburb,"—at the foot of a nearly hidden trail that rose hundreds of yards into the forest above. Climbing out, she heaved on her backpack, grabbed her canvas bag and water bottle, and watched her father extricate his gnarled wooden staff and graying wicker basket from the profusion of gear in the back of the truck. He locked the doors, and in minutes they were on their way up the steep trail at a healthy clip.

"We will be hunting the mushrooms at just under 10,000 foot altitude," her father said. "Almost two miles above sea level. The little creatures are very particular about where they like to grow."

Her father seemed to Anna like a mountain goat, startlingly nimble for his age. The air was cool and sweet with the heady fragrance of Engelmann spruce and Douglas firs. A mountain squirrel scolded them from a treetop. A sharp-crested, gray-and-blue colored bird eyed them, hopping to ever higher branches.

"A Steller's Jay," her father said, stopping to point before continuing his stride up the path, somehow avoiding roots and rocks. "Soon, Anna, we will not be moving so fast. You cannot watch for *steinpilz* if you are running along. We will walk slowly, watching always from right to left, left to right, sometimes up ahead to see what is coming. Right to left...left to right..."

"But David," Anna gasped, doing her best to keep up. "What do these special mushrooms look like?"

Kunstler stopped and gazed at her thoughtfully. "It is true. I have not explained." He stabbed the point of his staff into the soft earth and leaned on it. "A proper one has a cap that is reddish brown, almost copper in color. The babies can measure an inch, and the grownups can be as much as eight inches across. With the big ones you watch for worms, a sign they may be overripe, though not necessarily."

"Worms?"

"Don't worry—they're tiny and you don't taste them," he said, grinning. "So…the *steinpilz* have a thick white stem that is thickest at the base and narrows as it joins the cap. Its chunkiness is what reminds the Italians of a porky pig, which is why they call them *porcini*. The underside of the rounded cap will be smooth and white, with little pinprick holes called pores. You will never see one with gills—if you do it is not a *steinpilz*." His eyes narrowed. "And if the stem turns blue when you cut it, you don't bring it home. It will give you a stomach ache."

They clambered up the mountainside, Anna trying not to think about wormy mushrooms. When she'd been a child in Florence, Anders had tried to convince her and her brother that worms in mushrooms were nothing to worry about, that the Italians ate wormy *porcini* with gusto. Of course she did not want thoughts of Anders to intrude on her time, now, with her real father.

They soon began finding a variety of mushrooms, early as it was. They passed clumps of tiny orange and white ones, some on rotting logs, some in large and small circles. Others stood alone, shaded by low evergreen branches, or out in the open. Still others jutted like rounded white shelves from the trunks of dead aspens. Some were large with white stems, their brilliant red caps embedded with what looked like white crystals.

He wagged his finger at her. "If you eat those they will make you sick. You will experience hallucinations."

"I've seen those in pictures, even in children's books. I didn't know they were poisonous."

"Bad children's books," he said with a wink.

Soon they were finding their first chanterelles, their graceful orange trumpet-shapes seeming to bloom from the earth. Kunstler deftly harvested them with his pocketknife, holding one up to the dim light that filtered through the spruce branches. To Anna it resembled a miniature sunburst.

"You see the texture of the skin?" her father whispered. "How delicate and tender? It is like the glowing skin of a young woman." He gave her a loving glance. "You may ask why I want to paint you nude. It would be to fix your special beauty to canvas for all time, to make it permanent. It is the making of art, Anna."

Anna frowned. It was not a subject she relished. "But wouldn't realist nude portraits be wishy-washy art?"

His rapt expression faded, and his hand holding the mushroom fell to his side. "Anna, painting a lovely woman in her natural state is the same as painting life itself. It is the antidote to the Grosse Fugue testimonials."

Anna gazed at the tiny *chanterelle* stumps left in the ground. "Would painting me remind you of the woman whose name slipped out of your mouth last week…the woman, Kate?"

Kunstler glanced at her out of the corner of his eye. "Kate is gone. You are here."

"Do you ever think about Kate?" she asked, quietly. "Do you wonder what happened to her?"

"*Ach*, women. Always jealous. I have no idea what happened to her."

"Why would I be jealous? No, I was just wondering." So, Anna realized—her father and mother had lost touch over the years. He didn't know about the accident on the *autostrada*. But there was another matter. "David, I happened to mention wishy-washy art because..." she began. "Last week when I was in your studio, when you went out to make tea, I was curious about the art you had turned to face the wall."

"Yes?"

"I thought it might be unfinished work, not ready to be sent to Donald. Or maybe they were nudes you did of other women. I was curious to see how you painted them."

A shadow seemed to fall across his face. "And so what did you do?"

"I confess I turned a few around. They seemed finished, but they were the sort of work you called wishy-washy that day when you came to the poetry reading." She glanced at his face, which was darkening. "I'm confused."

"Let us look for mushrooms," he mumbled, and strode off uphill.

"David, please don't ignore me," she pleaded. "If you want me to pose that way for you, I will need to understand you. Right now I don't."

Kunstler stopped and stared at the ground for what seemed minutes. "They're commodities, that's all," he murmured. "Those paintings of mine you saw...they are like coffee or orange juice, wheat or barley. Sold in markets. You understand?"

Anna nodded. "I know what commodities are."

"It is okay to make a living, yes?" he asked quietly, as if

to the trees. "Sharpe likes to sell these things. They are easy to do—not serious, of course, but harmless. Not against the law."

"Do you know what he does with those paintings?"

"Do you?" His stare was probing, demanding. "No, you don't. It is not our business what he does with them."

"He pays you to…"

"Yes—that is all."

"All?"

Kunstler looked up at the sky and sighed. "Have you ever heard of a man named Theodor Adorno?"

She thought for a moment. "No, I don't think so."

"He was a German philosopher well known in Europe. He was a piano prodigy—also a *mischling*. He got out of Germany before the war. He once wrote that the day art turned into a culture industry and became marketable…how did he put it? 'The purposelessness that was the key to its autonomy was eliminated,' he wrote. The art became so much bacon or orange juice. *Fetish* was his term."

"Fetish?"

"He meant the *gesellschaftliche Schätzung*—the social valuation that consumers mistake for the merit of artwork."

"But I think of a fetish as a charm—like the ones the Indians make. An object of superstition. That doesn't sound like orange juice."

Her father shrugged. "Think of money, the most obvious commodity. If it isn't an object of superstition I don't know what is. It is just paper or metal, after all. Nothing but social valuation."

"And so you paint these fetishes, as you put it, and allow Sharpe to sell them?"

He gazed at her curiously. "Of course."

"I see. And your Grosse Fugue work—*that* doesn't sell well because it is no commodity, but true art?"

Kunstler laughed. "You are making fun of me. The Grosse Fugue work is no commodity, because it reaches for something in the human soul. It is *schöne Kunst* in German. Literally, *beautiful art*. It goes far beyond simply 'pretty.' Paintings that are only 'pretty' sell like orange juice, in Adorno's view."

"I see," she said.

"He was famous for another comment on art. He said that to write a poem after Auschwitz was barbaric. He got a lot of notice for that."

"I can imagine."

"He later corrected himself. He said that perennial suffering has as much right to artistic expression as the tortured have to scream. And that," he said quietly, "is what my Grosse Fugue art is about—the right to scream." He turned to the steep slope. "Let us search."

Anna followed. Yet she felt she couldn't let go of this. "David, what if you found out that your commodity art had become a cover for illegal activities?"

"What are you talking about?" he said without stopping.

"What if Sharpe was using your work, or copies of your work, to smuggle drugs?"

"Copies of my work? Copies? What are you talking about?" he asked, staring up into the trees as he walked, as if questioning the jays and the squirrels.

"Wouldn't that be immoral?"

Finally he stopped and turned. "Donald is a bit greasy, I admit. He cuts corners. But he is not a criminal."

"I've seen…"

"*What* have you seen, child?"

"I saw the broken frames from the paintings. I smelled the powder that drug dealers use to cut drugs."

"You must be imagining things," he said, shaking his head. "Did you ask him? Did you confront him, give him a chance to explain?"

"I didn't dare. Not yet."

"Listen to me. I'm sure you have misinterpreted things. But even if you were right, that he does illicit things, what would be my responsibility? Think about it. Drugs are smuggled inside the fenders of trucks. They are smuggled inside violins and cellos. They are smuggled in the vanity cases of women and inside men's canes," he muttered, raising his staff. "They are transported inside the stocks of shotguns and rifles. There is no end to the objects which can be made to smuggle drugs."

The expression on her father's face was so fierce that Anna was forced to stare at the ground. "But did you know?"

"*Ach…der liebe Gott*! You assume he is guilty, and that I am his eager accomplice. I tell you, an artist has no control of his art after it is sold, any more than a maker of cars can control how they are driven."

"But if you knew he did this, would you continue having him as your dealer?"

Kunstler gave an exasperated sigh. "Probably not, but are we not dealing with a… with a hypothetical?"

They continued, searching the ground for mushrooms. Anna wondered—could she be mistaken? Could the frames have been broken en route? Could the talc have been for Sharpe's hands, chafed by opening the crates? Even if Sharpe *were* smuggling drugs, did that make her father a criminal? What muddied things for her was the fact that she did not *want* her father to be a criminal—even by extension.

"Look!" Her father was crouched, pointing under a tree,

his basket on the ground. "Here are four of them. *Steinpilz!* Little ones, all together!"

As Anna reached him she saw the expression on her father's face. It was the expression of a child—a child at Christmas who has just spotted the wrapped presents. Questions of ethics slipped away. Was it this openness to spontaneous joy— the ability to seize unlikely delight—that allowed this man to survive everything? Had he really not guessed how Sharpe might be using his paintings?

She watched him now as he kneeled and sliced the stems of the mushrooms, tenderly placing them, one by one, in his wicker basket. The gray wisps of thinning hair on his scalp quivered in the faint breeze. This father of hers, this David Kunstler, seemed so vulnerable. There would be no more questions for now. Vindication—and trust—would have to wait.

Chapter Twenty-Seven

"One thing I've wondered…" Anna asked her father as they drove back down the long, winding road after the day's mushroom hunt. His basket and her canvas bag, both half-filled with *steinpilz*, lay in the back of the truck on top of the knapsacks, rain gear, boots, empty water bottles, and other equipment. "How did you escape Meckler?"

"*Did* I escape him?" Kunstler answered. "I often ask myself that. But you mean physically—literally. That is a long story." He was quiet for a minute and sighed.

"I suppose it began in 1945—that March. The Russians were advancing faster than the Germans expected. We could hear the boom of their guns in the distance. The SS guards were ordered to move the archives and other contents of the camp to more secure places—mainly to hide criminal evidence. At the same time, they sped up the exterminations." His voice went flat. "They gassed many babies and pregnant women that last month. They were the last of the 92,000 women and children who died in Ravensbrück, that vacationland of forests and lakes."

Anna tried to grasp not only the implications of her father's words, but also the emotions that lay hidden behind them. He spoke in monotone, as if he was reciting by rote the instructions for operating a machine. For a moment he was reliving life in the camp, she realized. Being present at the killing of thousands of women and babies, he must have had to shut down all feeling just to keep going. Only one of the most damaged patients in her practice had suffered anything like such a dissociation.

"How you must have suffered," she murmured. "Helpless to do anything about it."

"Helpless, yes. And suffered, yes. But think of my mother's suffering—and the suffering of the others. I was fortunate. I survived."

As the road descended, bending left, Anna stared through her open window at the aspens and spruces covering the mountainside that sheered off to her right. The forests of Northern Germany must have had trees this beautiful, she thought. But nature was oblivious. Birds would have sung in those German trees decades ago. "When you and your mother stepped off the train into such lovely surroundings, did you have any idea what awaited you?"

"No, but when the SS guards greeted us with yells and beatings, we knew it was going to be anything but a vacation. My mother hoped it would at worst be a typical internment camp with scarce food and harsh discipline, where we might stay for a while, or however long the war lasted. There were frightening rumors, but I remember her attributing them to people's paranoia. Who could imagine otherwise?" he said, shaking his head. "By the time we arrived in November of 1944, the camp was well organized and running smoothly. Obersturmführer Eugen Meckler had already been there for almost a year. I think I told you that he had requisitioned somebody's summer cottage a quarter mile from the camp."

Anna could hear her father's breathing deepen. "Yes, you did."

"Well, I got to know the inside of its cellar quite well. During the day, Meckler was apparently busy deciding which mothers and children from the trains should die and which were still healthy enough to work for a few more weeks or months. In the evening he had me soothe his strained nerves upstairs, as I played his piano. I suppose it may have been difficult for him to erase from memory the stares of the condemned, even if those eyes belonged to the racially inferior. He could not have avoided those eyes any more than he could have avoided the odor from the crematoria. Even a dedicated SS officer cannot command his nose not to smell. Even when he was in the cottage, listening to the tones of his Bechstein, that odor would have remained in his nostrils."

"How horrible. What could you know of all that, as a child?"

"At first, nothing. But even though I was an eleven year-old, under certain circumstances you grow up quickly. I could see his nervousness, his rigidity, in that dead fish stare of his. These were qualities of a man under extreme pressure. Sometimes, when he returned from his duties, he would take a hot shower for an hour or more in the evening. I could hear the water running in the pipes above me."

Anna shook her head. "As if to wash away what he had done. Yes, I can imagine."

"But there's only so much you can wash away. For example, there were these SS *Einsatzgruppen* units that followed the main *Wehrmacht* divisions during the invasion of Russia. Their mission was to wipe out thousands of small villages, mostly Jewish, shooting the innocent villagers at close quarters, including women and children. Hitler had them cleansing Ukraine of its people to make room—*Lebensraum*, he called it—for the superior Aryan race. Many of those *Einsatzgruppen* soldiers came down with colitis and other psychosomatic diseases from their deadly work. Some were hospitalized, some were suicides, such was their stress. That was when Himmler took it on himself to replace shooting squads with gas."

"Yes, I can imagine such reactions," Anna murmured. "So, Meckler took showers to relieve the stress, and you had to play the piano for him."

"Yes, every day he was responsible for condemning women and children to death. If I had arrived a year earlier, when he was full of energy, freshly inspired to fulfill the sacred mission of the Reich, he probably would not have needed a young *mischling* pianist to relax him."

And she, Anna thought to herself, would not be on this planet.

"You have to understand…" He stopped, and for some minutes seemed lost in thought, perhaps focusing on the descending road as he steered through the hairpin turns. "Why," he groaned, "am I telling you all this?" He glanced at her, and his shoulders drooped. "Every two or three weeks," he continued, "Commandant Suhren and the SS doctors Schwarzhuber and Pflaum would select the women who were too sick or weak to work, for the transport to Mittweida, a sub-camp of Flossenburg. The women were forced to lift their skirts above their hips and run before those criminals. Those whose feet were swollen, injured, or scarred, or those simply unable to run, were selected for the Uckermark Youth Camp for recovery. Being shut in sealed barracks without medical care, food or water until they died was what the SS considered recovery."

He took a deep breath and sighed. "Of course, many of those sick women selected for Uckermark never even made it there. Their transport vans' exhaust pipes were…" He uttered something under his breath. "They were connected to the interiors of the vans. I was told that it took fifteen or twenty minutes for them to die from carbon monoxide."

Anna was no longer gazing at the forested mountainside. Her eyes were trained on the pavement that seemed to roll under them like a conveyor belt.

"At the time, locked in Meckler's cellar, I knew none of these details. I learned of them later. I thought only of my mother. Fifteen or twenty minutes in such a van, when she finally realized what was happening, with the screaming, it would have been unbearable for her."

Anna could only stare at the road ahead.

"And then I learned what they did to the children." He shook his head. "As I told you, Meckler promised me that when I played a few of Schumann's *Kinderszenen* exceptionally well—these piano pieces from childhood—that the next day he would save the life of one child."

Anna held her breath. She did not want to hear what they did to the children. Except that this was her father's testimonial. He seemed to need someone to understand what he had gone through.

"Children were used for what they termed medical experiments. Hundreds of little girls, sometimes only eight years old, were sterilized by the lengthy application of powerful x-rays trained on their little abdomens. Newborn babies were taken and drowned in front of their mothers. Or thrown into a sealed room where they died. Witnesses testified to children being thrown alive into the crematory, or buried alive, or poisoned, or garroted…"

"*Enough*," Anna groaned. "No more."

He glanced at her. "I know. And to think that we were discussing the morality of selling paintings." He shook his head. "No, forgive me. That is a very different scale of morality."

The reproach in those first words stunned her. But something was stirring in her, some dark suspicion. "About those Grosse Fugue paintings, David. They are so evocative of such painful things. Almost like documentary records. The details of mutilated human beings are so vivid. Yet you were locked every day in Eugen Meckler's cellar."

Kunstler went silent, his knuckles white on the steering wheel. "I have a good imagination. I visualize things I read about or heard about. Is that so surprising?"

"No, I suppose not," she answered. "You must have a terrifying imagination. But I keep wondering. Again, how *did* you escape Meckler?"

"Escape?" He began to shake, almost imperceptibly. "Meckler locked me in the cellar that final day before the Russians arrived. Then he ran away with the rest of the camp administration. The Russians found me and saved me."

"And then?"

He was quiet, staring straight ahead. "I was small even for my eleven years. The Russian soldiers made me their mascot. They brought me with them all the way to Berlin, where I watched them shoot the German men and rape and bayonet their women." He turned to Anna furiously. "*That* is where I saw those atrocities I later painted—the mutilations of living people, their limbs ripped from their bodies, children strangled. Do you want to hear more?"

"No," she said, her brain fogging over. "No more."

They rode that way for some minutes, neither of them speaking, the air between them heavy, as before a storm.

"All right," he finally growled. "You ask how I knew so much? You want the details? I didn't want to tell you. Yes, I was a prisoner of Meckler. I played piano for him in the evenings. It was difficult to play those keys with my fingers cramping after hours of helping push corpses into the crematoria. I was small but I was strong, and exhausted by each day's end. So now I make a confession to you. Before being a mascot of the Russians I was a pet of the Nazis, who thought it was very funny that a child could be a *Sonderkommando*." He was speaking very rapidly now, as if he had to get it all out in one breath, a breath he had been holding for a long time.

Anna was staring at him. His stiff posture, the rigid way he held his head, all spoke to her of immense stress. He gave her a blank smile.

"You know what is a *Sonderkommando*?"

She shook her head. She did not *want* to know, though she couldn't bring herself to stop him.

"We were selected by the SS guards not to *do* the killing, which was their job, but to clean up *after* the killing. *Special command* they called us, with their Nazi humor, as if we were an elite corps. Yes, we were elite, as we dragged the corpses of women and children out of the gassing vans across the courtyard and shoved them into the crematoria, the arms and legs always difficult to manage as they went every which way. My only blessing was that I did not have to drag my mother's corpse. They must have gassed and burned her weeks earlier."

Anna stared straight ahead, through the windshield. Instead of shock, she felt a kind of numbness. Was her mind trying to shield her, as an eleven-year-old boy's mind must have tried to shield him as he was forced to do these terrible things?

"You may ask why," he said, his voice shaking. "How could we do this? How could I participate in the whole macabre operation? It was to save our lives, of course, even for a few days or weeks." He glanced at her. "Do you think you would do differently?" He asked it accusingly, as if daring her to deny that she would.

"I don't know." Her own voice sounded to her alien, disembodied.

"That's right, you don't know. You never know until you are face to face with it. Then something takes over. You stop thinking. There is no decision to make. You just do whatever you must do. You *survive*." He laughed a bitter laugh. "Of course every few months all the *Sonderkommandos*—dozens of us—were made to lie on our stomachs, and one by one we were executed, a bullet to the back of the head. We knew too much. We couldn't be trusted. And so we were replaced by a new generation selected from the new arrivals. The first chore of the new arrivals was to drag the bodies of their predecessor *Sonderkommandos* to the crematoria."

"My God. But *you* were spared."

"Yes." His grin was ghastly, like a rictus, painful to see. "I was spared because I was Meckler's pet. I was useful to him. I was his prescribed sedative. I was his *Sonderkommando* puppy dog, under his wing, too valuable to be shot like the others." His shoulders sagged, his fingers barely grasping the wheel, the vehicle slowing. "By Ravensbrück standards I was immortal."

For Anna, the trees, as they drove through Black Canyon, seemed to have lost their color, as if the green had been drained out of them. "But how do you manage to keep going, after what you have been through?"

"...and *done*?" he snapped. "I paint. Hour after hour, day after day, week after week, year after year. First only the Indian scenes, for many years. Then, recently, I found myself doing the Grosse Fugue work."

"The suffering…"

"I would have committed suicide, as many did. But I was convinced my mother and my father would have wanted me to live, when they could not."

"Maybe *meant* to live?"

"Meant? By whom? God? Divine Providence?" He laughed grimly.

There was a long silence between them. Anna listened to the hum of the tires on the road.

"David," she began at last, lacing her fingers on her lap. "Have you been able to trust anybody after what you've been through?"

"Trust?" He enunciated the word as if trying to recall its meaning. "I trusted my parents. And once, someone else."

"Someone else?"

"Yes," he said, his voice barely audible. He glanced at her. "After Ravensbrück, words such as *trust* had no meaning. Only until years later, with a woman, I had such a feeling. This woman, her name was Kate…Kate Summers."

It took her breath away to hear him say the name. "That's remarkable. And love?" she said, her voice faint. "You loved her?"

"Love? I found I had a *fever* for her. Passion—like a whirlwind. Is that love?" Slowly he shook his head, as if such ideas were incomprehensible.

"What would you call it?" she murmured.

"I had no choice," he said, giving her a haggard glance. "The power of the passion, it erased all reason. It was a torment. All my yearnings were for Kate's love."

Anna couldn't take her eyes off him. His face was dissolving into tears. It may have been her mother, she realized, whatever her intent, who saved this man. Kate Summers may have drawn David Kunstler away from the world of the dead.

Chapter Twenty-Eight

By the time Anna and Kunstler arrived back at his studio she had become awed by the inner strength that had allowed her father to survive. Yet she knew the price had been steep—probably a deep cynicism about people, about all life. How had he summoned the wherewithal to court the young Kate Summers—or manage *any* relationship? But he had, despite everything, managed to keep a spark alive inside him.

"I remember your telling me," Anna said, as she sat sharing tea with Kunstler in his studio, "that you could touch Kate physically...but not in another way you wanted. A deeper love, perhaps?" She was more and more comfortable asking him such questions, since he seemed more and more comfortable answering them.

Her father had rolled a cigarette and was searching in his pockets for a match. "It is true," he said.

"Yes?"

"How can I find words?" Finding a match, he lit his cigarette and blew a plume of smoke into the air. "There was a time..." he began, instantly coughing. He began again. "Do you know the fresco on the ceiling of the Sistine Chapel in Rome—the one by Michelangelo?"

"I've seen pictures of it."

"You will recall that God stretches out his hand to give Adam the spark of life, a touch which is not quite a touch.

The spark must leap the small gap between God's forefinger and Adam's limp hand." Kunstler gazed at the end of his cigarette. "It recalls for me the way the synapses work in the brain, the way electrochemical charges are sent across tiny gaps."

Anna nodded. "Yes?"

"It is not a perfect comparison," he said, lowering his eyebrows, "but imagine the life spark of the Sistine fresco's gap as leaping in *both* directions. It gives life not only to Adam but also to God. I am sounding Nietzschean—Man as God—and blasphemous besides. But that's the idea. Such a charge would illuminate God as much as Adam. It is the touch I always hoped for from a woman."

"You're a Romantic, aren't you? In spite of everything."

He smiled and coughed. "Maybe. Anyway, that is how I would describe it. Now I'm like Rilke—great ideas on love between a man and a woman, never able to pull it off myself."

Not lost on Anna was that this Romantic created the spark for her own existence. "Now that we are speaking of Michelangelo's God, *was* there a place for God in your life after Ravensbrück?"

"Impossible," Kunstler said, shaking his head. "Many of those dead children I was forced to dispose of were my age. They had said their prayers at bedtime just as I had."

She was overcome at the thought. How would—how *could*—he be with grandchildren? Would he welcome Katey and Tommy, or would they be a reminder of the abyss? "I have a little girl and boy of my own, as I think I told you," she said hesitantly.

His face brightened. "So you told me. And I look forward to meeting them. I want to hear your little Katey play *Träumerei*." He pointed his cigarette at the covered piano.

"I've been thinking I might try to revive that instrument. Have it tuned."

"Katey would be delighted," she whispered. "So would I." Anna took a sip of her tea. "But I keep wondering about Kate Summers. How did you and she manage a love relationship, with such radically different experiences of life?"

Kunstler rubbed his eyes as if suddenly tired. "You are a curious one, aren't you? All right. I must tell you more about myself. For a year after the Russians let me go I wandered postwar Europe. I lived from day to day. Weeks went by and I forgot where I was and where I might go. It was my Uncle Daniel, the American brother of my mother's father, who found me and brought me to New York. He sort of adopted me—I became the son he never had. He owned that piano over there, covered as it is with paints and brushes. He left it to me when he died. He was the one who saw my talent and forced me to practice at that piano for hours and hours after school. He must have guessed that it might give me the will to go on living, as if the discipline would be a kind of mental armature—like that in sculpture. Years later I was accepted for study at a Conservatory in New York."

Exactly, Anna thought to herself as she gazed at the bulky shape of the grand piano under the profusion of art materials. *That is where you both met.* She remembered her mother's endless practicing in North Carolina and in Italy—her ambition to restart her moribund career. "Your uncle must have been a student of human behavior."

"Just so," Kunstler said. "He taught me to reduce everything to the mastery of each individual key. The action of the keyboard, the markings on the musical scores, only those things mattered to me in the world. Everything else was shut out, past, present and future. At least *that* could be accomplished."

He leaned forward and stubbed out his cigarette. "At the Conservatory there was grueling competition with other young pianists, some more gifted than I was. And there was my performance anxiety to deal with. My nerves."

"It's a miracle you were capable of getting that far," she said. "And so, is that where you met Kate?"

He looked at her in surprise. Then he nodded slowly, as if recollecting a dream. "Kate was my first inkling that there might be a woman for me in my life. Piano playing was becoming everything, you understand. It was for me a kind of flywheel, as in an engine. It kept my closed world going. Then like a revelation, Kate appeared. I could not go back to my tiny closed world after that."

"You hadn't had romantic experience to speak of?"

"I had never allowed myself to consider it. The importance of a piano career consumed me. It allowed me to shut everything else out."

"But how did you and Kate meet? Were you in the same class?"

"I was practicing Chopin Études one day. We all had to learn the Études of course—they were our bread and butter. The door to my practice room opened, and in she walked. 'I'm Kate Summers,' she said. 'I heard you in the hallway outside, and I like your playing.' That alone was very generous. There was so much rivalry, so much ego, such sharp elbows in the atmosphere at the Conservatory."

"And then?"

"I was intrigued. She had that soft Southern way of speaking. And such a frank manner, with that sparkle in her eyes. Before long we were taking walks. Little by little, I crawled out of my cocoon."

"Life opened up for you?"

Kunstler smiled. "I opened up to *her*," he said, reaching for his rolling papers and tobacco. "Maybe in the beginning she thought I could be a safe friend while her boyfriend—I remember his name was Anders—was away in the Army. She may have thought I wasn't the type she would get involved with, that I was just an interesting character with a foreign accent to have around for a while."

Anna nodded. So, her father remembered Anders' name. "Yes, life continually surprises, doesn't it?"

Kunstler drank some tea and frowned at her. "I remember your telling me that you left your husband because of his infidelity."

She couldn't avoid feeling a pang. "He took up with a woman who soon came around, begging to become my patient. I suppose she invented demeaning things I had supposedly said about him during our therapy sessions. Of course, revelations by a therapist to a patient about her marriage would have been unlikely and unprofessional. But a man infatuated with a young woman might believe anything."

"What kinds of things would she have fabricated?"

"Oh, perhaps that I thought he was a bore. That sort of thing."

"And your husband—you saw no reason for him to want to turn to her?"

"Reason?" Anna thought back over the last loveless years of her marriage, to the quick-snatched breakfasts, her dinners alone with the children as Sanderson worked late. She remembered the invisible wall that seemed to separate the two of them—nights when he would return and slip into bed as she pretended to be asleep. "Sometimes a spark dies, and we don't know why. You were never married, were you, David?"

"No, never married, so I don't know." He smiled wonderingly. "I like it when you call me David."

"Really?"

"Something about your voice. Almost like Kate's. You even have a little of her Southern accent."

"Well, we're both from the South," Anna said, smiling. She reached for her cup and took a long sip. "So," she continued, "you were an idealistic young man. A Romantic. Love, a divine spark between a man and a woman. Such an agreeable thought." She caught herself veering toward flirtation. *Don't...*

Kunstler lit his newly rolled cigarette and inhaled, then let the smoke curl from his nostrils. "Love was an epiphany—a revelation. Maybe I had an idea that love might be a way we humans could redeem ourselves—from the wreck we had made of ourselves as a specie."

"You thought this as you were falling in love with Kate?"

"Not consciously, I suppose."

Anna cocked her head. "It's a high standard you set—for both of you. But I wonder. Did the fact that she was unavailable—did that attract you? Like the Provençal poets who composed love poems for ladies who were married and out of reach?"

Kunstler stared at her. "How do you know she was unavailable?"

"You just told me that her boyfriend was away, in the Army."

He frowned. "Yes, but she *might* have been available. She didn't have to go back to him."

"That's what you were hoping," she said softly. "And when he came back, what happened then?"

"She left me and married him," Kunstler clipped the words off, as if to dispose of the fact.

"And that was it?"

He gave her an unhappy glance. "Not quite. In the summer of—I can't quite remember—Kate telephoned me out of the blue. She asked how I was. She said she missed me. She was depressed, she said. She suspected her husband of being unfaithful. They had been married seven years." He sighed. "Of course I had never stopped loving her. I cannot express what it was to hear her voice again."

Anna lowered her voice. "And then?"

"I thought she would leave him. We were back to a mad love for three months. I thought she was mine at last. Forever." He sat and smoked for several minutes, as if to control his emotions. "Madness. It was as if there had been no seven years. I couldn't eat or sleep, only thinking of her and how I could make sure she would not go back to her professor husband. One afternoon she did not show up. Then the next day, and the next. I was crazy with anxiety. She called a week later. She said she couldn't continue to see me."

"How miserable for you. Did she give a reason?"

He tilted his head back and stared at the Quonset ceiling. "She said that it would never work with us. That we were so good in bed because it was the only place we could relate. She said I was too obsessed with her, that she was feeling trapped and we weren't even married. It was true, of course. Toward the end, as I felt things shifting, I had to know where she was every second."

"Of course it was your first love."

He sighed, shifting in his chair. "Jealousy, possessiveness, it was all there. She must have felt threatened. Our sex was… getting desperate," he said, stopping. "These are such personal things I am embarrassed to tell you. Except that you are a therapist. I suppose you are used to hearing such things."

He smiled ruefully. "In any case, I can see she was right. As I became more and more dependent on her I had the idea that only sex could hold us together. Sex was everything. Maybe she felt the same."

Anna's mind was doing somersaults. Her father couldn't have known that his Kate broke things off because she found she was pregnant. "Did you ever try to reach her," she asked gently, "after that?"

He stubbed out what remained of his cigarette. "Once, I did, almost a year later. When I reached her she told me that her mind had not changed. That our lovemaking had been so intense because we longed for what could never be. She asked me not to call again, to forget about her."

"That must have been so difficult for you," Anna said, restraining herself from asking whether Kate had hinted at a child.

"That's when I had the breakdown."

"Oh, no."

"My Uncle Daniel put me in a hospital. They said I didn't speak for almost a year."

Anna gazed at him gravely. How cruel for him to have been rejected by the first love that brought him out of his shell, after the devastation of the camp, his hopes crashing down, the hospital, the full catastrophe. She felt her tears welling up.

"In the hospital I recovered slowly," he said, reaching again for his tobacco and papers. "I couldn't speak, but I managed drawings of houses and landscapes on paper they gave me. Watercolors, too. Later there was oil painting. I began spending hours mixing oils on my palette, painting tables, chairs, even other patients. I was a maniac. When I came home after a year, my Uncle Daniel understood that

I would never be a concert pianist and that I must pursue other things. Those days, when I wasn't working as a waiter at a restaurant, I was drawing and painting. My uncle gave me a place to live, even provided me with a small studio in Brooklyn. He helped pay for art school. He was very good to me, my Uncle Daniel."

Yes, Anna thought, *a parental figure you could trust and love*. "But how on earth did he manage to find you when you were wandering in Europe?"

Her father lit his cigarette and inhaled deeply. "Actually we found each other. After the war ended, the Nuremberg Trials were being broadcast every day on the radio. The world was learning what had gone on in the camps. My uncle decided he must find out what had happened to his German relatives, especially my mother. For myself, after months of spending nights in people's houses and barns in Germany and France, I remembered, one morning, my mother speaking of her Uncle Daniel in America. I contacted a group in France who were trying to reconnect Holocaust survivors with relatives abroad. Since he was also searching for me, the group connected us quite quickly."

"What luck."

"Of course, I spoke no English, and so my first year in New York was frustrating. But at least I was alive and safe. Uncle Daniel's wife, my Aunt Bertha, was very kind. They had a big old apartment on Manhattan's Upper West Side. I got to sleep in the maid's room. I even had my own tiny bathroom. It was a real cubby hole."

Anna pictured her father in his American sanctuary, orphaned and uncertain. "I can imagine," she whispered.

"And so after the hospital it seemed there might be a place for me in the world after all. I painted everything I saw—buildings, people, street scenes, the Brooklyn Bridge, the waterfront, the boats, everything. And yet behind it all was this…this longing." He took a long pull on his cigarette and blew a series of smoke rings, snapping his jaw, as he sent one after another whirling overhead. "I never quite forgot that it was a world that contained Kate. She was somewhere living, eating, breathing, apart from me, unknown to me."

"You had settled such hope on her," Anna murmured.

He nodded. "Every so often I still wonder where she might be." He stared up at the Quonset ceiling. "I suppose she would be in her eighties now. It is hard to imagine Kate that old."

"If she's still alive."

"Of course. If she's still alive."

Watching her father wrestle with his past, it came to Anna in an intuitive flash that her father was a decent man. Not perfect, but decent. Besides earning him a living, painting had kept his demons at bay. That was its main function, his therapy. He was not in thrall to the earning of illicit profits through the drug trade. Sharpe was using him. Could she criticize her father for not digging deeper into his gallery's dealings? Not if he existed so totally in his own world, bent only on remaining sane. His wanting her to pose nude might be little more than a futile attempt to recapture the Kate Summers of his youth. No, she would not take her clothes off for him. She would claim modesty if necessary. She was on the cusp of revealing that she was the love child Kate conceived during their affair in that long ago summer. How would he react? She had to prepare him.

Chapter Twenty-Nine

Kunstler soon returned with a fresh pot of tea. As he refilled her cup, Anna watched the bubbles rising to the surface. She stirred a teaspoon of sugar into her tea and waited for her father to settle back in his chair.

"Your life story reminds me that since we can't erase our pasts, we must accept them and move on. You've done that with your painting. At least some of us can make the most of our misfortunes."

"Very true." He was quiet, gazing into space. "When I was little, in Germany, I had a cousin on my father's side who was born deaf. He also had spinal deformities preventing him from walking. I remember how preoccupied my aunt and uncle were, always fearful that he would catch a virus or a fever. We would occasionally visit them, and my parents would tell me how lucky I was to be born healthy. '*We thank God...*' they would say. I have a picture of little Hermann, along with family pictures from the old days. Maybe you would like to see them?"

"I would," Anna said, smiling. Not only did she love old photos, but these might be of her grandparents. "How did you manage not to lose them during the war years?"

"My mother gave her most precious belongings to her best

friend the day before we were sent off to Ravensbrück. Just in case. After I was liberated I looked up Frau Müller. She gave me the pictures, as well as Mama's jewelry. I had to sell the jewelry piece by piece to stay alive in the months afterward, but I kept the photos."

"If you were homeless, couldn't you have stayed with Frau Müller?»

"Her house had been bombed, and like so many, she was living hand to mouth in a corner of what remained of it. Her husband and her sister had been killed, and so she was alone. The son of even a best friend would have been a burden. Given her circumstances, it was very kind of her to hand over my mother's jewelry. But," he said, standing up, "let me get the pictures. I will show you."

Returning with an old green shoebox, Kunstler placed it on the table before Anna with the care of one about to reveal religious relics. "Many of these were taken with our family's Zeiss camera." He chuckled. "I remember so well the smoothness of the leather case, molded to the shape of the camera." He removed the top of the box. From where she sat, Anna caught a musty smell. One by one he lifted out the small black and white photographs and set them in three rows before her. The brittle, curled prints were in the small format of those years, two by three inches, some with edges that were scalloped, others straight-edged.

She was incredulous. It was almost as if Kunstler sensed she was his daughter. He seemed to her to be saying, *Anna, here are a few of our ancestors*. The first photo was of a young couple with a small boy. The man, wearing a suit and tie, appeared to be in his thirties, dark-haired and handsome, his expression serious. The woman, slightly plump and wearing a square-shouldered dress, was half-smiling for the camera.

The boy stood erect between the man and the woman, his little shoulders thrown back, his expression confident and proud. He was wearing what must have been his school uniform—a jacket, shorts and long stockings.

"That was me, with my parents," Kunstler murmured. "You can see our Auto Union Wanderer in the background. We were about to take it for a drive. I think Papa got Herr Müller to take that picture."

She picked up the photo. As tiny as the image was, Anna couldn't believe how much the young David resembled her own Tommy. The nose, the eyes, even the shape of the head—it was uncanny. "How old were you in this picture?"

"I think seven."

The boy was two years older than Tommy, but his face was almost the same. It had crossed Anna's mind that her mother might have lied to Anders during that fight in the Italian farmhouse, falsely confessing to adultery out of revenge at his philandering. But there must have been a candid tone to her voice that led Anders to record it in his journal as true. The photograph was proof, if any was needed. Anna peered at the others. Some of them were of David with his parents, some were of the boy alone, and several were of her father's mother smiling coyly for the lens—*her own grandmother*. And finally there was a print of a sickly looking child, propped in a chair beside a woman who must have been the child's mother.

"That is little Hermann, the boy I told you about, with my aunt. I learned from Frau Müller that he was taken away one day by the State after my aunt had pleaded for more of his medicine. Medicine was scarce." He shook his head. "The Nazis had their master race eugenics. Hitler had no room in the new Reich for the crippled."

"The horrible brutality of it all," Anna said. "And your aunt and uncle? What happened to them?"

"My uncle had been drafted into the Wehrmacht and was killed during the Allies' offensive in Sicily. It was Frau Müller who told me that my Aunt Tilda was not right in the head after losing him—so soon after losing little Hermann. And then there was the bombing, the Americans during the day and the British at night. Essen was a big target of the allies— the center of the industrial Ruhr. Frau Müller told me that one day my aunt went for a walk amid the rubble of the city. She never saw her again."

Anna tried for the hundredth time to come to terms with what humans were capable of doing to each other. "But these pictures and histories—I'm struck at how much little boys can look alike. When you were seven, you could easily have been mistaken for my own Tommy."

Kunstler took the photo from her and held it up to the light filtering through the windows. His expression didn't change, but his eyes glittered.

Anna had just come around to look at the photo over her father's shoulder when the sound of knocking echoed from inside the house.

"That must be Donald," Kunstler said. "He said he would come by to pick up my new work at four o'clock." He quickly gathered the photos, put them in the shoebox, and replaced the lid. "I'll be right back."

Moments later he returned with Sharpe, who was brushing the dust from his tailored leather vest. Spotting Anna, Sharpe flashed her a sardonic smile. "So, has the model finished posing today?"

"No modeling today, Donald," Kunstler said. "I have your paintings ready. All Grosse Fugue work," he added mischievously. "They should sell well if Anna is doing the selling."

"That stuff?" Sharpe snapped. "I asked you for a half-dozen pueblo villages."

"Stuff? You call it stuff?" Kunstler's face was flushing. "If you want *stuff* you can have your pick of these," he said, sweeping his hand at the row of canvases leaning against the wall.

Anna couldn't help smiling at her father's defense of his Grosse Fugue work. He was nobody's errand boy. Sharpe had just stepped over to check the leaning canvases when there was a sudden pounding on the front door, louder than the last time.

Kunstler frowned at Sharpe. "Who did you bring?"

"Nobody," Sharpe said, dismissively.

Kunstler hurried into the house as Sharpe checked the first of the canvases.

Seconds later Anna heard a loud voice. "Out of my way, old man." That voice—not her father's—could it be?

The front door slammed and there was a scuffle. Then Kunstler's *"whoever you are, you are not welcome…"*

To Anna's shock it *was* Lant walking through the doorway, her father close behind.

"Donald," Kunstler demanded, "do you know this man?"

Sharpe seemed startled. "Unfortunately, yes. What do you want, Wolverton?"

"Besides the twelve thousand you owe me? But that's not why I'm here."

Anna felt Lant's eyes bore into her. She could tell he'd been drinking, or doing drugs.

"I've been following you, gal—watching and waiting. I figured if a Donald Sharpe can walk in here, then by God, Lant Wolverton can too."

Sharpe took a step toward him. "What are you doing here?"

"I'm after the lady. She's my tenant. Ran out on me."

"If she ran out on you I'm sure she had good reason."

"What the hell would *you* know about it?" Lant hitched his thumbs in his belt and glanced around the studio. "Nice place for a party. Seems I never got the invitation." Again he was staring at Anna.

"It seems you didn't need one," she said carefully. The tension was crackling all around her, threatening to explode.

"Donald," Kunstler shouted, "who is this man?"

Sharpe shrugged. "Last I knew he was a burnt-out drug dealer."

"*Who's* the one pushing drugs?" Lant snarled. But his focus remained on Anna. "Why're you working for this rattlesnake? And who's the old man?" he said, looking Kunstler up and down. "Everybody taking advantage of the lady?"

Anna was trying to think—how to defuse the situation? Was it time? Now? "This old man as you put it—he happens to be my *father*."

Kunstler turned and stared at her, wide-eyed.

"It's true," she said, softly.

Lant laughed. "*Your father?*" He dug a knuckle into his right eye and rubbed furiously. "You expect me to believe this dried-up old Chile pepper is your daddy? He took you up in the mountains to tell you bedtime stories?" He squinted at her. "You think I'm *stupid?*"

Anna recoiled. Lant had followed them from the motel into the mountains? Spied on them as they hunted mushrooms? "It's no lie, Lant. I took the job at the gallery because Donald shows my father's work. I hoped to meet him."

Sharpe snorted. "So you used me. Just like a woman."

Anna looked again at her father. "My mother never told you there was a child?"

Kunstler couldn't seem to take his eyes off her. "You're my Kate's daughter? *Our* daughter?"

"Hah!" Lant slapped his thigh. "The old man doesn't know what you're talkin' about. And I'm your long-lost uncle. *I'm your Uncle Lant.*"

"My father didn't know until now," she said fiercely. "I was waiting to tell him."

"Waitin' for what? Why would you be waitin' to tell your father you're his daughter? That's like me telling Sharpe here I'm gonna sit right down and wait a couple o' months to tell the Feds about his dope business." He whirled on Sharpe. "I could use that twelve thousand you owe me."

But Sharpe had reached into his boot and his hand came up holding a revolver. "You've got nothing coming from me," he hissed, leveling the barrel at Lant's head. "Now get your ass out of here before this thing goes off."

Lant took a step back. "So you think I'm here for leftovers?" He cocked his head and studied Sharpe's gun. "Okay, you want to play it that way. I'll be moving along. We'll settle another time." He turned and left, his boot heels pounding the floor all the way out.

As the front door slammed, Anna turned to her father. She found him still staring at her, his face flushed.

"Why didn't you tell me?" he asked, sounding confused.

"I couldn't just announce it," she said, searching his face for forgiveness. "I had to find out who you were. My resemblance to Kate—it didn't cross your mind?"

"My feelings for you...I was so confused," he said, taking a hesitant step toward her.

"So many years I thought of you, wondering where you were." There was so much she wanted to tell him.

"Is it possible?" Her father seemed in a trance. "Kate's child," he murmured. "I had no idea there was a child. She never said…"

"Not a word?" Anna said, tears coming to her eyes as her father stepped forward to take her in his arms.

Sharpe was watching them, his revolver pointed at the studio doorway. "I'm going to go lock that front door," he muttered.

Anna hugged her father as Sharpe ran into the house. A door slammed. Men's voices shouted and cursed. Anna pulled away as Sharpe reappeared, walking backwards through the studio door. Lant was advancing on him. He had a rifle pointed at Sharpe's chest.

"Drop it," Lant growled. *"I said drop it."*

Sharpe made a quick arcing movement with his right arm, as if to toss the revolver away. But midway through the arc he fired it, and Lant's rifle blast seemed almost an echo of the revolver's.

Anna, deafened by the concussions, saw Sharpe's body leap as if yanked by a rope, then stumble away, the revolver hanging from his hand. Half turning, he raised the pistol. Lant fired again, working the rifle's lever action at hip level.

Anna saw glass fly from the window behind Sharpe. For a second she thought Lant's bullets had missed. But Sharpe was suddenly on his back convulsing, his legs splayed out. Had the bullets gone *through* Sharpe before smashing the windows? He was making choking sounds, his blood pooling on the paint-flecked floor. The acrid smell of gunpowder was everywhere. Horrified, Anna took a step toward the stricken man.

"Stay right where you are," Lant shouted, pointing his rifle at her.

"That man is dying!"

"Nothing more than he deserves," he growled, glaring at her.

Anna heard her father mumbling a few feet away. She took him by the arm and helped him into a chair. She kneeled beside the chair, holding him.

Lant walked over and stared down at Sharpe. "Don't need your money as much as I need you dead, you sorry bastard. Always did enjoy shootin' snakes."

"...*der mörder*," Kunstler muttered. "...*der mörder...*"

"What's that, old man?" Lant demanded.

"...*verdammt...*" Her father's lips kept working. "Damned..."

"Whatever you say, old man." Lant glanced down at his own shirt and pulled at it. He brought his fingers to his mouth and licked the blood. "Bastard got me. Didn't even notice."

Sharpe's choking sounds had become strangled coughs. Then he went quiet.

"Dead?" Kunstler said, absently. It seemed to Anna he was addressing nobody in particular, his eyes roaming the Quonset studio. "Why...?"

"Just killin' varmints, old man," Lant said, squinting at Anna. The blood was now dripping from his shirt onto his jeans. "Now I'll take your so-called daughter off your hands. We've got plans, the two of us."

Anna jumped to her feet. He had *plans* for her? "Lant, before you do anything you need to go to a hospital."

Lant laughed. "Maybe it looks bad but it doesn't hurt much." He shuffled over to her. "Not going to any hospital. Here, take my hand."

But as Lant reached for her, Kunstler lunged, grabbing his wrist.

"You've done enough living, old man?" Lant yelled, stumbling. "Is that what you're telling me?" He raised his rifle. "Want me to blow your brains out here and now?"

Kunstler raised his hand, but he was too weak or too late, as Lant swung the rifle butt, catching him behind the ear. Kunstler's head rocked and he sagged forward.

Anna cried out and fell protectively over her father's body.

"C'mon," Lant growled. His fingers grabbed the back of her neck like a vise. "We've got road to cover."

Chapter Thirty

Out of the corner of her eye Anna saw that Lant was driving the pickup at just over forty miles an hour, slower than it seemed with the wind blowing in through the open windows. The road through the forest from Ojo Sarco was winding and hilly. Lant had his left arm propped on the windowsill as if to steady himself. Steering with his right hand, he glanced over at her every half minute, as if to be sure she was still there. Anna was intensely aware of the rifle in the gun rack bolted to the cab behind their heads. That rifle had just killed Donald Sharpe.

She absorbed these impressions dully, a stunned spectator to her own catastrophe. She was fighting a fog of shock to maintain the energy she would need to escape. For the moment she would be going nowhere. The doors were locked. She sat slumped, her hands tied painfully behind her, a rope running from her wrists to her ankles. Out of the corner of her eye she watched Lant's blood slowly drip from his jeans onto the seat's black vinyl. Would she survive whatever he had in mind until he lost enough blood to pass out?

"I have two little children, you know." She was surprised how weak and small her voice sounded against the wind and engine noise. "They'll be here in a week."

Lant seemed not to have heard her, as if only the road ahead existed. "Yeah, well they'll have to go back to where they came from," he barked. "When things quiet down maybe I'll let 'em come live with us."

The words chilled Anna. The man was deranged. He had just killed a man. Was her father going to die, too? Dear God, she thought—please no! And here was Lant, thinking life was going to go back to whatever he considered normal, *with her*.

"My father…" she began. She tried to look at Lant, but just the sight of him, slouched there with his Stetson pulled down to his eyebrows, a slight smile curling his lips—it made her sick, and she had to look away. "Do you know that my father was tormented by the Nazis for years in an extermination camp? He suffered terrible things, Lant. And after all that, you might have killed him?"

Lant seemed to be focusing on an approaching curve. "I don't know he's dead. If he isn't, he'll have a hell of a headache when he comes to."

She tried to stay calm. "Lant, he could die in a matter of hours without medical care. He might have a cerebral hemorrhage. The least you could do…" She stopped, choking on sudden tears. "Could you at least call 911? Give the paramedics his home address? I would but I can't, with these ropes."

"Don't think so." He gave her a sidelong look. "He shouldn't have gotten in the way."

"He was only trying to protect his *daughter*," she shouted. But she knew she had to suppress her outrage. Now was not the time to offend Lant.

He concentrated on the road for another minute. "Why're you still sticking to that line o' yours that he's your daddy?"

"He *is* my father." She shifted in her seat, trying to ease the pressure on her wrists. "Will you be good enough to please call 911 on your cell and give the paramedics my father's address?" Her tone was forceful yet pleading. She had to appeal to the trace of humanity she saw in him that night he'd told her of his Vietnam experience.

"What makes you think I've *got* a cell? You're doing all this worrying about this man you call your daddy," he drawled, "instead of worrying about your own situation."

She would say no more. She would lose her father as she lost her mother, as she lost her brother. There was no bargaining with evil. Evil did not negotiate. It just took possession.

"I just shot and killed a man." Lant looked over at her. "Ended all he is and all he'll ever be. Got that from a movie I saw once."

She stared ahead. A movie. The banality of the man. Sharpe was no angel, but he didn't deserve to be killed. They were entering Truchas from the north, with its small art galleries and its adobes with their rusted metal roofs. She wondered— should she scream and attract attention?

As if Lant had read her thoughts, the cab's windows rolled closed. Again Anna felt his stare. With the doors locked and the windows up, she was trapped like an animal. Out of the turmoil of her fear and frustration rose a desperate spike of anger.

"Yes, you killed a man." Her own voice sounded almost strangled. "Maybe two. How does that make you feel?"

"Just so you remember," he continued, as if he hadn't heard her. "I told you about my 'Nam experience. Showed you the scar. I've been shot before. I'm a survivor. Survivors don't die."

"I wasn't talking about *you*," she said under her breath.

It was quiet. Lant steered the pickup slowly down through Truchas. The shut windows made Anna feel they were in a moving bell jar. "Guilty survivors may not die, Lant," she said, "but the paths they take afterwards can be so tormenting they wish they had."

"What do *you* know about torments?" he snapped.

"I've seen people destroy themselves."

"Like who?"

"Patients of mine. They would tell you, if they were here to be asked."

Lant tried to laugh, but it was cut short as he winced from the pain of his wound. "You don't know the choices I had when I got back from 'Nam."

"I know about Sallie Ann. And I know about your brother."

"Had to be Betsy told you that." He gave her a fierce glance. "So she told you while I was in 'Nam getting shot, my big handsome brother got rich and stole my woman?"

"Yes, she did. Lant, I will only comment that a woman who betrayed you like that would have made you miserable."

"How the hell would you know?" he shouted.

Anna decided she wouldn't stir that pot. "Lant, would you please do me a favor and loosen this rope? My wrists hurt. I'm not going to run away."

"We only got another fifteen minutes."

Lant made a sharp right turn, leaving Truchas behind. As the road dipped down past a string of decrepit roadside adobes, Anna gazed out across the vast valley that stretched below. Piñon and juniper dotted the badlands that shimmered in the summer haze. Would she survive wherever it was he was taking her? Would she ever see her children again? She shifted in her seat, trying to ease the pressure of her body's weight against her arms and wrists. Did he say fifteen minutes? She took a deep breath. "Where are we going, Lant?"

He mumbled something and explored the wound above

his hip with the tips of his fingers, as if he hadn't heard her. "Why'd you go on listening to Betsy when she told lies about me? You think she's all blameless and innocent just because she's a woman? Like she'd give you the straight story?" He coughed. "What else she say about me?"

Lant wasn't going to tell her where they were going, she realized. And lingering on his past would only agitate him and make him more dangerous. "That's all," she said. "Betsy only told me that in passing."

"Yeah, Betsy's perfect. A real angel. Goes around selling folks houses they can't afford. Shows 'em how to lie to qualify for the mortgages so she can get kickbacks from the mortgage brokers. She's a fine one, my ex-wife," he muttered. "Yeah and she hates my guts."

Anna glanced over at him. Lant's face was a snarl of anger. If he kept talking, would he expend energy, and lose strength? She glanced at the widening puddle of blood on the seat. Yes, she needed to keep Lant talking. "Why would Betsy hate your guts?"

"'Because she knows what I know about her. Like when I caught on to her being a lesbian. Found her in bed with one of her supposed lady friends. I never let her forget it. When I came home evenings I used to call out, "How's my little diesel dyke?' She didn't think that was funny. You bet things went downhill from there."

"Discovering that about her must have been difficult for you."

Lant didn't answer as he drove. He seemed to be concentrating on the long curving descent into the valley. "My brother lied to Sallie Ann about what happened to me in 'Nam. He told her I was making it all up—in my letters back home, I mean. Said I dreamed up surviving Ho Chi Minh's boys. Said I invented it, trying to act the hero. Friends *told* Sallie Ann that Sam was lying, but she believed him. She had to have Sam's big money, Sallie Ann did." He shrugged and winced again. "The world's full o' lies and liars. I guess one more doesn't matter." He glanced over at her. "What about you—are you true blue?"

True blue? Anna's mind flew back in time to Thomas, to her patients. "I just try not to hurt people."

"That's all? Here I thought I had me an angel," Lant murmured, glancing at her. "So what keeps you from being an angel?"

Should she disabuse him? His notion might be keeping her alive. "I haven't met any angels on this earth yet, Lant. But I believe I'm a good person, worthy of life."

"Yeah," he said resignedly. "Sallie Ann—I thought she was good, too—till she ran off with Sam. Only thing Sam was better 'n me at was lying. Mama and Daddy's fair-haired boy. He couldn't do wrong. They believed it all the way up to the day they died. All the while, Sam's kid brother Lant was scrabbling around, suckin' hind tit. Story o' my life."

"It's never too late, Lant. Even now."

"Hah! They catch me they'll give me the hot needle. Or put me away for life. I'll never let 'em catch me." He slid her a glance. "I've got you. You're my ticket, either way."

Chapter Thirty-One

The trailer was an old tan vinyl-clad, raised on a cinder block foundation. Its walls were streaked with dirt and rust, and its windows had been blacked out. It would have been indistinguishable from the dozen or so other trailers except for its location. It sat parallel to the back edge of a steeply sloping dirt wall that had originally been bulldozed out of the hillside.

Lant parked next to the trailer and turned off the engine. Anna could hear salsa music though the truck's closed windows. Its steady beat seemed to be coming from another trailer, perhaps thirty feet away. Was there anybody outside, she hoped, who might see them, become curious and come over?

Lant leaned toward her, reached down and untied her ankles, leaving her wrists bound behind her. In the minutes it took Lant to free her feet, pull her from the truck, and drag her up the trailer's steps, she never saw a soul.

Once inside, Lant wrapped one arm around her waist and planted a long kiss on her neck. The odor of his breath nearly overpowered the chemical smells that filled the trailer's interior. Lant half-pulled her down the narrow hallway to the trailer's tiny bedroom. He heaved her onto the bed and dropped down beside her. Slumping, his chin on his chest, he seemed to forget she existed.

She looked around her. The trailer's ceiling was sagging with age. The walls were stained from roof leaks. The sheet she was sprawled across could not have been laundered for months, if ever. The smell of old sweat mingled with that of the caustic chemicals Lant must have used to cook up his drugs. Surely this was his meth lab, and meth was his habit. She drew her breath as shallowly as possible. The chemical and unclean smell of the place, closed-up and without air, was already giving her a headache. Her shoulder sockets hurt and her wrists burned from the chafing of the rope. Her hands were numb. Was this where she was going to die? Would newspapers blare details of an art gallery employee's murder by a depraved drug dealer? Was this how Katey and Tommy would lose their mother?

Lying there on her side, she watched Lant carefully, studying his vital signs. He had to be exhausted. Every few minutes he seemed to stop breathing—then his head jerked, he snuffled and gagged, and his eyes opened. The blood had soaked through the side of his shirt, but there was less than might have been expected from a gunshot wound. The explanation had to be the meth. Two of her patients had been addicts, and she knew from her research that methamphetamine was a vasoconstrictor. Lant's blood vessels must have narrowed, reducing his blood loss. It might have been just enough to keep him from slipping into shock. Was he going to be too weak to pull her clothes off—too weak to go further than that? She could only hope.

Lant jerked out of his trance and stared at her. "I don't want you getting away on me." He lurched to his feet and staggered down the trailer's hallway. He returned with a piece of rope. He looped it around her ankles several times, pulled it tight, and knotted it. Again he left. Anna heard a cabinet door open and slam. There was cursing, then silence. It was the first time he had left her alone since the shooting.

Anna worked her way upright. Her headache spiked with every movement. From her new position she was able to see down the hall. There was no sign of him. She knew she had to get the ropes off her wrists and ankles. If Lant nodded off again, she might then be able to run outside and scream for help. Would he follow her and shoot her? Where was the rifle—had he left it in the pickup? She couldn't remember.

Dizzy with fear, she scanned the trailer bedroom for something sharp to cut the ropes. There was only a small lamp with a torn shade on a tiny, makeshift bedside table. The bulb? Could she somehow break the bulb? Small chance, but there was nothing else. She wriggled across the bed toward the lamp, inch by inch. The soft lumpiness of the mattress made movement difficult. Pain shot through her shoulders and wrists. She paused and closed her eyes to allow the pounding ache in her head to subside. Time was everything.

Again she moved, slowly and deliberately, trying to ignore the squeaking from the bed's platform. Would he hear it? She stopped. No footsteps, no other sounds. She began again, slowly maneuvering so that her back was at the edge of the bed. She groped behind her toward where she calculated the lamp would be. But the mattress was soft, and she nearly toppled off the edge. Regaining her balance, she scrunched herself up and slowly extended her fingers toward the unseen lamp, her face pressed against the filthy sheet.

"What do you think you're doin'?"

Though she couldn't see him, Lant was only a few feet away. She twisted her head around. There he was, staring down at her, his eyes wide and bloodshot. He had stripped off his shirt and taped a bandage onto his side. Why hadn't she heard him come in? Had he pulled off his boots? "I'm just getting in a different position," she pleaded, "to ease the pain, Lant. If you had any kindness you'd take these ropes off. They're cutting off the circulation, and my hands are numb."

"You're trying to get away," he mumbled. "Can't have that."

"But you've got me tied up. How could I get away? You'd stop me in a second."

He sat down on the bed and studied her. He seemed wide-awake. He'd probably done more meth, she realized. He grabbed her thigh, and she flinched at the touch.

"Just testing to see how solid you are, woman. You're not so weak. And me in my shot-up condition." He frowned and scratched his head. "I could loosen 'em up though," he murmured as if to himself. "Then I could…"

Could what? It didn't matter. "That would help," she said hopefully. Anything would help. If she could get her legs free she could kick, if it came to it. Kick his wound…or his crotch…again and again. *No, he has a gun.* "Yes, that would help, Lant."

He began at her wrists. She could feel his fingers fumbling with the knots behind her back. He cursed often. She felt his breath on the back of her neck.

"Done," he finally muttered. She felt the heat of his body as he sagged against her. Was he passing out? Dying? She waited. His breathing was rapid now. She was beginning to feel her hands again. It was a relief, even with the sickening heat of his breath in her ear. Carefully, she straightened her legs.

"I dreamed of holding you like this." His words came slowly and emphatically.

"My ankles still hurt so much, Lant," she said, louder than she intended. "If only you could loosen the rope a little more around my ankles."

"Ankles?" He didn't move, as if pondering the thought. "So you can run away?"

"You've got me locked up. How could I? My ankles hurt so."

He pulled away from her. "Gotta get something."

Anna heard him make his way down the hallway, heard the trailer door unlock and open, then shut. All was silent now, except for the salsa music she could still faintly hear through the wall. Twisting around, she began to work her way toward the lamp again. Her back felt wet. Lant must have leaked blood on her. Before she could reach the lamp the trailer door opened and closed again. She heard the click of the lock. In moments he was back. Out of the corner of her eye she saw him lean something against the wall. It was his rifle. Anna choked back her terror. Her mouth was dry, her throat constricting.

"What are you going to do with that?" she managed, twisting around enough to be able to see him.

He wiped his mouth with his sleeve. "Don't know yet. But if the law gets here faster than I figure, they'll have a fight on their hands." He glanced down at his side, touched his bandage with his free hand, and winced. "Damn. But I'll tell you, darlin', if they do come, I'm not goin' down easy." He made a wheezing sound. "Got to protect my intended, don't I?"

She stared at him. "Your intended?" Her voice was almost a croak.

"Won't let you get away this time."

"This time?"

"Don't act innocent. Like when you ran off with my brother."

"Lant," she shouted. "I'm not Sallie Ann. I'm Anna. I'm not your intended. I rent your guesthouse."

He slumped down on the edge of the bed and studied her as if trying to make out who she was. His bloodshot eyes kept wandering off to one side or the other, unable to focus on her. His breathing was shallow and rapid. Finally he seemed to give up, and he began smoothing the wrinkles out of the dirty sheet. "Don't suppose it matters anyhow," he murmured. "Can't tell one from the other. Women all the same, wanting to do just one thing, mess up a man's life."

"That's not true, Lant. Maybe some women, but not all. Most women respect men. Admire them." Coming out of her mouth, the words sounded jarring, this talking sense to a deranged meth addict, but what else could she say? "Secretly they do. It's true, Lant."

"Secretly?" He sounded slightly interested.

"They don't let it show." She turned away so that her eyes wouldn't betray her.

"Uh-oh," he grunted. "Look here."

He had found the blood on her back. She could feel his fingers exploring the wetness. She shut her eyes against the sensation.

"Got my blood on you now. That says…that says you're mine forever."

Anna had no idea how to respond.

"Reckon that makes it different. Got to help you now." He turned her so that once again she was partially facing him.

In a moment she felt his rough fingers picking at the knots at her ankles. He was breathing hard, probably concentrating on making his fingers work. "Admire us?" he mumbled.

"But you all beat us hands down. We're at your God-fearing mercy." He stopped to rub something—his nose? He was snuffling, his breathing quick and noisy. Then she felt the knot come apart, felt him attempt to unwind the rope. She lifted her feet to help. His hands lingered on her ankles, and he began rubbing where the rope had chafed.

Anna's heart stood still. Seconds lurched by. He continued to rub her ankles, slowly and methodically. Then he began rubbing her calves through her jeans.

"Poor shapely little legs, got to make 'em feel good again. Too bad I had to tie you up. Had to. Couldn't trust you, women running off the way they do." He was massaging the full length of her right calf now, up and down, slowly and lightly. "Got to do something about these pants of yours."

She felt his hand work its way under the right leg of her jeans, then go halfway up her calf. It felt like a small, weasel-like animal working its way along her leg.

"Feels nice," he whispered. "Real nice."

Anna's mind was madly sorting through her options. What could she say—or do? She had to play for time. People in Ojo Sarco must have heard the shots in the studio. They were earsplitting. People in such a small hamlet would have paid attention to gunshots. She remembered seeing an old *campesino* standing near the road as Lant's truck had thrown up gravel, skidding out of there. The old man would have reported a description of a white pickup after hearing the shots, wouldn't he? Possibly got the license plate?

"Lant," she said, "you're upsetting me. If I'm your intended, you need to respect me."

"Respect you? I *do* respect you." The tone of his voice was a caricature of sincerity.

His hand had not stopped its exploration. He tried to slip

his other hand under her left pant leg. Again he was breathing hard—she could smell the tobacco on his breath and the odor from his meth-dry teeth.

"Got to get these pants off," he mumbled.

He tried to turn her onto her back. Stiffening, she resisted. He leaned into her and heaved her over. He began tugging at her belt, cursing softly, his fingers fumbling at her buckle. That was when Anna heard it—a police siren in the distance. Was it her imagination? A hallucination? But Lant seemed to hear it too. He stopped fumbling at her belt. The siren grew louder. Could it be the state police in Chimayò or Española, answering a call from Ojo Sarco? Would that be too much to hope for? But the siren was already beginning to fade. Even if they'd learned where to find Lant Wolverton's trailer, they wouldn't be back before half an hour at the earliest. Anna listened. The siren sound was gone. But no, there was another siren. They must all be headed for Ojo Sarco, she realized. She glanced over her shoulder. Lant was leaning over her, grinning.

"The law's goin' on a wild goose chase, darlin'."

"They'll be back, Lant. Don't make things worse for yourself. Aggravated rape carries a life term."

"Rape? Who's talking about rape? I've just got a little time with my intended before I bleed to death, or the law gets me."

"But you don't have to bleed to death. And if the law comes you can claim self-defense. Remember, Sharpe shot *you*. He tried to kill you."

Lant seemed lost in thought. "No my little darlin'. When they put two and two together—when they find eight pounds o' crystal and all the makings I got stashed here in the trailer, well, they'll know I'm dealing. They'll lock me up for whatever years I got left. Better to die than rot in a cell."

"But it doesn't have to be that way."

"Yeah it does," he said, grinning. "Now I want to make you feel *good*. Something to remember Lant by. Here...help me get these jeans down. How's this buckle work?" His fingers were finding the secret of her belt's double brass rings, and he loosened them, the leather slipping through. Slowly, button by button, he undid her jeans. His breath was coming in pounding gasps. In moments he was tugging at her jeans, trying to pull them down over her hips.

Anna stiffened. She bowed her legs just enough to stymie him.

"Now, darlin', you got to help me here."

But Anna heard...was it possible? Another siren. Returning from *the other direction*. "They'll be here soon, Lant," she warned. "They must have radioed the patrol car to turn around."

Lant sat straight up, listening. He gave her a wild glance, his eyes flame-red. "Well, I told you you're my ticket. One way or the other."

Lant sprang off the bed quickly for a wounded man. He grabbed his rifle and stumbled away. When he reappeared he was dragging a light wooden chair. He placed the chair facing the bed. "Got no time," he mumbled. In seconds he had fumbled the rope from her wrists, freeing her hands. He lifted and wrestled her along the bed until she was sitting with her back against the trailer wall, facing—across the width of the bed—the chair.

"Now," he said, grabbing the rifle. "The only thing as good as making love to a beautiful woman is dying by her hand. Born by woman, die by her loving bullet. And that, darlin', is what you're going to do. I'm going to sit right down in this chair here and you're going to sit there, and aim right here," he said, pointing to his chest, "right in the heart. An' you're going to pull this hair-trigger of my favorite .30 caliber Henry Repeating Rifle "

"Lant, no…"

He levered a round into the chamber and handed her the rifle, stock first. "Now I'm going to count to five. When I hit five, you pull the trigger. Easy as pie."

The rifle felt incredibly heavy in her hands. "But I've never shot a gun," she lied. "I couldn't."

"That case I'll get up real close," he said, pulling the chair to within a foot of the bed. He sat back down. "Now you lean back there against that wall, nice and steady. Can hardly miss now. When the law gets here you tell 'em I tried to rape you. They'll let you off."

"No!" She shouted. "I won't do it."

"Yes you will. By God, I prepared for that." The siren sounded much closer now. Lant jumped up, reached under the mattress, and pulled out a large revolver with a long barrel. He sat back down in the chair and pointed the revolver at her. "Now, it's going to be either me or you. I got nobody but you. But you—you got two little ones. What'll happen to them with their Mama dead?" He waited a second, smiling crookedly at her. "Now here's what we're going to do. I'm going to count to five and when I hit five, I'm going to wait another second for you to pull that trigger. If you don't, well then I'm going to pull mine," he said, grinning. "Put a .41 caliber bullet right through your pretty little heart."

"You wouldn't…"

"Sure I would, darlin'. Of course it wouldn't be as good as getting killed by you, because with you dead I'd have to swallow my own barrel and blow my brains out. But it'd be better than getting cut down by the law. Get my drift?"

Anna was paralyzed into silence. She raised the rifle and aimed it at Lant's bare chest. Her finger found the trigger. She couldn't think. She would not do it. But Katey and Tommy…

"One, two…" Lant counted.

She couldn't miss. Her rifle's muzzle was barely two feet from his chest. She would *not* murder this man. "Lant, please. If you love me you won't ask me to do this."

"Three, four…" he counted.

"*I won't do it,*" she screamed.

"*Five!*" The blast from his revolver knocked her back as if she'd been hit by a giant fist. Gunpowder burned her face. She blinked. She had not fired the rifle. And she was alive.

He was grinning at her. He cocked the revolver and aimed again. "*At my heart, woman!*"

Another revolver blast rocked her against the wall as the rifle leapt in her hands and Lant disappeared.

Anna dropped the rifle on the bed and stared at it. She rubbed her hands against her jeans, trying to rub off something horrible. Had she really fired it? Had it gone off by itself? Where had *his* bullets gone? From where she sat she could see only the tops of Lant's knees beyond the edge of the bed. One knee was twitching. The other was still.

In a daze, she shifted to look at the wall beside her. There were two holes at least a foot from where she was sitting. The edges of the holes were shiny where the bullets had peeled the paint on their way through. *He was so close he couldn't have missed.* She scrambled forward across the bed and looked down. Lant was on his back, his knees flexed over the seat of the turned-over chair. Blood was bubbling from the corners of his mouth. His eyes were wide open, unblinking, staring straight up.

The siren was close now.

Chapter Thirty-Two

Four weeks later

Sitting in her father's studio with the children, Anna was watching shafts of September's morning sun slanting through the glass of the newly repaired window. Particles of floating dust were bobbing on unpredictable currents of air. They reminded her of the Brownian Motion she'd studied in college biology. Microscopic particles in water randomly bombarded by what? Molecules? Atoms? That was how she often felt now—bombarded. Her mind was still going off like this on brain-numbing tangents.

Her father had just said something whose meaning she missed. Her mind was elsewhere, but she couldn't say where. Mornings had been this way for a while now, after many nights' bad dreams, since she pulled that trigger in the trailer. How strange of her right index finger to have given her life such a wrenching twist. She'd killed a man. Every once in a while she glanced at the finger with wonder and misgiving. *If thy eye offendeth thee…*No, she thought, that finger saved her. She did not die. The trained therapist part of her stood aside, nodded sympathetically, and pronounced such thinking primitive and magical. It was what the mind did after a bad shock. At least the lights—the flashes of tiny sparks that appeared so suddenly—came less often, now only at night, when she lay in bed trying to sleep. She knew that such flashes were not uncommon after severe trauma. They could go on for years.

She had been jumping at loud noises since the shooting, noises as innocuous as the dropping of a book on a tile floor. It had happened yesterday at home, when Katey dropped her Schirmer's music book—the mere shape and weight of a magazine, but so *loud*. Small explosions seemed to lie in wait around every corner. Perhaps that was why she'd begun taking close notice of details her restless brain could tag as warnings.

The police had finished questioning her for the third time. She had described everything again, as it happened. What was important, the police said, was that she had not been killed in the gunfire, either by Sharpe or Wolverton. Her children had not lost a mother. She would probably have to testify in court, something she was not looking forward to. Donald had barely survived, and would be in rahab for quite a while. What would happen with the gallery? Her mind traveled back and forth this way, back and forth.

She remembered that Peter had called several times and left messages. He was worried about her, he said. What could she tell him, when each day she felt like a different Anna? But she would call him soon. He was not like other men she had known. He really seemed to love her, and that was something. She remembered their making love, remembered losing herself in the passion. It seemed so long ago. She missed him. He deserved another chance. So did she.

Anna wrestled her attention away from the dust particles. Something important was about to take place. She, her father, Katey, and Tommy were sitting around the table for a special occasion. Katey, holding her Schirmer's, was prepared to play the piano. She had just declared that she would play Robert Schumann's "About Strange Lands and People." Her grandfather was smiling and nodding. He murmured something in German.

Katey frowned. "What, granddad?" They had all spent time deciding what his grandchildren should call him. "Granddad" seemed a good compromise between simply "David," which Kunstler felt lacked proper respect, and the German "*Großvater*."

He pronounced the title of the Schumann piece again, spelling it, "*V-o-n f-r-e-m-d-e-n L-ä-n-d-e-r-n u-n-d M-e-n-s-c-h-e-n.*" He smiled. "Maybe by and by you will learn a little German with your music—the language of *good* Germany, before…" His voice trailed off, his expression changing…"before the bad years."

Anna was relieved that her father no longer wore the large bandage on his head. A large red depression remained where the rifle stock had hit him. He complained of headaches, but otherwise seemed strong, though he still coughed. Anna looked at Tommy. He had on his little blue-striped soccer jersey and blue jeans, and his ash blond hair was tousled. Ma-i was on his lap. Tommy had been carrying Ma-i around with him ever since he got home from Ohio. For some reason the kitten didn't object to the boy's handling—in fact he seemed to enjoy Tommy's attention.

"Shall I play now?" Katey asked.

"Yes," her grandfather said to her, "it is time. Now, do as I told you. By the time you become a concert hall pianist it will all be second nature."

Anna watched eight year-old Katey rise and walk across the floor to the piano. The ebony grand piano seemed to her to be crouched in the far corner of the studio like a wild animal. The instrument had lost its carapace of tarp, paintbrush cans and canvases. From where Anna sat, its curved profile seemed naked, almost ruthlessly clean.

Katey marched eagerly across the paint-specked floor. She carried herself proudly, Anna thought, in her new navy blue school uniform—proud, yet frail and vulnerable. The world would test her in so many ways.

Reaching the piano, Katey turned and straightened, throwing her narrow shoulders back. "About Strange Lands and People," she announced. Her features were serious and intense. "I will play a piece from *Kinderszenen*, by Robert Schumann, composed in 1838." She tipped her head to the side. "Part of his fame came from his marriage to the brilliant pianist Clara Wieck." She grinned mischievously, and her grandfather chuckled with amusement.

Katey settled onto the black leather piano seat and flamboyantly adjusted its height with its two knurled knobs. She began playing, the first notes coming uncertainly as she struggled for proper tempo. In seconds the warm phrases of Schumann's music was flowing across the studio space. Watching her daughter's profile, Anna sensed a new poignancy in the melody, even after the many days she'd heard Katey practice at home on the new upright. Many of the *Kinderszenen* were composed not only for children, Kunstler had told Katey, but also for adults who themselves had been children. It was easy to imagine a child's wonderings about far-off lands and strangers known only from pictures, and tales told before bedtime.

The piano had been resurrected with difficulty. After years

of neglect it required several tunings to raise the strings to pitch. Three of the strings had snapped, unable to bear the sudden new tension, and had to be replaced. It was the way Anna felt these days. Old moorings inside her seemed to be giving way. But electro-chemical brain circuits could not be replaced like piano strings. New paths had to form, the doctors said, and that would take time.

Katey played the final repeat. At the end, she allowed the tones to die away with the soft *retard*, as her grandfather had taught her, only then lifting her fingers from the keys. She released the pedal, and from her perspective, Anna could see the corner of her daughter's mouth turning up in a smile.

Stepping out from behind the piano, Katey rose and took a deep bow. The audience of three—Tommy releasing Ma-i for a moment—applauded. Anna was imagining how her own mother would have loved listening to her namesake granddaughter performing with such talent.

She turned to her father. "What do you suppose my mother would have thought if she could have heard her granddaughter play like this?"

Kunstler raised his eyebrows. "Maybe she *is* here and *does* hear it."

"Now you play something, granddad," Katey exclaimed.

"One of these days, perhaps, I will try something," he said. "But now my fingers are stiff from not playing for so many years. So now, what else will you play for us?" he asked, as if he hadn't been coaching Katey for this day for weeks.

"*Träumerei*," she said, triumphantly. "In English it means "Reverie."

"Ah really? You can play that difficult piece of dreaming music, *Lento, con gran espressione*, as the composer directed? Slow, with great expression?'"

"Yes!"

"Well, in that case you will have to prove it to me and to your mother—and your brother and Ma-i too."

Katey was once again at the piano, perched on the edge of the piano seat. After the first plangent chord, the notes ascended gently to the F octave.

Anna closed her eyes, trying to imagine how it must be for her father to hear this music. No light flashes were haunting her just now. For once her brain was quiescent. Could these same notes have soothed her father as he played for Meckler so many years ago? No, she thought, he would have been too terrified to miss a note, to break the spell that bound the SS officer to his playing.

But why think of Meckler? Was it because she now knew the feel of blood on *her* hands? But Lant was a drug dealer—a criminal. He had forced her to shoot him. He'd given her no choice. He'd manipulated her into pulling the trigger, having her, in his own twisted way. He'd counted on a mother's instinct to protect her little ones. And she was left in the aftermath with trying to convince herself that it was the violence of his revolver's blast that caused her finger's reflex on that trigger. She needed to put it behind her, to move on. How to erase the crooked smile, the knowing expression that seemed to say, "*Woman, you will do exactly what I want you to do.*"

Anna gazed across the table at Tommy, at the little hands that were holding Ma-i so fiercely, as if unwilling to lose a creature so precious. Tommy had been having nightmares, waking up screaming in the night. It seemed that in Ohio, Heather had read to the children from Grimm's Fairy Tales. Tommy had become obsessed by the tale of Hansel and Gretel. He dreamt that the witch was pushing *him* into the oven.

Katey finished playing. She rose proudly and bowed, smiling at the applause. Again, her grandfather clapped with the full weight of his arms. Anna could see that her father and her daughter had won each other over, and she was pleased. But there was Tommy.

"Did Ma-i enjoy '*Träumerei?*'" she asked her little boy.

"When are we going home, Mommy?"

"But we've just begun to be here, my love. And we still have dinner to eat."

"Ma-i wants to go home. He's lonely."

"But he has you."

"No he doesn't."

"What do you mean, darling?"

"He just *thinks* he has me. He doesn't really."

"I don't understand."

"When I put him down I might be gone."

Katey came over and sat down next to her brother. "Tommy is sad," she said, confidently. She put her arm around him and smiled at Anna. "I'll take care of him."

Tears came to Anna's eyes, and she looked at her father. He seemed moved. But moved by Tommy, or by the music? He was humming the "*Träumerei*" theme, gazing at Katey.

Anna knelt in front of Katey and Tommy, taking them into her arms. As she did so, she felt a chill. It was from a dream she'd had last night. She had been lost in the *barrancas*, alone in the desert peaks and valleys of dried lava and sediment. She had been searching for the children. She'd heard their cries, but always from different directions—first from the road, where tires roared on the blacktop, then from shadows where she saw coyote shapes. Then she saw them, and began running toward them, but the children didn't see her, and began running the other way, toward the mountains and the caldera.

“Mommy, you’re hugging me too tight.”

Was it Katey? Tommy? Both? Anna released her children and looked at them. Their faces were bright, illuminated by the late morning sunlight pouring in through the studio window.

“This will take time, dear ones,” she murmured. “This will take time.”

The End

Acknowledgements

I have had the benefit of generous commentary on the part of Santa Fe writers Colin Barker, Glenna Boyd, Charlie Romney Brown, the late Marigay Grana, Margaret Mooney, Jim Roghair, Tori Shepard, Tamar Tomson, and the late Margaret Walsh.

I am in debt to the late Susan Stern, Santa Fe teacher of fiction writing, and to Lynn Stegner, now teaching at Stanford University.

Finally, I am in debt to my son, Greg, for his fine edit of *Desert Electra* two years before he died.

About the Author

Born in New York City in 1941, Bruce Moss grew up in the Northern Westchester town of Bedford Hills, N.Y. He graduated from the Harvey School, The Gunnery School, and Washington and Lee University, then served in the U.S. Army in garrison in South Korea in 1965 and 1966. He then worked at Manufacturers Hanover Trust in New York for several years. In the early 1970's he moved to Tuscany for two and a half years with his wife and small son, writing fiction and studying the Italian language at Florence's Dante Alighieri Centro Linguistico Italiano. His research in these years provided material for his novel, *A Death in Florence*, (published in 2023). Returning to New York in 1974, he worked for twenty years for the publisher Standard Rate and Data Service. In 1994, Bruce moved to Santa Fe, New Mexico, where he now lives and writes. *Desert Electra* is his latest novel.